THE DOJANG

A novel

Marek Handzel

"Good luck to the whole lot of them"

Elizabeth Handzel

1991

THE MINI CAB PULLED UP in the middle of the industrial estate's car park, puncturing its soft silence. The driver switched off the lights and cut the engine. He got out of the car and stamped a cigarette out with the heel of a polished brown shoe. Two other men followed him out of the cab.

One of them had three teardrops tattooed below his left eye. The other man's long dark hair was tied back in a ponytail.

The driver opened the boot and took out an empty sports bag. He hung it over his shoulder. Then he handed the other two men a crowbar and a wrench. He took a hammer out for himself and locked the car.

They walked up to one of the estate's units. The man with the ponytail smashed a lock on a door and broke it open. It was dark inside. The driver stumbled over some boxes as he entered the unit.

'Where's the light in this place?' he said. The man with the ponytail found his way to a wall and patted it, searching for a switch.

'It's somewhere here,' he said. 'I only saw it the other day.' A few seconds later a long fluorescent tube light flickered into life, revealing a storeroom full of cardboard boxes.

The man with the teardrops scanned their surroundings. 'Does he usually have this much stock in? You wouldn't be able to find this many jars of gherkins in the whole of Warsaw.'

'Well he's doing alright for himself, isn't he?' said the driver.

'And he still can't pay? Come on, let's go and straighten the whore's son out,' said the tattooed man.

They walked through another door into a large shop floor area where long rows of tall aluminium shelves were stacked high with groceries. A dim light at the far end of the store acted as their guide. The tattooed man tapped his crowbar against the shelves as they walked down an aisle. The noise it made echoed through the building.

When they reached the end of the aisle he stopped tapping. 'You in here Feliks?' he said. 'Come on chief, it's time to say hello.'

—

'He's in his office,' said the driver, pointing his hammer at some light creeping under a door opposite them, about 20 metres away. He started walking towards it. The other two men followed him.

'Hey Feliks,' shouted the tattooed man at the door. 'This better be open.' He pressed the handle. It was firmly locked.

He put his face to the door. 'Are you going to open up or do you want us to smash it down?'

There was no response. He banged out a crescendo on the door with his fist. 'Last chance to open up.'

The seconds ticked on his watch. Silence. He brought his crowbar down against the handle and kicked the door, but it remained shut.

'Are you two going to just stand there with your dicks in your hands?' he said. The man with the ponytail barged the door with his shoulder. After a few more hits, the lock broke. The door almost came off its hinges as it swung into the shop's office and rebounded off the wall.

Inside, Feliks, the shop owner, was sitting behind his desk, facing the door. Two other men were propped up against either side of the desk. One of them had his arms crossed, the other one was chewing on a toothpick. They looked at the intruders as if they were cleaners who had come in to give the office a quick vacuum.

The tattooed man stood still for a moment. Then he said, 'Who the hell are you?'

The men on either side of the desk said nothing.

Feliks stood up slowly, using a crutch that had been hooked on the arm of his chair. 'Hello Maciek,' he said, raising a hand as if he was taking an oath. 'I thought I'd invite these two friends of mine to come and meet you.'

'You've got some nerve old man,' said Maciek.

'What's the matter? Don't you like making new acquaintances?'

Feliks pointed to his right. 'This is Tomek, and this is Wojtek,' he said, pointing in the other direction.

'Tomek and Wojtek eh? What is this, some whoring comedy sketch? You've got yourself some faggot bodyguards?'

Feliks smiled faintly. 'Like I said, I'm only trying to make some introductions.'

'Shut your mouth,' said Maciek. He glanced at the driver who was stood next to him. 'Taxi man. Open the bag.'

The Taxi man unzipped the sports bag and threw it towards Feliks. It landed on his desk.

'We'll keep this simple,' said Maciek. 'No more negotiation. We've come to collect.'

He pointed the crowbar at the men. 'So start putting everything you have in the bag, or Tomusz and Wojtusz are going to be spending a couple of nights in one of the wards down at the hospital.'

'Can't we talk about this?' said Feliks. 'Nobody needs to get hurt.'

'We've already talked too much. Get on with it.'

'I'm sure we can come to some sort of an arrangement if we all sit down and talk,' said Feliks. He laughed a little, and pushed his glasses up his nose, looking at Wojtek.

'Do you boys want a drink? I've got some Wyborowa here. I keep it nicely chilled for when suppliers come to visit.'

'You've got five seconds,' said Maciek.

Feliks touched his glasses again, eyeing Tomek and then Wojtek. They stared straight ahead. 'There's no need for this aggression Maciek, I'm sure we can talk, like I said –'

Maciek marched towards Tomek. He raised his crowbar and swung his arm back. Before he had the chance to bring it down, Tomek leaned back slightly and kicked Maciek in the chest, winding him and putting him on his knees.

The other two hoodlums froze. Tomek and Wojtek walked towards them. The Taxi man raised his hammer, holding a hand out in front of Tomek. 'Don't come any closer. I'll open your head up. I swear.'

Tomek didn't stop. The Taxi man swung out, missing him. He felt one of his legs go from under him and he fell backwards, dropping the hammer. The ponytailed man tried to hit Wojtek with his wrench, but Wojtek stepped into his path, and struck him with an open palm to the nose, followed by a ridgehand to his neck. The ponytailed man knocked over a swivel chair on his way down.

Tomek kicked the Taxi man's hammer across the office floor. 'Don't bother getting up,' he said.

Scrambling to his feet, the Taxi man threw himself at Wojtek, who stepped to one side and punched him in the temple. Reeling, the Taxi man crashed into a bookshelf and collapsed.

—

Wojtek turned around. Maciek was back up. He threw a haymaker. Wojtek ducked and aimed a side kick towards his knee, sending him down again.

Tomek picked up the weapons and put them on the desk.

'What now?' said Feliks, taking a few shallow breaths.

'These gentlemen are going to go back to where they came from,' said Wojtek. And they're never going to come back here again.'

The three hoodlums took their time to stand up and make their way towards the office door. The ponytailed man helped Maciek to his feet. Before limping out, Maciek raised an outstretched arm and aimed a finger at Feliks.

'You've made your last mistake,' he said.

Tomek and Wojtek followed them at a distance. They waited in the storeroom as they watched the gang stagger back to their car.

'I'll get something to fix this up for tonight,' Wojtek said, inspecting the door. 'You go make sure Feliks is OK. We'll take him home in a bit.'

Outside, as the three men reached the mini cab, the ponytailed man said, 'Who were those whores' sons? They've broken my whoring nose.' He took his leather jacket off and threw it onto the roof of the car. Taking his shirt off, he pressed one of his shirtsleeves up against his bleeding nose.

'Did you not see how they fight?' said the Taxi man.

'So?'

'So take a wild guess.'

The ponytailed man paused. 'Are you being serious? Here? Since when? It can't be.' 'Shut it,' said Maciek. 'Have we got a '64 in the car?'

The Taxi man hesitated. Maciek backhanded the Taxi man in the chest. 'Are you deaf? I asked if there's a '64 in there?'

'It's strapped under where you were sitting,' said the Taxi man. 'On the left.'

Maciek opened the passenger door and put his arm under the seat. He took the pistol out from under it.

The Taxi man gripped Maciek's wrist. 'Leave it,' he said. 'We can sort this out another time.'

'There won't be another time,' said Maciek, brushing him away.

'Those guys are serious.'

'Yeah? Well, I'm serious too.' He released the safety catch on the gun and starting hobbling back in the direction of the industrial unit.

'Maciek, come on, you're not thinking straight.'

He carried on walking, dragging his wounded leg with him.

'He's going to do it, isn't he?' said the ponytailed man.

'Looks like it. Come on, we'd better go with him.'

Maciek pushed through the door into the storeroom. Inside, Wojtek was standing on a stepladder, looking for something to help secure the door for the night. He turned his head. Maciek shot him. The force of the shot sent him down, clattering into a box of gherkin jars. He cried out in pain, holding his shoulder. Blood seeped through his fingers.

'Do you like that tough guy?' said Maciek, kicking some smashed glass at Wojtek. 'You want to play with us hero? Huh? What, you think you're some sort of whoring war hero?'

Maciek placed his foot on the injured shoulder and pressed down on it. Wojtek clenched his teeth and roared in defiance. Maciek pressed harder.

'How do you like it now, hey?' He started laughing. 'Check out our whoring hero,' he said to the Taxi man and the ponytailed man, who were in the doorway. 'Doesn't look so tough now, does he?'

He kicked Wojtek in the stomach. 'You thought you could come here and interfere with our business? You should have read the script. It ends badly for whores' sons like you. Always does.'

He lifted the gun up and aimed it at Wojtek's stomach, before falling like a felled tree. His head bounced off the concrete floor and then he lay still.

Tomek crouched over him and hit him twice more in the head with a black baton. He looked up at the other two men. 'You want the same?'

They backed out, feet over feet, arms outstretched for balance. When he got in the car, the Taxi man was shaking. He fumbled in his jacket pocket for his keys.

'What about Maciek?' said the ponytailed man, pulling his leather jacket off the roof of the car. 'Are we leaving him there?'

'He left himself there,' said the Taxi man. Before the ponytailed man had time to close the passenger door, the Taxi man started reversing.

—

He drove into a bin, put the car into first gear and accelerated out of the industrial estate.

Twenty years later

PIOTR GAZED AT THE FLAG. Fresh paint filled his nostrils.

'It's crooked,' said Jacek, who was standing next to him.

'Crooked?' Piotr titled his head to one side. 'You sure?'

'Look at it. The bit with the three straight lines is higher than the one opposite it.'

Piotr took hold of a stepladder that was next to the wall, climbed up to the flag's height and adjusted it.

'There. Better?' he said, looking back down.

Jacek took two steps back to get a better view. He stuck his thumbs up. 'Perfect.'

Piotr got down from the ladder and walked back over to where Jacek was standing. They looked up at the flag again, hands on hips.

'It's the symbol for heaven by the way,' said Piotr.

'What is?'

'The three lines in the top left corner. They represent heaven. Then the ones opposite, with two broken lines, represent water. The three broken ones below are earth, and the ones opposite those, under heaven, they represent fire.'

'Yeah? I didn't know that.'

'Sabum would have told you at some point. You've just forgotten.'

'Maybe I missed that lesson,' said Jacek.

'You know what the symbol in the middle is, right?'

'Sure. The Taeguk. Yin and Yang.'

Piotr smiled at his friend. 'You haven't forgotten everything then.' He circled, admiring the hall. 'So, you like what's been done to the place?'

'It's great,' said Jacek. 'There's loads of space. Nice high ceilings. It's wide too. We can get some decent sparring going.' He started to shadow punch lightly, shuffling across the hall, away from Piotr. Then he threw two reverse turning kicks in quick succession as he moved back towards him.

Piotr threw a half-hearted side kick to warn him off. 'When are you going to quit with all that Hollywood stuff?'

'I'm only messing.'

'You're spending too much time with your MMA buddies. Come here, I'll show you the equipment cupboard.'

Piotr took a set of keys off his belt and searched through them for the one he wanted. He opened the door to a built-in storage cupboard and switched the light on. The small room was filled with kick shields, punching pads and foam mats. Behind them was a large wooden breaking-board holder and a punch bag with a faded logo and loose stitching.

'Hey, it's all Sabum's stuff,' said Jacek, leaning against the door frame.

'What did you expect it to be?'

'I don't mean it like that. It's just a bit hard to look at. Brings back the memories, you know.'

Piotr put his hand on the mats. 'Yeah, it does.'

'So how many are coming then?'

'Eight. Including you.' Piotr, threw a kick shield at Jacek, who caught it and grasped it to his chest.

'Hey, steady, I didn't say I was going to get back into regular training.'

'But you're here now. And you've brought your dobok with you. So you'll at least train today. Anyway, you should start training regularly again. The dojang needs you.'

'You've heard something then?'

'I'm always hearing things.' Piotr threw some more kick shields at his friend.

'So we've had some concrete enquiries?'

'That's right.'

'About time. Is Krzysztof coming?'

'He said he was.'

'Is he still pissed off?'

'A bit, I guess,' said Piotr. 'But he'll get over it.' He walked out of the storage cupboard and lined the kick shields up against the wall.

'Do you want to help officially open the dojang then?'

'How?'

'With a *tul*, what else?'

'Which one?'

'*Juche*. Seems appropriate. Controlling our destiny and all that.'

'You could have picked an easier one, I feel stiff as hell.'

—

'Well warm up a bit.'

'OK. Give me five minutes.'

'Let's get changed first.'

They left the main hall and went into the male bathroom in the corridor. It smelt of fresh paint and lemon, from the deodorizer blocks in the two urinals. Jacek used one of them. When he finished he washed his hands with soap and warm water in a chrome sink. He then rubbed his hands together under a powerful dryer.

'Makes a change from the old piss-stained walls and that towel dryer doesn't it?' said Jacek. 'That thing had more holes in it than the road from Krakow to Zakopane.'

Piotr laughed. 'It's a bit of culture shock, eh?'

'Best not turn us soft,' said Jacek, taking off his T-shirt.

They put on freshly cleaned and ironed white doboks. Piotr took extra care with his belt, tying it tightly and making sure the knot sat in the centre of his abdomen.

Before they walked back out, Jacek said, 'How comes we're in here anyway? Do we get changed in the same place with the white belts now?'

'Don't worry. It's only until we get the key to the kitchen. It's not quite finished yet.'

When they came back out into the main hall Piotr waited while Jacek limbered up. When he was ready, they stood in front of the flag again and bowed to it.

'*Junbi*,' said Piotr.

They both stood up straight and placed their fists on their hips, with their elbows pointed out. Taking a deep breath, they prepared to deliver the first move in the *tul*, a block.

'*Seja*!' shouted Piotr.

They performed a series of strikes, punches, blocks and kicks in one fluid, synchronised motion. On each execution of a move, they exhaled sharply.

Four men entered the hall. They stood against a wall and watched the two black belts, listening to the crisp snapping sound of heavy cloth as they struck blows at their imaginary adversaries.

They finished the last move with a loud war cry. It resonated off the walls as they stood motionless, holding their final stance.

After a few seconds Piotr said, '*Junbi*.' They returned to their original positions, facing the flag.

'That was a bit rusty,' said Jacek.

'It wasn't that bad. You didn't hold your kicks out for long enough a couple of times though. And you were dropping your arms too low for the knifehand guarding block. Here, let me show you.'

Piotr stood in front of Jacek as he formed the block again. He took hold of Jacek's wrist and pushed his left hand up until the fingertips were in line with the top his shoulder. 'There, like that.'

Piotr turned his attention to their spectators. 'Evening boys. Glad you could make it,' He walked over to them. 'Have you dyed your hair Sebastian?' he asked one of them.

'I got it done for the summer.'

'Well don't get it done permanently. It makes you too memorable.'

One of the other men, called Jan, said, 'Sabum, this is my friend, Szymon. The one I told you about.'

'Right. Welcome,' said Piotr. They shook hands. 'You were with a dojang in Nottingham right?'

'Yep. I've had to move for work. Our training was dropping off a bit up there. So I'm a bit out of shape.'

'No problem,' said Piotr. 'Ease yourself into it. We're all a bit off the pace ourselves.'

A few more men arrived and Piotr told them all to change into their doboks. When they were done, Piotr checked the time on his mobile phone. 'OK,' he said. 'It's seven thirty. Line up.'

The men stood in two rows facing Piotr, with Jacek on his own, in front of them, on the right.

Jacek turned his head and scanned the white belts. Satisfied that they were in formation with their hands behind their backs, he faced forwards again. He stuck his arms out to the side of him at a 45-degree angle with his fists clenched, and commanded the class to bow to its teacher. They all did so, in unison.

Piotr took them through some warm-up exercises. He instructed them to circle their necks, arms, trunk, hips, knees, and ankles, one after the other.

As they were jogging on the spot, a black belt walked in, adjusting his belt as he went past the white belts to the front of the hall.

'Sorry I'm late,' he said.

Without looking at him, Piotr said, '50 burpees Mr. Florek.'

'Yes Sabum.'

The black belt dropped down into a press-up position, thrust his legs forward into a squat and then jumped up into the air as high as he could, tucking his knees up as he did so.

When he was done, he bowed to Piotr and joined the rest of the class. Piotr ordered them to partner up for some conditioning. They swung their arms across their bodies, clashing forearms. Bone on bone, gritted teeth.

They dropped into a low horse stance and punched each other in the stomachs, beginning lightly and then building up the intensity. They did the same with their thighs, kicking them inside and out, finishing with their shins. In between striking each body part, they performed 20 knuckle press-ups each.

With their limbs numb, Piotr got them to run up and down, performing more knuckle press-ups, sit-ups and burpees at each end of the hall floor. Every time they got to one end Piotr would shout out an exercise and then the number of repetitions they had to perform. By the end, they could only run at half pace and were gasping for air.

To finish the warm up they picked up the kick shields. Every student performed 100 front and side kicks with each leg.

Piotr gave them a short break. They put the kick shields back in the storage cupboard and took some mats and the breaking board holder out. Nobody spoke, apart from Piotr, to give instructions. After carrying out the breaking holder with another student, Szymon walked to the end of the hall and got a bottle of water out of his bag.

Piotr approached him. Out of anyone else's earshot, he said, 'There's no drinking until the end of the session.'

'Sorry,' said Szymon, putting the bottle away.

When they resumed, the white belts broke boards with various techniques. Piotr, Jacek and Kris sparred, two on one, taking turns to be alone. For the last half an hour they went through some tuls.

The session complete, they lined up in rows again, sat down and stretched their legs. When they were done, Piotr said, 'Close your eyes. Think about today's training.'

One of the students wiped the sweat off his face with the sleeve of his dobok.

'Stay still,' said Piotr.

After a couple of minutes, Piotr said, 'Szymon, do you

remember the tenets?'

'Yes Sabum.'

He called them out. The class repeated them in one confident voice.

'*Ye Ui!*'

'*Yom Chi!*'

'*In Nae!*'

'*Guk Gi!*'

'*Baekjul Boolgool!*'

After the session, the black belts stood outside the hall chatting and waiting for everyone to leave, so that Piotr could lock up. Jan, Adam, Sebastian and Szymon walked out of the hall together.

'How are you feeling?' Piotr said, looking at Szymon.

'Pretty battered, but pretty good too.'

'That's what we like to hear. So you want to keep training with us? Your level's good. Especially for someone who's been out for a while.'

'Definitely.'

'OK. Bring your ID in next session and we'll do the usual checks. And it's £10 a month to help cover the church hall fees. Is that OK with you?'

'Yes Sabum.'

Piotr crouched down, produced a notebook out of his training bag and held it out. 'Actually, to speed things up a bit, write your full name and date of birth in here will you? And you don't have to call me Sabum out of the dojang. Call me Piotr.'

'OK,' said Szymon. He jotted down his details and left to catch a bus with Jan. Adam and Sebastian drove off shortly afterwards in Adam's van.

Piotr locked the door and the black belts walked down a small road to the side of a church, which hid the hall from the main road.

'Listen, sorry about being late,' said Kris.

'Don't worry about it,' said Piotr.

'Did you have to give me that punishment though? I really was stuck in traffic. And I texted you.'

'What do you mean? Everyone has to do their exercises if

---

they're late.'

'Yeah, but come on, I'm second in command now.'

'Even more reason then,' said Piotr. 'You know the rules.'

'You could have cut me some slack. It was the first session back.'

'What was I supposed to do? Late is late. I'd expect the same treatment myself. And I expect you guys to do the same if I'm not here to take a session too.'

They reached Kris' car, which was parked on the main road in front of the church. Before Kris got in, Piotr said, 'We're going to grab a couple of beers, want to come along?'

'I can't. I have to go shopping with Magda. I'll see you on Monday.' Kris gripped hands with them both, jumped into the driver's seat and drove off, playing with the dial on his radio.

Piotr and Jacek took the bus back to Piotr's home. Piotr went inside to drop his bag off and had a quick shower while Jacek bought four Polish beers from a local store. He waited there until Piotr caught back up with him. He had a Yorkshire terrier with him. 'My Aunt's not in. He needed to get out,' said Piotr.

'Hey Gapczo,' said Jacek, bending down and ruffling the dog's hair. The dog stood up on his hind legs and put his paws on Jacek's knees. Jacek let him lick his face.

They walked for about a mile and a half, passing an underground station on their way until they reached the top of a hill, which stood proudly in the middle of rows of residential streets.

They sat down on the grass with their beers and watched the planes coming in and out of Heathrow. Below them, suburbia sprawled out like a never-ending carpet of semi-detached houses, gardens and lines of cars, broken up by the occasional supermarket or industrial estate.

Piotr watched a plane come in to land. 'Can you make out where that one is from?' he said, holding his hand over his eyes to shield them from the sun.

Jacek took a sip of his beer. 'They're too far away.'

'I think it's a LOT. You ever been on a LOT?'

'Nope. Only Air Polonia.'

'They went bust didn't they?'

'Can't say I'm surprised.'

The warm haze of the day drifted over them. Some children

were playing football behind them. One of them let out a loud cry and put his T-shirt over his head to celebrate scoring a goal. Piotr and Jacek both turned their necks to look at him. Gapczo lifted his head up off the ground to see what was going on as well, but soon put it back down. Piotr scratched Gapczo's belly as he closed his eyes and rubbed his back against the grass.

Jacek laughed at the kid, but when he turned back around he grimaced and held his shoulder.

'Still got that injury?' said Piotr.

'Didn't help today with Kris getting me with that crescent kick,' said Jacek. He placed his cold bottle against the back of his neck.

'You need to rest it.'

'Maybe I'll take it a bit easier at the gym.'

They sat for a few moments in silence, drinking, then Piotr said, 'So are you going to start training regularly again? I was being serious earlier. We need as many black belts as we can get.'

'I'll try my best. But I've got all my commitments at the gym. You know how it is. I need to do as many shifts as I can at the moment. Otherwise I'll never save enough for that flat deposit. Plus Monika says I'm not spending enough time with her and the kid. When things settle and I've got more cash I'll train more. I guarantee it.' Jacek held his bottle out and Piotr touched it with his. They drained their beers.

'Kris seemed pretty pissed off,' said Jacek. 'Don't you think it's best to keep him sweet for a bit?'

'Are you getting paranoid about him again?' said Piotr, shielding his eyes from the sun as he tried to look at another plane. 'What's he going to do? Turn up late and then whisper some crap to the students. So what? They know I'm the Sabum. He can't do anything.'

'I'm not paranoid. I just don't want something to happen like it did with Guzik.'

'That was completely different.'

'Was it?'

'Yes. It was. He didn't want anything to do with running the dojang. He wanted to take students away from us. Kris loves being part of it. He has new ideas, that's all. None of which will ever see light while I'm here.'

Piotr squinted, trying to make out the name of the airline that was coming in to land. 'Anyway,' he said. 'I've got more important things to worry about.'

'Like what?'

'Well, now that you've mentioned Guzik.'

'They wouldn't try anything again, would they?'

Piotr scratched Gapczo's chin. 'Who knows.'

'What, have you been warned or something?'

'It's nothing like that. But they must know I'm in charge by now. I get this feeling that something's brewing for some reason. It's making me edgy.'

'Maybe they want to see what happens. Wait it out. Make sure we stay out of their business. That's all they want us to do, right?'

'I don't know.'

Jacek took two new beers out of the bag. 'Ready for another one?'

'Sure brother. I'm not a communist.'

Jacek picked up his pocketknife which was lying on the grass next to him and flicked one of the blades open. He took the tops off two bottles and handed one to Piotr.

They drank and watched the planes for a bit longer. When they finished their beers Jacek stood up, rubbing his neck again. 'Right. I have to get back and go fix a washing machine for one of Monika's friends. Then she's cooking me pierogi.'

'You still haven't got me her recipe for her meat ones you know. Doesn't she want shares in Porski's?

'I'll get it for you today. Then you can give me a 25% share when you float on the stock market.' He picked up the empty bottles and put them in the plastic bag. 'In the meantime, getting back to reality, don't forget that we're going out tonight.'

'We are?'

'We're celebrating the opening of the new hall, remember?'

'Where are we going?'

'The Redback. Where else?'

They parted ways at the bottom of the hill. Piotr walked through a park on his way home. He passed three young men sitting on some swings in a children's playground, smoking and chatting. They had a Staffordshire bull terrier with them. It was running around freely. It saw Gapczo and ran straight towards him. Piotr could sense his aggression. He picked up Gapczo and walked on with him in his arms, but the dog kept circling them, barking. One of the men by the swings shouted at the dog.

'Bruno! Get back here. Now!'

It ignored him and kept prowling next to Piotr.

The owner shouted again, swearing at the dog. 'Now, I said.' The dog hesitated for a second and then ran back. Piotr watched it return to the swings.

The owner said, 'What are you staring at?'

'At your dog. You should kept it on a lead.'

'Piss off, gypo. I'll do what I want with my mutt,' he said, turning his back.

Piotr put Gapczo back down on the ground, stroking his hair gently as he did so. 'Hey, it's OK,' he said. 'Good boy.'

As he unravelled Gapczo's lead from his arm, he glanced back at the men. They were busy talking to each other and laughing about something. Piotr had a feeling that it was about him.

THEY HAD TO QUEUE UP to get into the club. After standing in line for ten minutes in the same spot, Piotr went to buy some beer.

When he got back he handed Jacek a can. 'Couldn't you have got something a bit stronger?' said Jacek, reading the label.

'It was on offer.'

'But it tastes like piss.'

'Just drink it,' said Piotr. 'You can't even tell the difference.'

Jacek opened his can. The beer frothed up out of it. He held the can to his mouth and tried to drink the beer, but most of it spilt onto his shirt. He wiped his mouth with his sleeve.

'What the hell's wrong with you?' said Piotr. 'Have you been on it all afternoon?'

'Monika's friend gave me a couple of cans after I fixed her washing machine. You know how it is.'

'A couple? Maybe you need to ease up a bit.'

'I feel fine,' said Jacek, taking a big gulp of beer. 'Oh by the way,' he said, handing Piotr a piece of paper. 'Here's the recipe for the pierogi.'

'Thanks,' said Piotr, looking at it briefly and putting it into the pocket of his jeans. He stuck his head out of the queue to see whether there was any movement at the entrance. 'Do you reckon we'll be in before the band starts?'

'We've got plenty of time,' said Jacek, inspecting the marketing material on the back of the beer can. 'Hey, it says here that you can win a pick up truck if you get three of these red coloured tabs from a can. Maybe we should start drinking this stuff regularly.'

'You sure you only had a couple? You sound like you've had a whole barrel,' said Piotr. 'That offer is only for people living in Poland.'

'Right,' said Jacek, looking at the can again. 'No wonder it was cheap.'

When they got in, they went straight to the bar and ordered four beers. They were being sold at half their usual price until 10.

'I can't stand this Aussie stuff either,' said Jacek as they sipped their drinks by the bar. 'Weak.'

Piotr chuckled. 'Why don't you bring your own beer next time.'

A man in a tight rugby shirt approached the bar and ordered a large round of beers.

'Seen the size of this chief?' said Jacek. 'He could give Pudzianowski a run for his money.'

Piotr looked over at the man and the group of friends he was with. They were all wearing rugby shirts as well. Some of them were chest bumping each other.

'I'd say they've drunk about as much as you have already,' said Piotr.

'Hey, did you see his fight?' said Jacek.

'Whose?'

'Pudzianowski's.'

'No, I didn't. The guy should stick to lifting rocks and pulling trucks. He's an embarrassment.'

'He's in great shape though. And aggressive as hell. Plus he's picked up some skills. He did a lot more than in his first fight, I'm telling you.'

'What, more than running after a guy half his size, trying to kick his legs to bits while almost breaking his own, and then pounding his head into the canvas?' said Piotr. 'He's a freakshow.'

They drank their beers and Jacek ordered two more, alongside two double vodkas, which were also half their normal price. 'Might as well get our money's worth,' he said. He raised one of the shot glasses. 'To the new hall.' They touched glasses and downed one of the vodkas.

Jacek raised his second vodka. 'To your time as Sabum.'

'Cheers,' said Piotr. They drank the second vodkas as the band appeared on stage. The guitarist started the opening chords of a rock song they both knew. Piotr tapped his foot to the music.

They grabbed their beers and made their way closer to the stage, along with half the people in the club. Some of them stuck their arms in the air, a few started headbanging. Within seconds, Piotr and Jacek felt themselves being pushed further towards the band. The juddering sound of the bass guitar made its way from the floor up to Piotr's stomach. Jacek was shoved from behind by someone and spilt some beer on his wrist. He quickly sucked it up and then took another sip from his bottle.

'Awesome song,' he shouted into Piotr's ear. 'Did I tell you they're on YouTube?'

Piotr shook his head. The frontman spread his arms, soaking up the adoration of the crowd.

Piotr noticed three bouncers move to their usual spots when a band was playing. He had seen them do it numerous times. One of them took a position on a balcony on the right, to get an overall view of the dance space, while the other two stood at the back of the crowd, ready to move at any sign of trouble.

They stayed in the same place for six songs, after which the band went off for a break. A DJ to the side of the stage began playing some music.

Jacek elbowed Piotr. 'You want to talk to some girls?'

'OK,' said Piotr, noticing that the bouncers were on the move.

'Let's get some more beer first.'

'I thought you said you didn't like the beer.'

'I won't get the Aussie stuff this time.'

Jacek came back with two bottles of a South American beer Piotr had never heard of. He guided Piotr towards a corner of the club.

They stopped near four girls who were dancing together. Jacek asked one of them where they were from.

'They live in Willesden,' he said in Piotr's ear. 'One of them's South African and the one with the dark skin is from Mexico. The other two are from New Zealand.'

'One of them's a teacher. You know what that means?'

'No,' said Piotr, smiling at the girls.

'She'll be into kinky stuff. Trust me.'

When the band started up again, Jacek began dancing with the girls. He held his arms high above his head. Piotr kept smiling and sipping his beer. He leaned over to the Mexican girl and asked her if she had ever heard of the beer he was drinking.

'It's Argentinian,' she said, looking at him briefly, before turning to look at the stage again.

'Right,' said Piotr. 'You don't like Argentinian beer?'

'No, it's fine. My boyfriend is Argentinian. He drinks it a lot.'

Piotr joined in as they all continued moving to the music, along with most of the rest of the club. It was getting humid inside and Piotr felt some beads of sweat slide down his back.

When the band's singer announced another break, Jacek grabbed Piotr's arm. 'We need more drinks, and so do the girls.'

'What are we going to buy them with? I've only got ten pounds left. And it's past happy hour.'

'Here,' Jacek stuffed a twenty pound note in Piotr's hand. 'They're drinking those vodka lemonade things.'

Piotr flattened out the crumpled note. 'You got a pay rise at work or something?'

'Just take it.'

'I'm going to the toilet to cool down a bit first. Then I'll get the drinks.'

Piotr had to wait in line outside the toilet. When he got in, he stood at the far end of the group urinal. Some of the men in rugby shirts that he had seen at the bar were there. They all spoke with what sounded like Australian accents. They were shoulder barging each other while relieving themselves. One of them almost tripped over and bumped into another man. His stream hit the floor and his shoes. He swore at the rugby shirt who had knocked him sideways. The rugby men all erupted with laughter. Piotr finished as quickly as he could and went to the sink. He splashed his face with water and put his wrists under a cold tap, while watching the rugby shirts in the mirror. He decided he'd had enough alcohol for one night.

When he got back with the drinks, Jacek was even closer to the girls, and was talking to one of them. One of the rugby shirts was standing next to Jacek. He had a thick beard and was leaning down to talk to the Mexican girl. He had placed his hand on her upper arm. A bulging vein protruded from his large bicep.

'Sorry mate,' Piotr said as he squeezed past the man, clutching the bottles close to his chest. He handed some of the bottles of vodka mix to the girls and then pulled out a beer and a bottle of water that he had tucked into his belt. 'Hold these,' he said to Jacek.

He then took the last vodka mix drink out of his back pocket and reached over the man talking to the Mexican girl. 'Hey, here's your drink,' he said.

'Thanks,' she said, smiling at him. The bearded man ignored him.

'I think she's got her hands full with that rugby guy,' Piotr said to Jacek.

'His meathead teammates are all on the hunt as well,' said Jacek, pointing his bottle at some of the rugby shirts behind Piotr. They were talking to some other girls. 'They're all smashed as well.'

'I know, I saw them in the pisser.' Piotr glanced over his shoulder at them. 'Probably best to keep our distance.'

'You not drinking anymore?' Jacek said.

'I've lost my taste for it.'

'Fair enough.'

Jacek tapped one of the girls on the arm. 'Hey, listen,' he said in English. 'Alice doesn't believe that you're Polish.' The girl tipped her head back and smiled at Piotr.

'Why not?'

'Why do you think? Because she says you don't look it, that's why,' he said.

'Do you want me to show you my driving licence?' said Piotr. He took his wallet out of his pocket and found it.

'There you go,' said Jacek, pointing at the licence. 'It says he was born in Radom. See? That's like 100 miles south of Warsaw. You can't get more Polish. It's right in the middle of the country.'

'You guys are hilarious,' said the girl, giggling.

The DJ announced that the band would be back on in ten minutes. Two of the girls said they had to go to the toilet. They asked the Mexican girl if she wanted to go with them. 'OK,' she said.

'Hang on,' said the rugby player who had been talking to her, 'give us a cuddle before you go.'

The girl pushed his arms away playfully and tried to walk off with her friends, but the man pulled her back. She pushed him away again, but he held onto her waist.

'Come on babe. One cuddle, that's all,' he said.

Jacek cupped the bearded man's elbow. 'Let her go,' he said, in English.

'I'm only trying to get a cuddle mate,' said the man, reaching out behind her with his other arm.

Jacek, now in front of the man, put a hand on his chest. 'No, she wants to be left alone. Can't you see?'

'Piss off mate, what are you? Her father?' The man let go of the girl and shoved Jacek back. Regaining his balance, Jacek stepped forward and punched the rugby shirt, hard, in the solar plexus. He doubled over in pain.

Piotr rushed to Jacek, shielding him from the man's incoming teammates.

'What was that dickhead?' said one of the rugby players. He was flanked by six companions. He spread his arms out wide. Jutting his shaved head forward, he towered over them.

'He started it,' said Jacek.

The man with the shaved head stepped in closer, trying to get to Jacek. Piotr mirrored his steps, closing off his route.

'Calm down, mate,' Piotr said, noticing the man's large cauliflower ears.

The man got within a few inches of Piotr's face. 'You calm down. Mate!'

A few specks of his spittle hit Piotr's face. Piotr kept his position, looking back at Jacek to make sure that he hadn't moved anywhere.

'It's OK,' he said. 'It's a misunderstanding. We don't want any trouble.'

One of the other rugby players said, 'You two better get out of here before we tear you a new one.' He was smaller than the man with the shaved head, but more muscular.

'We're going, OK?' said Piotr, checking to see if any more of the rugby team were nearby. He had already counted nine of them.

Piotr walked backwards, trying to take Jacek with him, but Jacek brushed his hand away.

'Hey,' said Piotr. He held his friend by the back of the neck and put his index finger up to his face. 'That's enough.'

As he pushed Jacek backwards, a bottle flew past Piotr's head. He turned to see if anything else was about to come hurtling towards them. The rugby shirts were motioning at them to return and fight. Jacek picked up a half full plastic pint of beer off a drinks table next to him and launched it at the rugby shirts. It hit one of them.

Three of the rugby shirts rushed forwards before Piotr had a chance to react. He heard one of the girls scream and felt his feet come off the ground. The rugby player who had picked him up rotated before throwing Piotr as far as he could. Piotr broke his fall, rolling as he made contact with the floor, which was all sticky from spilt beer. He stood up again straight away, looking for Jacek.

The bearded man, who was now back on his feet, had joined the man with the shaved head and another of their companions. They were throwing wild punches at Jacek and trying to rugby tackle him. Jacek aimed a back kick at one of the men, but missed and lost his balance. Lying on his back, he managed to strike one of the rugby shirts in the knee, forcing him to buckle and giving himself the split second he needed to scramble to his feet.

Most of the people on the dance floor had stopped dancing or talking to watch the fight. As the bearded man swung another punch at Jacek, he stepped to the side, blocking his arm, grabbing his hand and twisting his wrist into a lock.

Five bouncers burst through the crowd. Two of them got hold of the bearded man and marched him towards the exit, while the other three got hold of Jacek and the man with the shaved head. Another two bouncers rushed in behind them and stood in front of the rest of the rugby shirts.

Piotr said, 'It's OK, he's my friend. We're leaving.'

'Has he got a jacket?' said one of the bouncers.

'Jacket? No, no jacket,' said Piotr.

'How about you? Have you got a jacket?' the same bouncer asked Piotr.

Piotr shook his head.

'I didn't do anything,' said Jacek, when they reached the cloakroom near the exit.

'Nobody ever does,' said another bouncer in a black bomber jacket by the door. He was chewing some gum. He had earrings in both ears and no neck, as far as Piotr could tell.

He poked a fat finger in Piotr and Jacek's direction. 'You're barred.'

When they were outside, Piotr said, 'You want to tell me what that was about?'

Jacek pointed at the entrance to the Redback. 'What? Are you being serious? Did you not see what happened in there? I was protecting that girl.'

'Protecting her? You don't even know her.'

'That chief was harassing her.'

'Come off it. It was harmless,' said Piotr.

The bouncer at the door shouted out at the two of them. 'If you don't get out of here we're calling the police.'

They started walking down the street.

'What the hell were you thinking?' said Piotr.

'Oh come on Piotrek, you're losing your touch. We could have taken those guys. I had two of them down before you even got up.'

Piotr stopped walking. 'You think, eh? You've got no idea. There were probably at least fifteen of them and a load of bouncers. Plus you were in trouble. One of them was about to strangle you before the bouncers jumped in. So not only was it totally uncalled for, it was reckless too. You've only been away a few months and you've forgotten the first oath already?'

'They threw a bottle at us.'

'So what? You walk away. Anyway, you started it all with the bearded guy.'

'That girl looked like she needed some help, you've got to admit that.'

'She was fine.'

'Did you see that lock I put on that meathead though? Smooth as anything.'

'Whatever. Did you get hurt?'

'Not a scratch. You?'

'Don't think so. Come on, you need some food.'

They crossed the road and walked towards a kebab house.

'So how do you know there were fifteen of them?' Jacek said.

'I'm guessing, but that's the number they have on a rugby team.'

'What about subs? And they could have been a rugby league team. They have 13 players, not 15.'

'What the hell is rugby league?' said Piotr.

The kebab house was busy. Jacek sat down and Piotr ordered two doner kebabs and two cans of soft drink.

A man in front of him had just been given his kebab over the counter. He was wearing a replica shirt of a local football team. He was swaying as he fumbled in the pocket of his jeans, before fishing out some money and handing it over. The assistant behind the counter gave him some change. As the man tried to put the coins back in his pocket, he tilted his kebab and half the contents spilt over onto the counter. He started picking the meat off the counter and eating it.

Another man behind the assistant was cutting slices off a large rotating piece of kebab meat. He laughed at the man in the football shirt. 'He's hungrier than a dog,' he said.

As Piotr was about to pay, he saw two of the rugby shirts walk in.

Piotr checked to see if Jacek had noticed. He was sitting down on one of the stools facing the wall. He was mumbling something to himself, with his head in one hand and his phone in the other, trying to type a text message.

One of the rugby players elbowed the other one, gesturing at Piotr. Piotr braced himself. A clattering noise broke his concentration.

Jacek was on the floor, his legs up in the air. He lay there for a second, motionless. Piotr went over to him and Jacek started laughing. Piotr shook his head, while the kebab shop workers and some of the customers jeered.

The rugby players were holding their stomachs, howling. Piotr couldn't help but join in.

He hoisted Jacek to his feet, and the rugby men came over. They asked if he was OK. They all shook hands and agreed that they had acted like idiots in the club. The rugby players ordered their food and they sat down to eat together.

'How did you get so wasted man?' one of them asked Jacek. 'You been on the lash all day?'

'He's a lightweight,' said Piotr.

The rugby players were Kiwis. One was called Dan, the other Brett. 'Typical Kiwi names, bro', said Dan.

Piotr didn't think he'd ever met a Kiwi before. Jacek asked them if they knew his second cousin, Bartek, who had left Poland to live in New Zealand three years ago. They told him that millions of people lived in New Zealand.

Brett took a bite out of a green chilli and aimed it at Jacek. 'Where did you learn to fight like that?'

'Here and there. What about you guys. You know any styles?'

Dan swallowed a large mouthful of kebab meat and shook his head.

'Nah man, we don't need that kung fu stuff. We've got the haka.' He leaned forward and stuck his tongue out.

His eyes looked as if they were going to pop out of his head.

PIOTR HEARD HIS AUNT come in through the front door. Her perfume entered the living room before she did.

He stopped doing his stomach crunches and turned down the volume on the TV. She walked into the room and squinted at the MMA fight on the screen.

'Are you watching that silly fighting again?'

'Hi Auntie,' said Piotr. 'It's just a replay of a fight from last night. There's nothing else on. How was church?'

'Very good, thank you. There was a baptism, which is always lovely to see.'

She took her gloves off and put her handbag on the sofa, before adjusting her headscarf and taking her watch off. 'I need to get on with the soup.'

'Anything I can help with?'

'No love, I'm OK. I need to keep on my feet. You can do the washing after dinner,' she said, walking into the kitchen.

Piotr stood up and got into a low horse stance. He sat in it for a couple of minutes and then began slowly shuffling his feet away from himself, moving into a side split position. He was almost in a full split until he could spread no further. He bent forwards and clenched his fists, pressing them against the carpet while tensing his adductor and thigh muscles as hard as he could for five seconds. A second later, he spread his legs a little further. He repeated the process until he was in a full split position. Then, holding the position, he tensed the muscles for a full 20 seconds.

His Aunt poked her head around the door. 'Do you want me to cook some extra sausage so that you can take it to work tomorrow?'

'Sure, why not. Thanks.'

'OK, I'll put them in then and come and sit down.'

When she returned, Piotr said, 'Do you want me to change the channel?

'No, don't worry dear.'

'When are we eating?'

'In about half an hour.'

Piotr sat down on the sofa next to her. 'Don't forget your medication before we eat. You didn't take it yesterday. I checked.'

'I know. It's like I'm losing my mind sometimes. I get so tired, that's why I forget.'

'I thought the tiredness was supposed to stop when the chemo was done.'

'Well, I can barely keep my eyes open sometimes.'

The fight was over and the programme had switched to some men in suits in a TV studio.

'I've been meaning to ask you,' said Piotr's Aunt. 'What do you think of the new church hall?'

'It's great. Father Leopold has done it up really nicely. He gave me a tour before training. Seems like a good guy too.'

'Does he?'

'Sure. Why do you say that?'

'I don't know what to make of him yet, that's all.'

Piotr switched off the television and set the table. When dinner was ready his Aunt came in with the soup and said, 'I spoke to Mr. Stablinski in the cafeteria today. He's still got that vacancy open at his firm. I told him I would mention it to you again.'

'Right,' said Piotr, sprinkling some pepper on his soup.

'He's a good man, you know. He would be a fair boss.'

His Aunt said grace and they began to eat. She brought out some salad with the main course. Piotr spooned some of it onto his plate. 'Did you put sugar on this Auntie?'

She peered into the bowl and dabbed her finger onto a salad leaf. 'Goodness me, so I did.' She licked her finger. 'I don't know what made me do it. I must have not been thinking. I'll go and prepare some more.'

'No, don't,' said Piotr. 'There's no need to make another lot. If Uncle liked it, then it's probably not that bad.'

They ate in silence while Piotr thought about his Uncle. A picture of him sat on top of a cabinet by the TV. His big smile shone down on them.

Piotr woke up early the next morning. He went straight to the bathroom and tried to avoid urinating into the pool of water in the toilet. He put the lid down before gently pulling the flush.

He washed his hands with equal care, not turning the tap on full, as he was worried that the old pipes would rumble into life. Looking in the mirror, he noticed that the bags under his eyes were darker than usual. He told himself that he would get some early nights during the week. He walked downstairs circling his head and rubbing his shoulders, making sure that he missed the three creaky steps that were in the middle of the staircase.

He put the kettle on and went into the living room. Pulling a chair from under the table, he put his right hand on the backrest, with the seat facing away from him. Turning his body to the side of the chair, he started swinging his left leg up into the air, in a controlled motion. He did the same on his right and then repeated it on both sides. With the water boiled, he poured some into a mug with two heaped teaspoons of instant coffee. As he waited for it to cool, he performed some slow motion kicks at various targets in the kitchen. His toes almost touched a calendar hanging from the wall. It had a picture of John Paul II on it. He was waving to a huge crowd inside a sports stadium and holding a silver papal staff. It had a crooked cross on the end of it.

Once he had drunk his coffee and eaten some toast, he grabbed a bag with two large cooked sausages in it, some bread, and an apple. He put them all in a plastic shopping bag. He then went back upstairs and brushed his teeth as quietly as he could. He sprayed some antiperspirant on his armpits and then put on a T-shirt and jeans. Thirty seconds later he was out of the front door, heading for the bus stop.

Piotr sat upstairs on the double decker bus, in his usual spot. He took his earphones out of his jacket and plugged them into his MP3 player. He stuffed his hands into his jacket and listened to the music.

Two Somalian men who usually caught the bus at the same time as Piotr sat near the front of the bus. They were dressed as if they worked at a supermarket. They always sat together and talked to each other in low voices, as if in deep discussion. Piotr wondered what they were talking about. Football? Women? Maybe they were discussing politics, or even philosophy. He had heard that people came over to England from places like Africa with medical and engineering degrees, but had to work in shops or as taxi drivers, because their English wasn't good enough, or their qualifications weren't recognised in the UK.

When he got to the car wash, the gate was still shut. A couple of the guys, Dennis and Andrzej, were waiting outside, leaning against the makeshift fence that bordered the car wash. Both of them had a can of strong beer in their hands. They were from Ukraine, and Piotr could converse with them in a Slavic-English hybrid dialect.

They were hungover. Andrzej's brother had come to visit. They had not seen him in over a year and had drunk two bottles of vodka to celebrate.

'Is it working?' said Piotr, nodding at one of the cans.

'Does it every time, for me,' said Dennis, sipping some beer.

Andrzej was reading the sports pages of a newspaper. 'Heard the news?' he said.

'What's that?' said Piotr.

'Your manager. He might drop your keeper for the friendly at Wembley. You know, the one who plays for Arsenal.'

'He probably wants to give someone else a chance before the Euros.'

'Think we'll both make the final?' said Dennis. 'I mean, we are the joint hosts and everything.'

'Not the way we're playing,' said Andrzej. 'Our strikers wouldn't be able to score in a brothel right now.' He crushed his empty can under his heavy boot.

The owner of the car wash turned up just as Dennis finished his beer. He was wearing the same Chicago Cubs T-shirt that he had worn when Piotr had first met him. He said hello to the three of them without looking up as he walked over to open the gate to the site. He wore some stubble and his hair was unkempt.

'What's this whoring branch doing in front of our sign?' he said. He climbed the fence by the gate and started pulling at the branch.

'Don't all help at once,' he said, struggling with it.

Dennis scrambled up the fence and grabbed the branch at another end. They both pulled it until it snapped. Dennis dragged it down and stamped on it, breaking it into three pieces.

'Piotr,' said the owner. 'Give that sign a clean before we open up will you?'

'Sure,' said Piotr.

The owner had some buckets in the back of his car.

'What's with the buckets?' said Andrzej.

The owner searched for a key from a bundle he had fixed to his belt. 'They're from the Northolt site. I shut it down yesterday.'

'How come?' said Dennis.

'How come? Because there's too little work coming in. That's how come. I made the decision last night when I went there to collect the week's earnings. Down again. For the sixteenth week in a row. Sixteenth. I couldn't believe it.'

He pushed the gates open and walked towards the cabin. 'I had to cut the deadwood before it started affecting everything else.'

Piotr fetched a ladder and scrubbed the sign with some soapy water. When he was done he took a moment to check that there were no marks on it.

Dr. Car Wash
No vehicle too dirty – let the doctor heal your car so that it looks brand new!

The owner stayed in his makeshift cabin for most of the morning. When Piotr walked passed it and peered in he could see him stooped over his desk, studying some papers and sipping a cup of coffee.

Later, when there was a lull in their work, Piotr went out with Dennis to get something to eat. As they walked down the road towards a parade of shops, Piotr rubbed his left shoulder and swung his arms forwards and backwards, trying to get some of the soreness out of them.

When they were getting closer to the shops, they crossed the road. The traffic was stationary and some drivers were sounding their car horns.

'The Sheriff must be out directing the traffic again,' said Dennis.

They went around a corner. Twenty metres ahead, a man wearing a big blue ski jacket, grey combat trousers and Doc Marten boots was standing in the middle of the road, waving his arms frantically in every possible direction, with a large smile on his face. He kept turning to face the traffic on both sides of the road.

A black man towards the front of the line of traffic got out of his SUV and started walking towards the Sheriff. He was wearing a baggy T-shirt and a thick gold watch. Piotr studied his body language. He didn't think that he was going to ask the Sheriff to get off the road politely. Piotr nudged Dennis. 'We'd better hurry up,' he said.

They got to the Sheriff before the man reached him.

'What are you doing on the road again Gandhi?' the black man said, pointing at the Sheriff. He had two studs in his ears and a large gold ring on his right hand.

'It's OK. I know him,' Dennis said, in English. He put one hand on the Sheriff's shoulder, and another on his forearm, leading him towards the pavement. Piotr followed behind them.

Dennis said to him, 'Hey Sheriff, come on, you're doing a great job today mate, great job. But you must be tired now, eh? Don't you want a break? Come on, we can get some tea.'

'That's right. Get Gandhi off the road before I run him over,' said the man in the suit.

'It's OK, we've got it,' Piotr said. 'He can't help it.'

'He should be in a spastic home or something,' said the man. 'He's always pulling the same stunt, holding up the road.'

Piotr stood still, facing the SUV driver. 'It's OK, he's moving now, see?'

The man kissed his teeth and went back to his car. He pressed hard on the accelerator before releasing his handbrake and speeding off.

Dennis ushered the Sheriff onto the side of the street and sat him down on a bench at a bus stop. Piotr put his hands up apologetically at some of the cars that had been waiting as they drove by.

'You want some tea Sheriff?' said Dennis.

'Takeaway,' said The Sheriff in a thick accent, shoving two pound coins into Dennis' hand while staring straight ahead at the dispersing traffic.

Dennis checked the money. 'OK. But don't move from here until we get back. Understand?'

They went into a café right behind the bus stop and ordered a tea in a polystyrene cup and some sandwiches for themselves.

Dennis handed the tea to the Sheriff with some sachets of sugar and small milk pots. Piotr gave him his change. The Sheriff prepared his tea and then put it down on the ground. He took a cigarette out of his jacket pocket and a box of matches from another. He put the cigarette deep into his mouth, so that most of the filter disappeared from view, and lit it. Piotr and Dennis stood next to the bench.

The Sheriff puffed away on the cigarette, without taking much of a break between inhalations, as if he was scared that someone would take it away from him. When he had smoked about two-thirds of it he threw it on the ground and stamped it out. He then picked it up and put the remains in the pocket of his jacket.

'What you drive?' he said, sticking his middle finger out towards Piotr.

'What do I drive?' said Piotr, looking at the Sheriff's long yellow nails. 'I don't have a car right now. I just wash them. Down there, at the car wash,' he said, thumbing in its direction.

The Sheriff slurped his tea and grunted. 'You should be careful when you drive.'

'Right,' said Piotr.

The Sheriff took his glasses off and looked at Piotr, before putting them back on. 'You need to protect yourself from people who drive too fast,' he said. He scratched his grey stubble and sipped some more tea as he turned away from Piotr to watch the traffic again.

Dennis circled his forefinger next to his temple.

'Well, when I get a car I'll take it steady. I promise,' said Piotr.

The Sheriff wagged his finger at Piotr but kept looking at the road. 'You can't be too careful,' he said. 'You can get killed on the roads if you don't watch out. If you don't look ahead of you. And behind you.'

Dennis checked his watch. 'We need to get back,' he said to Piotr. He bent over to look at the Sheriff. 'Are you going to be alright?'

The Sheriff lifted his cup up. 'No problem.'

'Don't go out on that road again, OK?' said Dennis.

'German cars. They're they worst,' said the Sheriff.

On their way back Piotr said, 'I must have told him that I don't drive about five times now. But he keeps telling me the same thing. Why does he do it?'

'Don't worry,' said Dennis. 'You aren't that special. He says crazy stuff to everyone.'

The owner was standing in the entrance to his cabin when they got back. He had some bank statements in his hands. 'Where have you two been? You're late. Only 15 minutes break,' he said.

Piotr looked at Dennis, who then looked at his watch. 'Only one minute late, sorry boss. We were helping the Sheriff.'

'Are you car washers or social workers?' said the owner. 'I pay

32

you to clean cars, not help out mental home crazies. If you want to help people then go join a seminary or something. And don't call me boss. Some of the patients might hear.'

'Sorry Doc,' said Dennis.

Towards the end of the day, after the rush hour run had died down, Piotr and Dennis cleaned the buckets and brushes together.

'Sheriff had a close call with that drug dealer, eh?' said Dennis.

'Drug dealer?'

'Yeah, you know, the guy in the SUV.'

'What makes you think he was a drug dealer?'

'Come on man, he may as well have tattooed his job title on his forehead. You saw how he was acting, didn't you? He was into some dodgy stuff, no doubt about it. He stepped away from you quick enough though. What did you do, let one off when he was near you?'

'You're only saying that because he was black.'

'No I'm not.'

'Are you sure?'

'Listen. If I saw a white guy or an Arab, or whoever, come out of a car like he did, with all his bling or whatever it is the hip hop guys call it, I would say the same thing. Sorry, but I say it how I see it. You saw the way he was and what he was wearing. It didn't look to me like he was on his way to a sales meeting.'

'He could be anyone. We don't know.'

Piotr grabbed the clean buckets and took them over to the cabin. He stacked them and dropped them on the floor. When he walked back to where Dennis was, he kept his eyes away from him, wiping his hands on a towel.

'Listen, Piotr, I'm sorry,' he said. 'I didn't mean to. You know.'

'Forget it,' Piotr said.

When he got home his Aunt was in the kitchen, chopping up vegetables. The smell of browning beef filled his nostrils. His stomach rumbled. His Aunt stuck her head out of the kitchen.

'Piotrusz?'

'Hi Auntie,' he said, looking in the mirror at a large sweat patch on the back of his T-shirt where his rucksack had been.

He put on fresh clothes in his room. Taking his dobok out of his cupboard, he carefully placed it into his training bag. He then took his folded black belt off the bedside table and placed it on top of his dobok. He zipped the bag up and picked up his training notebook, which he had left on his bed that morning. Before he went back downstairs, he switched on his laptop and opened up an email account. It had one message in it. He opened it, read it twice, and deleted it.

When he came back downstairs he placed his notebook on his bag by the front door and walked into the kitchen. He picked up a couple of carrot pieces and popped them in his mouth.

'The stew smells amazing,' he said, reaching for a glass from a cupboard and filling it with cold water from the tap.

'You can have some when you come back from your training,' said his Aunt. 'I saw this lovely braising steak at the butcher's. I thought it was best to stock up. There's plenty in the freezer.'

Piotr used a wooden spoon near the stew pot to try some of the sauce. His Aunt flicked her tea towel at him. 'Get out of there,' she said. 'It's not ready yet.'

Piotr put his hands up. 'Sorry, couldn't resist. How are you feeling today anyway?'

'I had a nap this afternoon. I've got some energy now.'

'That's good. Just leave any dishes. I'll do them when I get back.'

ZIGGY WAS SITTING ON THE CAR PARK WALL outside the dojang, listening to music through some large headphones.

'You're early,' Piotr said.

Ziggy pulled his headphones off. 'I'm down on the cleaning rota for this week.'

'Good that you remembered.' Piotr grabbed his large bundle of keys out of his training bag and unlocked the door.

Inside, he turned a winch handle to open some windows that separated the walls from the ceiling. Ziggy began moving some chairs and tables that had been left out in the middle of the hall. Piotr took a broom out of the kitchen. Ziggy stopped when he saw Piotr sweeping.

'What's the matter?' said Piotr.

'I thought you didn't do any cleaning.'

'Class starts in 15 minutes. I'm helping you get it done a bit quicker.'

Once Piotr had swept the floor and Ziggy had moved all the chairs and tables to the back of the hall and stacked them, they washed the floor with hot water and some soap. Ziggy then got down on his knees and used a large cloth to dry the floor.

Piotr went to get changed. The only sound in the building was the jangling of Ziggy's bracelets and the occasional clunking noise his long silver chain made when it hit the floor as he dried it.

After a quick warm-up, Piotr instructed everyone to pad up and spar. He told them to try to catch their opponents with a shoulder or hip throw.

Szymon was too slow in avoiding a counter-attack from Sebastian and started bleeding from his nose. He went to the toilet to get cleaned up. He bowed to the hall before walking through the door, cupping his nose with his hands to prevent any blood from dripping onto the floor.

When Szymon came back in, he had some toilet paper rolled up his nostrils.

'Are you OK?' Piotr said.

'I think so.'

'You need to work on your footwork a bit.'

Piotr called Kris over. 'Get him to concentrate on his footwork will you? Hands behind his back to start with. Not too heavy with the strikes.'

He turned to Szymon. 'He's going to try and hit you. You've got to move out of the way, or into his way. If you get my drift.'

After class, Jan and Szymon approached Piotr.

'How's your nose?' said Piotr.

'It's OK. No major damage.' Szymon felt it as if he was checking to see if it was broken or not.

'So, what's up guys?'

'There's a tournament taking place in a few weeks,' said Jan, glancing at Szymon. 'We were wondering if we could enter.'

'A tournament?'

'It's open styles. Punches allowed to the head and sweeps. But no knees or elbows.'

'Sounds a bit boring,' said Piotr, smiling.

Szymon said, 'It's closed doors, invitation only. I've got a friend who could get us in.'

'You do, huh? What's got you interested in it?'

'We thought that it would be good to go to for the experience,' said Jan.

'What made you think that?'

'Well, I guess it's good to test yourself right? And it seems like the dojang isn't being called upon as much as it used to. So we thought that maybe you'd want us to keep sharp.'

'We keep sharp in here don't we?' said Piotr.

'Yeah, but this would be under a bit of pressure.'

'Do you want me to put more pressure on you?'

'It's not that, it's more about adrenaline I guess.'

'I know what you're saying, but you both know that the Kwan doesn't go in for that stuff.'

'We're itching to get some real action,' said Szymon. 'Like some other dojangs are doing.'

'You'll get some action, don't worry about that.' Piotr put his hands on the small of their backs and walked them towards the corridor. 'We can't talk anymore about this right now. I have to close up and speak to the bousabums. But if I was you, I'd forget about these sorts of fights. They're ugly. And the people who run them are even uglier.' He patted Szymon's shoulder. 'You get some ice on that nose.'

Piotr watched them walk away, thinking. When they left the hall he went to get changed in the kitchen with Kris and Jacek.

'What did they want?' Kris said.

'Some underground set-up they've been told about. They were asking if they could enter.'

'Where did they hear about that?'

'I didn't ask.'

Jacek sprayed some deodorant on his chest and armpits. 'So what did you say?'

'I told them they couldn't enter. What else was I going to say?'

'What if they go for it anyway?' said Kris.

'Then we'll probably know about it when they come in with black eyes or on crutches. Don't worry, they'll forget about it soon enough.'

Piotr took off his belt and started folding it up. 'I've heard some more news about those muggers at Greenford station,' he said.

'It's usually three guys. They wait until it's dark. Normal stuff, women on their own, anyone looking vulnerable. They've taken phones, jewellery, handbags. Flashed a blade a couple of times.'

'Another non-priority file?' said Kris.

'Looks like it. The police interviewed a couple of victims when they finally got to it. But it's still happening and there are still no coppers hanging around.'

'Our lot?' said Jacek.

'Two Polaks. And one Lithuanian they reckon. They're known. All three got involved in petty stuff back home.'

'What's the plan then?' said Jacek.

'Standard. They may be there tomorrow so we'll meet up. I'll text you the details.'

His Aunt placed a hot plate of stew in front of him. 'Here you are love.'

She was about to sit at the table, then she said, 'Oh, before I forget.' She went into the kitchen and came back with a small sheet of notepaper. 'Here's the number for Mr. Stablinski.'

She put it down it by his plate. 'I called earlier and he even gave me his mobile, so that you could contact him any time if you want. He'd be happy to hear from you.'

'Thanks,' said Piotr. He blowed hard on a spoonful of stew.

'He hinted that he couldn't keep the trainee position open for ever. He only mentioned it at the end of our conversation. We were talking about the next parish meeting. He works so close to here, it's only down the road. You could walk there and not have to get up so early. You could have a nice leisurely breakfast every morning.'

'I'll think about it Auntie.'

'Should I tell him that you'll call him then?'

'I don't know yet. Can I think about it a bit more?'

'Of course dear. But not everyone knows what is best for them you know. Sometimes you have to try something and give it a chance.'

Piotr took a slice of bread from a chopping board in the middle of the table and dipped it in the stew before taking a large bite out of it.

'You don't want to work at a car wash all your life, do you? This could be a great opening for you. There are thousands of young men who would jump at the chance to take this job.'

Piotr chewed slowly on a morsel of beef. 'You make it sound like he'd give me a job straight away.'

'Well, maybe he would. He's very keen to meet you.'

'I'm sure he is Auntie, and I don't mean to sound ungrateful, but I still want to do my own thing.'

'And you can still do that. Taking a job like this doesn't mean that you can't be you own boss one day. You're the one who's in charge of your career. It wouldn't be a prison sentence. Goodness, it could even help more than anything else. All that experience working with numbers and other businesses, seeing what is profitable, and what isn't.'

Piotr took some more bread and tore it up before dropping the piece into the stew.

'I don't know why you're so reluctant. You've got nothing to lose from talking to him.'

When he was finished Piotr went into the kitchen and washed the dishes. His Aunt followed him in and made some peppermint tea for herself.

'You know Auntie,' said Piotr, trying to squeeze out some

washing up liquid from a bottle. 'I'm not sure I want to do some sort of apprenticeship and be stuck having to take exams and all that stuff. I just want to set up my own business and get on with it that way. Then I can help run the dojang better, because I can pick and choose my hours, you know, have more freedom. I'll be able to devote far more time and resources to it once I'm up on my own feet.'

His Aunt took two tablets out of a small pot and swallowed them with a little water. 'Yes, but you may find that you have even less time for the dojang if you have to worry about a business,' she said.

'You only worry if you've got a bad plan or you're not making money. And the idea we've got has got a good chance to do well.'

'Selling food is not easy. Especially our type of food.'

'People like pierogi. They taste good. Plus lots of countries have similar dishes, so they can recognise them. They'd be a hit here in London.'

'Piotrusz, you've never even worked as a chef.'

'I know, but Henio has. And Jacek's given me the recipe that his sister uses. Her meat pierogi are amazing.'

'Have you cooked any together yet? What about your other recipes? Are they ready?'

'We're working on it. Once it's off the ground, it'll fly.'

'Who told you that? Henio?'

'Oh come on Auntie. He's a good guy. He's ambitious, that's all.'

'He puts silly ideas into your head.'

'I can think for myself you know.'

His Aunt put her hand on his forearm. He stopped scrubbing a pot. 'Don't dismiss the job just yet. Please,' she said.

'Think about it for a couple of days. I know you're always looking to the future and you're young and you want to do so much. I understand that. But your Uncle used to say that if you concentrate on the now, then the future would take care of itself. This job could be a stable platform for you. To build whatever you want on top of it.'

Piotr went back to cleaning the base of the pot. The residue was hard to shift, so he put a few more drops of washing up liquid into it.

'Does it pay well?'

'I'm sure it pays better than the car wash.'

'I'll think about it,' he said. 'I suppose if it pays OK then I could buy you a dishwasher.'

THE DOC WAVED PIOTR over to his cabin.

Piotr walked over, throwing a ragged towel he had used to clean some bucket handles over his shoulder. 'Hey Doc, what's happening?'

'Happening? Nothing's happening. That's the problem.' He lit a cigarette and took a sip from a mug of coffee.

'We're down on numbers. Seriously down. You understand? We're losing custom to some whoring new outfit that have set up down the road, right opposite the town hall. They're in full view of the main road. All the traffic goes right by them, the whores' sons. I'd love to know how they got a spot like that. You know who I'm talking about?

'I never go in that direction,' said Piotr.

The Doc took out a suitcase out from behind him in the cabin doorway and dumped it in front of Piotr. He unzipped it and flipped the top open. Piotr stared at stacks of neatly packed flyers that were inside it.

'I've got a special job for you,' he said, grabbing a bunch of them and thrusting them into Piotr's hands.

'I want you to grab a load of these flyers and hand them out to people. Put them on car windows, through letterboxes, wherever. As many as you can. You've got the whole afternoon and then most of tomorrow. We have to get the word out that we're cheaper, and better then those chiefs down the road. You understand?'

'Sure, no problem. But I don't have a big enough bag to carry them in. Do I have to lug that suitcase with me?'

'I've got a couple of large carrier bags in the cabin, so all you need to do is stuff as many as you can in those and then carry another stack by hand.'

'Where do you want me to go?'

'Anywhere. Use your initiative. It doesn't matter, as long as they've got a car, who cares? And as you'll be on foot they'll all be within striking distance of us. One on each car, and one in each letterbox, OK? Don't waste them. Residential areas are the best way to go. If anyone asks you about them, tell them how good the remedies are on offer from Dr. Car Wash.'

'Right,' said Piotr, looking down at the flyers in his hands.

'Well don't just stare at them Piotrek. Start packing them. You can have a nice afternoon, out discovering the area. Think of it as an opportunity to help the business. If you're done before 5, come back. If not, then I'll see you tomorrow once you've got rid of them all.'

Piotr walked into the cabin to find a bag. He found one that was stuffed with microfibre cloths. He took them out and placed them on a shelf next to a picture of the Doc's wife and two children. They were all sat together on a park bench, feeding a squirrel. The Doc looked happy.

'This is really important,' said the Doc when Piotr stepped back outside. 'You understand? If we don't get more patients in I'm going to have to start letting people go.'

'I'll do my best,' said Piotr, holding up a flyer as he walked off.

He headed towards the town hall, leaving flyers on every car he passed. He asked a newsagent if he could leave one in his window. The newsagent said it would cost money. Piotr decided not to bother, in case the Doc wouldn't pay him back.

When he got to the town hall he crossed the road and took a look at the competition. Two bright blue banners, which stuck out from behind a barbed wire fence had the name *Car Wash* displayed on them in large yellow letters, with a little red car below the words. The washers all wore blue *Car Wash* T-shirts and baseball caps. The prices were cheaper. And they were busier.

He walked for three hours, checking over his shoulder every now and again. He passed parades of shops, went through leafy residential roads and walked up the staircases in several blocks of flats. He left leaflets under car window wipers and in letterboxes. He even gave out leaflets to some Polish builders who were renovating a large Victorian-era house.

Towards the end of the afternoon, he was tempted to put more than one leaflet on a car or in a letterbox, as he still had a big pile of them left, but thought better of it. He kept going, walking down one street after another, until all the leaflets had gone and he was lost.

He stopped at a bus stop which had a number of a bus he recognised on it. It took a route close to home. The next bus was due in 15 minutes.

There was a shop across the road. It had a Polish flag hanging in the window. It was called *The Red Duck*. Piotr rang his Aunt.

'I'm just outside a Polish shop. Looks quite good. Do you want me to get something there for you?'

His Aunt thought for a moment and then said, 'Maybe some gherkins dear. We could do with a couple of jars. Whichever pickled ones that you think look good.'

Inside the shop he walked through the aisles, looking at the produce. He noticed a brand of mustard that he had not seen in London before. It reminded him of home.

He pictured himself helping his mother to set out plates of food for a gathering they were going to have in their small family flat. She was busy stirring a large pot of bigos over the stove. His Dad was in his bedroom adjusting his tie and carefully smoothing his moustache down with his fingers. His brother was in their bedroom. All you could hear from behind the half-closed door was the gentle sound of a fat Italian plumber video game character bouncing off huge plants and squashing small animals in his quest to find a Princess.

'Can I help you?' said someone behind him, in English.

Piotr swivelled on the spot. A tall brunette stood in front of him. She was wearing a red apron with a black silhouette of a duck on it and a red sun visor. She wore her hair in a long ponytail that dropped to one side.

'I was just looking for some pickled gherkins,' Piotr said, in Polish.

She raised an already arched eyebrow. 'Any particular brand?'

'I'm not sure. How many types do you have?'

'I'll show you.'

Piotr followed the assistant down the aisle, into a small enclosed part of the shop. She pointed at a whole shelf of gherkins: large, small, pickled, soaked in brine.

'Great, thanks.' He smiled at her. She smiled back. 'My pleasure.'

As she walked away he watched her adjust her ponytail and expose the back of her neck. He put a couple of jars of pickled gherkins in his basket and went to pay for them. At the counter, he tried to catch another glimpse of the shop assistant. But she was gone.

On his way home on the bus he tried to think about what to do for the dojang's next training session. But he found his concentration slipping. All he could picture was the shop assistant's ponytail.

His Aunt was out that evening so he ate his meal on his own. She had made him a breaded pork chop and potatoes, a tomato salad and some sliced cucumbers in soured cream. He texted Jacek and Kris as he ate. He drank a pint of water after finishing his dinner and watched TV for half an hour. Before leaving the house he texted Jacek and Kris again.

They had arranged to meet in a fried chicken fast food restaurant opposite the entrance to Greenford station. When Piotr arrived, Kris was already there. He was sitting on a stool facing out of the restaurant's full-length front window.

'Any sign of them?' Piotr said.

'I've seen three guys walking up and down looking pretty suspect,' he said, pushing a bag of fries away.

Piotr sat down next to him and motioned at the fries. 'No good?'

'I've eaten too much greasy chicken already. You have them.'

'I've eaten. Are they there now?'

Kris leant forward, sipping from his cola drink. 'See that guy to the right of the dry cleaners? He definitely matches the description. He's even wearing the same blue tracksuit top that witnesses have mentioned. They're not exactly subtle are they? I can't believe they're dumb enough to keep hitting the same place over and over. And it's not even going to be dark for another hour or so either.'

'I've had some new info on that,' said Piotr, picking up a couple of fries and pointing towards the street with them. 'They move from place to place apparently. They've been spotted at Sudbury Town, Preston Road. North Wembley too.'

'I thought you said you weren't hungry?' said Kris, watching Piotr eat the fries.

'They smell too good,' said Piotr, grabbing a few more.

A minute later, Jacek walked in and slid onto a stool next to Piotr. 'You eating those fries?'

'Help yourself, ' said Kris, pushing the bag over to him.

'So what's the status?' said Jacek, with a mouth full of deep-fried potato. Piotr filled him in.

'Hey,' Jacek said, elbowing Piotr, 'Aren't those the other two guys?'

'Yeah, that's them,' said Piotr. 'Short brute with the huge forehead and the blond with the crew cut.'

They watched the three men huddle together and light cigarettes. The short man kept pointing in the opposite direction to the station as they talked. The other two followed his arm each time, as if their heads were connected to it by some invisible wire.

'What about the CCTV?' said Kris.

'Don't worry, they're not completely stupid. Look where they're standing,' said Piotr. 'They're out of shot from the station camera. They can take a victim down the alley behind them without getting filmed.'

A train rumbled over the bridge next to the restaurant. 'That's the one in from the city,' said Kris. 'It'll be busy. They might go for someone. We should get closer to them.'

'No, hang on,' said Piotr. 'Put your caps on, but let's just keep watching for now.'

Jacek picked up the last of the fries and threw them into his mouth, one at a time, chewing quickly. 'They look big from here,' he said, adjusting his cap. 'What do you reckon they could bench press?'

Piotr said, 'You're the one that works at a gym. You tell us.'

'I guess blue tracksuit can probably do a few 210kg reps. You can deal with him.' Jacek elbowed Piotr again and winked at Kris.

'We'd best not get into a wrestling match with him then,' said Piotr.

They heard the train leave as commuters began streaming out of the station. The three men outside backed themselves up to a wall by the dry cleaner's window. They were looking at the people walking past them.

As the crowd dispersed, two well-dressed women emerged from the station, arm-in-arm and laughing together. One of them was looking down at her phone.

The shorter man walked up to them and tried to talk to them, but they carried on giggling and waved his approach away. He stopped to let them walk on. As they did, the blond man and blue tracksuit slipped in behind them and grabbed each of them by an arm. They pushed them towards the alley.

'Let's move,' said Piotr. He followed Jacek out of the door. Kris sucked up a bit more of his drink and dropped it next to the half-eaten fries before running after them.

Jacek and Piotr got into the alley first. The short man was kneeling down, rummaging through their handbags on the floor, while blue tracksuit had one woman in a full nelson with his hands over her mouth. The blond man had a hand on the throat of one of the women, and had pinned her against the wall with his hand over her mouth.

Jacek punched the short man in the mouth, aiming upwards through his nose, before he had a chance to see him. The short man slumped backwards, dropping the handbag. As the blond man turned to look at Piotr and Jacek, he let go of one of the women, who screamed. Jacek hit him with a side kick to the thigh, forcing him to lose his balance. He struck him twice with a palm strike under his chin. The mugger fell to the ground.

Blue tracksuit threw the other woman to his side and showed Piotr a blade. Piotr lifted the back of his T-shirt up and took his baton out of his trousers. He flicked it open and it clicked into place as he kept walking towards the mugger. Kris flanked Piotr's left side. Blue tracksuit switched his knife so that the blade was protruding behind his clenched left fist. The alley was wide enough for Kris to move past Piotr and encircle Blue tracksuit, who had hesitated a moment and let him in. Piotr moved a step to the left to allow Jacek to move to his side as they trapped him against the wall.

Blue tracksuit went for Piotr, bringing his elbow up first and then thrusting the blade towards his chest. Piotr jumped backwards, outside Blue tracksuit's reach. He slammed his baton down on his arm, making him drop the knife and punched him in the jaw. Kris kicked him in the base of his spine. The mugger went down. Piotr stamped on his hands and Kris kicked him in the back again. He rolled onto his side, moaning in pain.

Jacek checked that the other two were still down. Satisfied, he turned to the women.

One of them was sitting on the ground, crying. Her friend was hugging her.

'Are you hurt?' he said in English.

'No, I don't think so,' said the woman who was comforting her friend.

'Have you got all your things?'

'Yes,' she said, shaking as she gripped her handbag.

'Go home,' he said.

'Thank you,' said the woman.

'Go now, said Jacek.

The women stood up and left.

Piotr spoke to the muggers in Polish. 'Next time, we won't go so easy,' he said. He collapsed his baton and tucked it into the back of his jeans and gestured at Kris and Jacek to follow him. They left the alley with their backs to the CCTV camera. They crossed the road and split up.

PIOTR TOOK THE BUS to *The Red Duck* early in the morning, hoping it would be empty.

When he walked in, the shop assistant with the brunette ponytail was standing behind the counter, flicking through a magazine.

Piotr picked up a shopping basket and read the shopping list that his Aunt had given him. There were two other people in the shop. He walked through each aisle slowly, picking what he needed. When the other shoppers had left, he went to pay.

He placed the shopping basket on the counter. 'Hi,' he said, grinning.

The shop assistant looked at him briefly, returning his smile. 'Hi.'

She started taking the items out of the basket and registering them with a handheld scanner. She flicked open a white plastic bag and put the scanned items in it. The bag had a large red silhouette of a duck on it.

When she picked up the beetroot, Piotr said, 'They look fresh.'

'We try to keep fresh produce,' said the assistant, tucking a strand of her hair behind her ear.

A bunch of flyers advertising a Polish disco night at a local pub sat next to the cash register. Piotr picked one up, pretending to read it. At the same time, he checked the assistant's right hand. There were no rings on it. His eyes darted to her left one. It was bare as well. 'Do you get them in every day?' he said.

'What, the beetroot?' she said, raising her right eyebrow.

He nodded.

'No, every few days. They're not that popular. Lots of people don't make their own barszcz, they buy the packets. Or they get the pre-cooked ones for salad.'

'Too busy earning a living I guess,' said Piotr.

'Aren't we all?'

Piotr put the flyer down and took a deep breath. 'Too busy for dinner?' he said.

She laughed, tucking her hair behind her ear again. 'You're not one to waste time are you?'

He grinned. 'It was too good an opening.'

She tapped some buttons on the cash register and studied a laminated piece of card that had a list of prices on it.

'So what do you think?' said Piotr.

'Maybe.'

'Well maybe I could call you or something.'

'Or something?'

'Well, I mean I could call you. If I had your number.'

A customer walked in, picked up a loaf of bread and queued up behind Piotr.' She grabbed a flyer and scribbling down a telephone number on the back of it. 'I'm free on Thursday,' she said.

'OK, great,' said Piotr. He held the flyer in his hand and stared at it, as if he was checking that the writing on it was real.

'That's £21.35 please.'

'Right, of course,' said Piotr. He fumbled in his pockets and handed over the exact amount in cash.

At the door, he said, 'See you later then.'

She gave him a little wave. 'See you later.'

When Piotr got to the car wash Dennis told him that the Doc had fired two workers.

'As soon as you'd gone off with the flyers, he thanked them for all their work, gave them an envelope each, and that was it.'

'Did they do something wrong?' said Piotr.

'Nothing wrong, no. I guess we've had a couple of quiet weeks. And the weather's been good. We should be flat out. It doesn't look great.'

'You think we're going to get shut down?'

'Well, he sent you out with those flyers didn't he? He's never done that. He's worried, that's for sure.'

'We're not advertising ourselves well enough,' said Piotr. 'That wash down the road? They've got huge banners telling people about themselves. We've just got that small sign at the front. I bet some people can't even tell that we're a car wash as they pass by.'

A trickle of cars came in until mid-morning, when a man drove into the car wash in a silver estate. He had a small Nigerian flag hanging from his rear view mirror. Dennis asked him what type of wash he wanted.

'I don't need a wash. My car has been cleaned very recently. Don't you remember me?' he said. 'I was here yesterday.'

'No, sorry,' said Dennis. 'It's hard to remember sometimes. We don't really notice the cars, we just look at the dirt on them.'

The Nigerian got out of his car. 'Well I was here. And one of you stole my watch. It was in my car when I came here. Then when I searched for it, it was gone. I have scoured everywhere, so the only option is you.'

'We don't touch any personal stuff in the patients' cars,' said Dennis.

'Then how do explain my missing watch?' said the Nigerian, thrusting a finger at him.

'I don't know, but we don't have no watch. We just wash the cars. We don't take anything, believe me.'

'Well you obviously do. Because as I told you, I came here with the watch but left without it. I want to see your manager.'

'The boss, I mean, the doctor, he's not here,' said Andrzej, who had walked over to them. 'He's away visiting one of his other surgeries.'

'Call him to come here then,' said the Nigerian.

Dennis said, 'Listen, we don't have no watch of yours OK? We are honest guys. You have to believe us. Come and check. You want to look in our bags?'

'I am not stupid,' said the Nigerian. 'You have probably taken the watch away already. So one of you who is the thief must go and get my watch and bring it back.'

Dennis turned away, shaking his head. Andrzej shrugged. 'So?' he said in Ukrainian to Dennis. 'Nobody here would have stolen a watch would they?'

'No, of course they wouldn't have. I'll call the Doc.'

He returned his attention to the Nigerian and said, 'I'm going to call the owner, OK? Do you want to sit down and wait in the cabin?'

'No, I will wait in my car,' said the Nigerian.

The Doc arrived about half an hour later. Dennis and Andrzej were waiting for him.

'Where's this chief?' he said.

'He's in his car,' said Dennis.

'Is he all there?' the Doc said, tapping his head with his middle finger.

'I don't know,' said Andrzej. 'But he's not happy.'

'I'll talk to him.' The Doc walked up to the silver estate and knocked on the window. It slid down. 'Are you the man in charge of these thieves?' said the Nigerian.

The Doc bent down to speak at the Nigerian's head level. 'Yes, I'm the head doctor. My colleagues told me you lost your watch.'

'No I did not lose it. It was stolen. By someone here. I know that because I was here yesterday with my watch, which I must have left on the dashboard.'

'We are all very honest here. You must believe me. We would not steal anything from any patients. I promise. Everybody here is a good Christian.' The Doc reached into the front of his shirt and pulled a gold cross out and kissed it. 'See? We know it's very bad to steal. Nobody here does it. We are honest hard workers.'

'Are you suggesting that I am a liar?'

'No, I'm not saying anything like that, I swear.' He kissed his cross again and left it to hang out over his shirt. 'Maybe you lost it in back of the car? Down the seat? I will help you look.' The Doc went to open the rear passenger door.

'Get away from the car!' said the Nigerian, opening his door and pointing at the Doc. 'I know you have my watch. Don't take me for a fool.'

The Doc held his hands up in the air. 'I'm helping you find it, that's all.'

'I said get away from my car!' The Nigerian took a step towards him and pointed at him again with his arm fully outstretched.

'OK, OK. Hang on,' said the Doc. 'What wash did you have?'

'What?'

'You know, what kind of wash did the car have? Was it basic body healing, all over body cosmetic surgery, or miracle cure?'

The Nigerian screwed up his face.

'You know, how much did you pay? Six pounds, eight or ten?' said the Doc.

'It was the most expensive one.'

'OK, right,' said the Doc. 'Boys,' he said, in English, turning towards Piotr, Dennis and Andrzej, who were standing by the cabin. 'Who was doing miracle cure yesterday at–' He turned back round to face the Nigerian. 'What time did you have the miracle cure?'

'About eleven.'

The Doc shouted out again, 'Morning shift – who was on miracle?'

Piotr and Andrzej put their hands up.

'OK, boys,' said the Doc, waving them over. 'Did you take a watch out of this patient's car?' He gestured at the Nigerian.

'No, of course not Doc,' Andrzej said.

'I didn't even see a watch,' said Piotr.

'See?' The Doc turned to look at the Nigerian. 'Nobody has even seen your watch.'

'They are lying,' said the Nigerian, glaring at Piotr and Andrzej.

'Listen, my workers are honest, OK?' said the Doc. 'We have no trouble. We clean cars, that's it. Come on, why would we steal your watch and cause trouble? What's the point? It's a bit stupid to do that when you are always here and someone can come back and find the thief. You understand? Makes no sense.'

The Doc ran his hand over his face, thinking. 'I can give you two free car washes to say sorry for your inconvenience. And we will look tonight, to make sure it's not fallen somewhere into a bucket or something.'

The Nigerian gripped the frame of his car door. 'Now you listen to me. Very carefully. I had my watch yesterday in this car. A very expensive watch. And now it's not here. I don't want anything from you but my watch. You understand?'

The Doc opened his arms out. 'What can I do? There's nothing I can do for you? I'm sorry.'

He walked back to his cabin. Piotr and Dennis followed him into it.

'What's he going to do now Doc?' said Dennis .

'How do I know? The guy's messed up in the head.'

'He's just standing there,' said Dennis, looking out of the cabin doorway. 'He seems pretty pissed off.'

The Doc went to the window and watched two of the workers wash the only other vehicle that was in the car wash.

'Hopefully he's cooling down and will head off in a bit. Anyway, don't worry about him. It's good you called me. We need to get some more flyers out there. Do you two want to earn a little overtime tonight? We need to get as many out there as we can. We've had a couple of people turn up with flyers in the past couple of days. So it works. But we need to do more.'

The Doc walked over to the suitcase of flyers he had left on a table in the corner of the cabin. He unzipped it and starting taking stacks of flyers out and placing them next to the suitcase.

'I think there's about 1,700 of them that we need to get out there,' he said. 'The sooner the better. So, can you both do it? I've worked out that the two of you could probably get these done in less than three hours if you...'

'Er, Doc, I think you need to take a look at this,' said Dennis. They all walked out of the cabin. The Nigerian had reversed to the entrance of the car wash and turned his car so that it blocked it.

'Is this chief for real?' said the Doc. 'I can't believe this whore's son.' He marched up to the estate.

'Hey, what are you doing?' the Doc said, knocking on the Nigerian's car window again. 'You can't park here. This is the entrance. You need to move.'

The Nigerian, in a muffled voice, said, 'You give me back my watch, or I stay here.'

'OK. I've had enough. The police are coming, you understand? I'm going to call the police.'

The only other car at the wash was being waxed. The driver, a man with short ginger hair in his twenties, got up from the plastic chairs where the customers occasionally waited.

'Is he going to move or what?' he said to the Doc. 'I got places to go, I can't be waiting all day for him.'

'Don't worry. I'm calling the police.' The Doc dialled 999 into his mobile. 'Sorry about this,' he said. 'I can give you a free wash to apologise.'

'Free wash? I don't want a free wash, I want to get out of here.'

The ginger-haired man paid Andrzej and got into his old Honda. 'I'll show you how to get rid of this tool.'

He drove right up to the estate, leaving only a few inches between his front bumper and the Nigerian's door and pressed his horn four times. When there was no reaction from the Nigerian, he blew the horn repeatedly. On the final blast he held his hand down on his steering wheel. The piercing sound went on for so long that its pitch seemed to alter, like an air raid siren from a war movie.

The ginger man got out of his car and banged on the Nigerian's front window. He had a large tattoo of a Celtic cross on his forearm.

'What are you doing?' he said, crouching down to look into the car. 'This isn't a lay-by you know. We're not back in Zimbabwe. Move out of the way you tool.'

The Nigerian stared straight ahead. The ginger-haired man banged on the window again.

'Move your car,' he said. 'Before I start kicking it in.' The Nigerian continued to ignore him.

'I've got to get to places you tool!' The driver's face was getting red, to match his ginger hair.

'Move your car or I'm going to start smashing it in, you hear me?' The Nigerian's mobile phone started ringing. He answered it.

The driver started swearing. He kicked the side of the Nigerian's bonnet. Piotr turned to Dennis and the Doc. 'I'll go and try to calm him down.' The Doc put his arm in front of Piotr. 'No, leave it. The police will be here in a minute.'

'It might be a minute too late,' said Piotr. 'It's alright, I'm only going to talk to him.'

'Piotrek man, he's a psycho. He might have a knife or something,' said Dennis.

Piotr made his way up to the entrance. He tapped the back of his jeans, realising that his baton was at home as he did so.

The driver was kicking the headlights of the Nigerian's car when Piotr reached him. Piotr stood behind him and said, 'Hey, come on. Leave the car alone. The police are coming, they'll sort this all out. There's no need for this.'

'Piss off chief,' said the man, kicking the car again, this time aiming at the wing mirror. He lost his balance and almost fell over, but Piotr caught him, putting his arms under his. He pretended to stumble as he did so, making sure that he took the man a few steps away from the car.

'Woah, we almost both went over there,' said Piotr, twisting the man further away from the car as he let go of him. Piotr put his hands on the man's shoulders. 'Are you OK? Maybe it's time to stop. This isn't going to make him move you know.'

'Get out of the way,' said the ginger-haired driver. He tried to more past Piotr, who mirrored his steps, keeping his arms out in front of him, palms facing outwards. 'Seriously, there's no point,' said Piotr, looking him straight in the eye. 'The police will be here soon.'

Dennis and the Doc were now by the ginger-haired driver's

Honda. 'Please,' said the Doc. 'We don't want any trouble here.'

Ignoring him, the man tried to side step Piotr again. 'Out of my way chief,' he said. Piotr blocked his path and took a short step into his personal space, while simultaneously pushing him in the shoulders. As he did so, he dropped his weight into his back leg. The ginger haired man staggered backwards and this time hit the ground. The driver gawped at Piotr, but said nothing.

The Nigerian climbed out of his car through the passenger door and went for the ginger driver. 'You bastard! I am going to sue you for damaging my property!'

The Nigerian tried pushing past Piotr, who stood his ground. 'Get out of my way,' he said.

'I can't let you pass. Go back to your car and wait for the police.'

The Nigerian walked away, muttering to himself.

Dennis and the Doc convinced the ginger-haired man to get back into his car and reverse it. Piotr and the Nigerian inspected his car. There were some boot marks on the bonnet but nothing was damaged. 'You got lucky,' Piotr said. He got a bucket and sponge and cleaned up the mud and boot polish on the paintwork. He asked the Nigerian to move his car and to wait in it for the police. Before the Nigerian did, he said, 'Why are you working with these people, eh? Helping them steal people's things from their cars. You should be ashamed of yourself.'

Piotr didn't say anything. He memorised the Nigerian's number plate. He had already banked the other car's registration number.

As the Nigerian parked near the cabin, the ginger-haired man fired up his engine and sped out of the car wash, barely stopping to see if there was any incoming traffic on the road.

The Nigerian got out of his car. 'Hey. Why did you let him go? He needs to be charged for attempted assault.'

'I've got his number plate,' said Piotr. 'We'll tell the police. They can track him.'

When the police arrived, they asked the Doc to shut the car wash. One officer began questioning the Nigerian. As he listened, he nodded and wrote quickly in his notepad. The Nigerian was shouting a lot and motioning towards the cabin.

The other officer spoke to the Doc, Piotr, Dennis and Andrzej. He took notes as well. Piotr told him the ginger-haired man's registration number.

'Good memory,' said the policeman. He paused. 'Don't I know you from somewhere?'

Piotr dropped his bottom lip. 'Me? I don't think so.'

'You ever been in trouble with us before?'

'No. Never.'

'Funny. You look familiar.' The officer shook his head and looked down at his notepad. 'Never mind,' he said.

When he finished questioning them, he went back to the police car and spoke to the other officer who had finished with the Nigerian. Piotr said to the Doc, 'Do you want us to deliver those leaflets? I don't mind taking them now. Who knows when they're going to let us open up again.'

'Alright. You might as well,' said the Doc.

Piotr and Dennis walked together. 'You dealt with those two fruitcakes pretty handily,' said Dennis. 'Where did you learn to push someone like that?'

'I got lucky,' said Piotr. 'Anyway, I grew up with two younger brothers who fought all the time. I'm used to being the peacemaker.'

When Piotr got home he got changed into an old T-shirt and some tracksuit bottoms, grabbed a large bottle of water and went to train in the garage.

He stretched his chest and shoulders for a minute or two by rotating his arms backwards and forwards and leaning his torso into the gap of the open garage door with his hands on either side of the doorframe for support. Then he got to work on the punch bag.

He threw some knifehand strikes and elbows before moving to kicks and knee strikes, building up the pace and getting into a rhythm. The dull thuds of his strikes made the bag swing as he pounded out a familiar warrior's beat. He hit the bag until his lungs burned and he could no longer maintain a high speed.

It was warm and muggy inside, but Piotr welcomed the heat. The sweat dripped down his face onto the garage floor.

When his breathing slowed down he performed four sets of 20 burpees with a minute's break between each one. He rested again, waiting for his heartbeat to slow down before doing some pull-ups, using a portable metal bar that he attached to the frame of the door. He then went through a *tul*, thinking about what the police officer had said to him.

When he was done, he sat down on a large wooden toolbox that his Uncle had constructed and drank some water.

He got up to leave after a minute, knocking the tool bench with his leg. One of the drawers opened slightly as it lent forward.

Inside it were some screwdrivers, a hammer, two rusty pliers and hundreds of nails. He picked up one of the pliers and held them in his hand. His Uncle had used a similar looking one to fix a pipe in his family's bathroom at home.

He and his Aunt used to visit them almost every year in Radom when he had been younger. They would spend two weeks together every time, visiting the countryside, walking aimlessly around town, eating ice cream in the park, having lavish home-made meals, and staying up late into the evenings while the adults would drink vodka and sing and laugh. His Uncle once took him to the swimming pool. That was where Piotr had first seen his long thick scar that stretched in an L-shape from the bottom of his neck to the middle of his back.

Piotr had once asked him how he had got it.

'I had an accident at work,' he had said.

'How did it happen?'

'I got a long nail stuck in it. Not very nice.'

'Do you like working as a builder?' Piotr had said.

'Sometimes. It means I can give your Auntie money to buy food and that we can go on holidays to come and visit you.'

'Maybe I could come to England and build with you.'

'You could. But it's hard work,' he had said. 'You'd be better off studying hard and getting some qualifications. You could become a lawyer. Or a doctor. Then you won't be getting scars like mine. You'll be stitching them up instead.'

Look at me now Uncle, he thought to himself. *Not much of a doctor am I?*

When he got back inside his Aunt was busy in the kitchen.

'Dinner is about ready,' she said. 'I've made gołąbki.'

Piotr went upstairs and changed his T-shirt for a fresh one. He washed his face and hands before coming downstairs and sitting at the table.

'How was work dear?' his Aunt said, spooning a huge ladle full of tomato sauce over his cabbage rolls.

'Eventful.'

'Why do say that?'

He told her about the Nigerian.

'Maybe someone is trying to tell you that you need to get yourself a better job,' she said. 'Away from so many crazy people, if nothing else.' She put the ladle down on the table and pressed her fingers to her temples.

Piotr stood up and put his arm over her. 'Are you OK Auntie?'

'I feel a little dizzy.'

Piotr led her to the sofa and sat her down. 'Here, stay there, let me get you a glass of water.'

After she drank it, he said, 'Do you want to eat?'

'I'm not hungry, but I suppose I should,' she said. 'To keep my strength up.' She got up and Piotr held her by the arm towards the table. He poured some sauce over her food and then brought her another glass of water. He ate slowly, looking at his Aunt all the time.

'Have you felt like that before?' he said.

'Not really,' she said.

'Is it a side effect of the drugs?'

'I don't know. I might check.'

'Maybe you should call your consultant tomorrow.'

'Yes, that's probably a good idea.'

She left half her meal and said she was tired and wanted to go to bed. Piotr led her upstairs. Her breathing was shallow when they got to her bedroom.

'Give me a few minutes,' she said. 'I'll get changed and then you can bring me some more water.'

Downstairs, Piotr checked the leaflets that came with her pills. They all said that they could cause drowsiness. He wondered if that was all it was.

PIOTR WAS STANDING AT THE BUS STOP on his way back from a shift at the car wash. He typed the number the shop assistant had written on the flyer into his mobile. She had written her name on it as well. He realised that he had forgotten to tell her his.

'Hi, Beata? It's Piotr here,' he said. 'The guy at the shop the other day? You wrote down your number for me. I'm sorry, I forgot to tell you my name.'

'That's OK,' she said. 'We were in a bit of a hurry. So how were the beetroots?'

'I haven't had them yet. My Aunt is using them for some barszcz. She didn't complain about them when she saw them though, that's usually a good sign. I think we're having the soup on Saturday.'

'Oh right.'

'I should explain. I live with my Auntie. I have done ever since I came over here. She's needed a lot of help. She's been ill. With cancer.'

'I'm sorry to here that.'

'It's OK. It's under control, for now at least.' He paused before saying, 'So anyway, I was wondering if you maybe wanted to go for a bite to eat. There's a new Polish restaurant that's opened up in Sudbury Hill. My Aunt never really eats out and my friends prefer to drink beer, so I was hoping you'd maybe like to see what it's like. If you want. Or if not we could go somewhere else. I'm not too bothered about it. I mean it would be nice, but I'm not hung up on eating there, if you know what I mean. Or I could come to somewhere near you. Or wherever you like. Within reason. Say a 15 mile radius.'

She giggled. 'It sounds good. I've never eaten in a Polish place in London yet. And it's not far from me. I live in Rayners Lane.'

'Great. I know you said Thursday the other day, but how about Wednesday evening?'

'Sorry, I'm not free on Wednesday. Is Thursday no good?'

'No, Thursday works. About 8? I can meet you at Rayners Lane and take the Tube with you. The place is opposite the station.'

'Don't be silly, I'll come and meet you at Sudbury Hill at 8.'

'OK. Great. I'll be there.'

'I'm looking forward to it.'

'Me too.'

Piotr pumped his fist. An old lady at the bus stop frowned at him. He turned away from her and smiled.

That evening Piotr, Kris and Jacek met early up before class.

'Any word?' Jacek said.

'No,' said Piotr.

'So we just wait?'

'That's right. If we hear that they've come back then we'll have to take another look at it. Anyway, hopefully we've done enough. They'll have probably realised that it was us. That's usually half the battle.'

'Yeah I guess, but remember those small time dealers in Harlesden?' said Jacek. 'They kept coming back to the same places to sell. Even after Sabum Zieliński put one of them in a wheelchair.'

'But they had backing,' said Piotr. 'We would have had to have broken the code to get rid of them.'

'More like they would have put a bullet in our backs if we'd carried on,' said Kris.

'Hard to argue with that,' said Jacek.

Piotr separated the white belts into three groups at the start of the training session. He asked Jacek to supervise breaking practice for the ones that needed it the most. Kris ran some of the more experienced white belts through some sparring. Piotr took the rest through their tuls. He decided to start with one of the basic ones, which they all knew.

Piotr called out the form's name. The white belts all bowed and prepared to start. He walked past them all to make sure they were in the right position.

'Left hand over right fist,' he said, adjusting one student's hands, pushing them up a fraction higher and squeezing them into place.

'*Seja!*'

Piotr's command echoed through the hall as they began the *tul*. He stopped them a few times to ask them the Korean name for the strikes or blocks they were performing and to explain how the move could be applied in combat.

One of the white belts kept repeating the same mistake in the middle of the *tul*. 'Come on, concentrate.' Piotr said. He made everyone repeat the same form until the white belt had fixed his error.

They took a break. Piotr asked them if they had any questions.

'Why do we have to learn tuls?' said Szymon. 'Isn't it better to spar and learn to use techniques that way?'

'Don't you like doing them?' said Piotr.

'It's not that, I'm just curious. I read that Bruce Lee said that there was no point doing them. He never used them after he set up his own system.'

'Bruce Lee was a movie star.'

'Yeah, but he was good, wasn't he?'

'I don't know. I never met him.'

'But you know what I mean Sabum, right?'

'OK,' Piotr said. He took a couple of steps back and stuck his thumbs under his belt, near the knot.

'For those of you who have forgotten, or perhaps were never really told, the tuls are the alphabet of our system. They're the building blocks of the art. Without them, you can't learn or understand it properly. And if you don't understand it, then you can't use it properly. Outside of this hall, you will be next to useless if you don't know the Kwan's alphabet and how to put it together when you need it.'

'Does that answer your question Szymon?'

'I guess that makes sense.'

When they were getting changed afterwards, Piotr asked Jacek if he could take the class on Thursday.

'Sorry, I can't. I'm on Thursday evening shifts at the gym all month. What do you need cover for?'

'I've got a date.'

Jacek whistled. 'Oh yeah? What is she – blind or desperate? Or both?'

Kris laughed.

'Yeah, yeah,' said Piotr. 'She's smart. That's what she is. How about you Krzysztof?'

'No problem. I'll be here. Anything you want me to cover?'

—

'Their forms,' said Piotr. 'Make sure they do them to death. Some of them seem to think that they can take them or leave them. They're also not using their combinations enough in *hosin sul*. So do a few drills on the mats too.'

'OK, will do.'

Jan walked with Piotr to the bus stop. They talked for a while about one of Jan's forms, as he was struggling with it.

'I've been thinking that maybe my *tul* training would make more sense if I could use some of the moves in a live situation,' said Jan.

'What do you mean?'

'You know, in an organised bout, like me and Szymon mentioned the other day. I also figured that it would help me to get ready for when I'm a black belt. To be able to fight when it really matters.'

Piotr propped himself up against the bus stop shelter, and scanned the street. 'Don't worry, when you need to be ready, you'll be ready.'

'What does that mean?'

'I'm not sure, but it's something that my old Sabum in Poland used to say to me. And he was right.'

'But that's just it. I don't feel ready.'

'Then you don't need to be yet.'

The bus took a while to get going after they boarded it. Piotr and Jan could hear the bus driver telling someone that they had to buy an adult ticket.

'You're definitely over 14,' the driver said.

'I ain't paying no adult ticket.'

'You can get off the bus then.'

A minute later, a young man stormed up to the top of the double decker bus, followed by two companions. 'I shouldn't be paying for no ticket,' he said.

He swaggered towards the end of the bus and sat at the back with his legs spread out. He started playing some loud music on his phone.

'How long have you been thinking about this all anyway?' said Piotr, stealing a glance back at the teenagers.

'I guess maybe the last couple of months. It sounds a bit more interesting than always doing forms and sparring the same people. That's all I've been doing for like, five years or something. Some action would make it a bit more bearable.'

Piotr sighed. 'Not you as well.' He sat upright, resting his elbows on the empty seat in front. 'That's what a martial art is. You want to do a sport, that's something else. Go and join a kickboxing club or the MMA gym that Jacek works at. They all do that. But it's not martial arts. The tuls are the art. It's what unifies us.'

'What about testing our skills against other martial artists?'

'Who says you'll meet any martial artists at a tournament?'

'Can I show you a video of one match?' said Jan. 'I've got it on my phone.'

'If you want.'

Jan got his phone out. He tilted the screen and held the phone horizontally to make the video projection wider. Two men stood facing each other with a referee in between them. They were wearing padded fingerless gloves but no other protective gear. Neither of them was wearing footwear.

'Where did you find this?' said Piotr.

'Szymon showed it to me. He said loads of dojangs are entering this kind of thing now.'

'He did?'

'Yeah. He said it's getting really popular. Some people earn good money from it too.'

'So where did he find it then?'

'On the dark web. You can't get this on the regular internet.'

Both men were of average height and similar weight and build. Piotr guessed that they weighed about 75kg. A large ring of men surrounded the fighters, pumping their fists and jostling for a clear view. Baying for blood.

The fight barely lasted a minute. One of the men kept coming forward punching and his opponent was unable to fend him off with his kicks. He was dropped with a hook punch to the side of his head. Before his hand was raised in victory, the winner had pounded his victim's head into the ground.

'What do you think?' said Jan.

'I think I know why it's hidden away on the web.'

'But it's pretty realistic. I mean, to what you'd encounter on the street.'

'Not necessarily,' said Piotr. 'But it is brutal and uncalled for. Where's the honour in taking part in it?'

63

Jan pocketed his phone. Piotr turned his head towards the teenagers who were playing the loud music at the back of the bus. 'See those kids over there?' he said, nodding towards them.

'Yeah.'

'Tall. Broad shouldered. Hostile.'

'So?'

'If they attacked you do you think you could defend yourself? Could you stop them from hurting you – or someone else? Someone you cared about, or wanted to protect?'

Jan shrugged his shoulders. 'I suppose so. I'd have a good chance.'

'Why's that?'

'Because I've trained for it, I guess.'

'And?'

'There's something else?'

Piotr smiled at Jan. 'I'd hope so.'

Jan thought for a moment. 'Because you're here too?'

'Exactly. There's always someone to back you up. Engaging on your own is crazy. Even in an organised fight. With the dojang, you've always got back up. Your friends are always with you. And you're only fighting if you absolutely must, and only to do good. Fighting for anything else is a betrayal of the Kwan.'

'Is this a test?' said Jan. 'Are you going to ask me to approach that guy?'

'No. Relax. All I'm saying is that you think you can protect yourself. And others. And I think you can too. You've already passed a sort of test, in a way.'

They didn't talk for a while. Then Jan's mobile rang. He talked on it for a few minutes to a college friend about an essay they had to write. Piotr stared out of the window as he talked, taking in all the cars that sat in the narrow driveways they drove by. He wondered how so many people had such expensive looking cars when their houses were so average-looking.

As Piotr got off at his stop he said, 'You're a good student. And you're getting close to your black belt. I wouldn't want to lose you. So do me a favour. Drop the competition talk, OK?'

HIS AUNT TRIED TO COME INTO THE KITCHEN to help cook breakfast, but he wouldn't let her.

'But I feel fine,' she said.

'Sit down Auntie, it'll be ready in a minute.'

After they ate he washed the dishes and his Aunt got ready for church.

When she came downstairs she sat in the front room with her handbag on her lap. She was wearing a dark blue beret and had an oval brooch pinned to her dress. A blue rose sat in the middle of its ivory centre, surrounded by gold trim.

Piotr was sat in the room too. He was reading one of his Aunt's recipe books and jotting down some flavour ideas on a notepad for pierogi and sauces. He noticed that his Aunt was breathing heavily.

'Are you OK?' he said, putting the notepad down on the floor.

'Yes dear, I just need to sit down for a bit.' She looked up at the clock. 'I hope Eric hasn't forgotten it's Sunday.'

'I think he's remembered,' said Piotr. 'I saw him tinkering with his engine this morning.'

'I'll invite him for lunch today I think,' she said. 'The poor man is getting thinner by the day. I have no idea what he eats.'

'Do you want me to do anything for lunch?'

'No. We can prepare it together when I get back.'

An engine started up outside.

'That'll be him,' said Piotr.

She stood up and walked to the door, where she hesitated for a moment.

'Are you sure you're able to go?' said Piotr.

'I'm fine,' she said. 'You don't need to worry about your old Auntie so much. I'll see you later.'

After Eric had dropped her off at the station she stood in her usual spot on the platform, waiting for the train. When it arrived she sat at the end of one the carriages and took her rosary beads out of her handbag. She took her gloves off and gripped them in her left hand, covering the beads with her right hand. She prayed for her nephew's conversion.

When she came back she put on her apron and they got straight to work in the kitchen. Piotr poured his Aunt a sherry and he opened himself a can of beer. His Aunt rubbed vegetable oil on a pork joint and sprinkled it generously with salt. Piotr peeled and chopped some potatoes, carrots and parsnips. Once they were in the oven, he put together a simple salad while his Aunt made mince meat croquettes to accompany the beetroot soup she had cooked a few days before.

'How was church?' Piotr said.

'Annoying.'

'How come?'

'Oh, I get very frustrated with Father Leopold. He's a moderniser. Can't help himself. He's allowed girls to serve at the altar. Nobody has taken up the offer yet, he only announced it today at the end of Mass. You should have heard how happy he was with himself when he told the congregation.'

'Maybe he's following orders,' said Piotr. 'Doesn't all that stuff come from the top anyway?'

'Oh no, he's the keenest of them all. You should have seen his face last week when we suggested bringing back kneeling at the communion rail. He told me and Mrs. Popowska that we needed to stop harking back to the 1950s. In front of the whole parish council.'

She put the meat in the oven and slammed the door shut. 'The gall of the man. The sheer gall.' She took a large sip of her sherry and leaned back on the kitchen work surface. 'I need to sit down.'

Eric had agreed to come to lunch. He brought a bottle of red wine with him. 'It's a screw top,' he said, as Piotr hung his coat up on a hook in the corridor for him. 'You can't go wrong with screw tops.'

They sat down to eat and Eric said, 'It's almost thirty-five years since I moved next door you know. Ten years before I officially retired.'

Piotr carefully sliced the pork. 'Do you miss not doing your job?'

'What, teaching the piano?' said Eric. 'I don't miss the feral kids much, I'll tell you that. Most of them never wanted to learn in the first place. It was like getting blood out of a bloody stone. Sorry, excuse my language dear,' he said, looking at Piotr's Aunt.

'I sometimes miss not playing at the hotel. Tinkling the old ivories for all these posh people who could afford martinis and whiskey sours at five-star hotels. But then that could be a pain in the arse too. The Americans were the worst. They'd always request a song. They wouldn't let you go through a repertoire.'

Eric smoothed his long white hair back into his loose ponytail and began eating. At one point, he crunched on some crackling and had to take his false teeth out.

'Sorry about that,' he said. 'I need to get a new set, these aren't up to the job of chewing much anymore.'

They had some coffee and cake at the end of the meal.

'Did your hear about those vigilantes then?' said Eric. 'All over the local news. Two girls saying that they were saved from being mugged by some heroes. They reckon they were Polish.'

'I haven't been watching the local news much,' said Piotr's Aunt.

'Did they say what they were like?' said Piotr.

'Who?' said Eric, wiping some cake from his moustache.

'The vigilantes.'

'Don't think so. They said it happened in a flash. Come to think of it though, they did say that they were wearing black baseball caps. Good on them though, I say. The police aren't up to much these days. All they do is sit by the roadside with speed cameras.'

When they had finished, Eric insisted on drying the dishes as Piotr washed them. He dropped one of the glasses on the floor and it smashed into pieces. He wanted to give Piotr's Aunt a ten pound note for the glass but she refused to accept it. They argued about it in the corridor for five minutes before he left.

THE RAIN CAME DOWN HARD, splashing up off the ground onto Piotr's shoes as he stood under the concrete roof in front of the entrance to the Underground station. He heard a train pull into one of the platforms below him and a familiar automated male voice urging travellers to watch their step in the inclement weather.

A minute later, a crowd rushed past Piotr like a herd of sheep being freed from their pen. They placed their smartcards on the barrier reader one after the other, causing it to beep every other second. He could tell that they had come off a train travelling from the centre of the city by their large number. Beata was coming from the other direction.

His phone rang. It was Adam.

'Hi Sabum, what's up?'

'Not much. I'm waiting to meet someone.'

'Oh right, sorry to bother you. It's just that the hall isn't open yet and I'm supposed to be cleaning the dojang.'

'Well Kris should be there any moment. It's 5 to,' said Piotr looking at his watch. 'He's got time. If he's not there in a bit then Father Leopold can open the hall. Go to the house next to the church and ring the bell. He'll let you in.'

'OK. Thanks. So you're not taking the session tonight then?'

'No. I'll be there on Saturday though. Oh by the way, do me a favour. Let me know how the lesson went will you?'

'Sure,' said Adam.

As the last of the city exodus dispersed, opening umbrellas and lifting hoods over their heads, he heard a train come into the opposite platform. His stomach jumped. He told himself to be cool. When Beata walked through the ticket barriers he gave her a casual wave.

Piotr raised his head to the sky. 'I don't have an umbrella. Sorry.'

'Not to worry, I've got one,' said Beata. 'Anyway it's only across the road isn't it?'

'Do you want to make a run for it?'

'Let's go for it.'

They raced over the road. Piotr tried to duck his head underneath

Beata's umbrella. He held the restaurant door open for her when they got there. A waiter greeted them inside. Beata apologised for getting the floor wet with her umbrella.

'It's no problem,' he said.

The waiter took them to a table in the corner and handed them two menus. He told them about the specials of the day, pan fried fresh trout and pierogi with fruit filling for dessert.

When the waiter had gone, Piotr said, 'I wonder where they get the trout from. Hopefully not the River Brent.'

Beata laughed. 'I've never seen the River Brent,' she said. 'Where does it go through?'

'Pretty near here. I go running along it sometimes, at the bit where it turns into a canal for a stretch.'

Piotr read the menu slowly and rubbed his thumb on the card that it was printed on. He looked around the restaurant and at the framed drawings of famous landmarks in Poland that hung on the walls.

'You seem very interested in this place,' said Beata.

'I'm kind of curious about restaurants.'

'Why's that?'

'I'd like to open one up some day. Not like this though. More a fast food place, but with a Polish twist.'

'What's the twist?'

'Well, it'll serve pierogi mostly. That'll be the attraction. I've got a name for it already – Professor Porski's Pierogi. The pig will be the face of the restaurant, but he'll wear spectacles. We'll sell four or five main types, maximum. With maybe three different types of sauce: Mushroom, barbecue, and spicy Chinese. You'll be able to order takeaway, or eat in. Like any fast food place. And there'll only be one or two desserts. Probably fruit filled pierogi and apple pie – both with ice cream. You have to have ice cream.'

'Wow. You've really thought about it then,' said Beata.

'They're not all my ideas. I've got a business partner.'

'Do you think the English would go for it?

'Everyone that's ever tried pierogi likes them,' said Piotr. 'As far as I know, anyway. If they're fresh, have decent dough and the fillings are good, then people go for them.'

The waiter came back. Beata ordered a chicken salad and the pierogi for dessert. Piotr chose the pork knuckle and the pierogi as well. 'I may as well test the competition,' he said. They both got beers. Beata asked for hers with a bit of raspberry syrup mixed into it.

When their drinks arrived, Piotr took a sip of his beer. As he did so, Beata noticed that the first two knuckles of his right hand were swollen. 'What happened to your hand?'

'My hand?' Piotr said, checking his right hand and then his left one. 'Nothing. Why?'

'Your knuckles look a bit swollen, that's all.'

He rubbed the top of his left hand. 'They've been like that for ages. On both sides.'

'Did you injure them?'

'I guess you could say that. I study a bit of martial arts. That's why they look like that. From knuckle press ups and hitting boards.'

'What about your fingers?' she said. Piotr had two bruised fingernails on his right hand. 'Is that from your martial arts too?'

'That's from work. I slammed them when closing a car door too quickly this week. I work at a car wash.'

'Do you enjoy it?'

'It's OK,' he said. 'A bit of money to keep me going for now, you know how it is. How about you?'

'Same. Staying at the shop isn't my long-term goal. I have some plans too.'

'Like what?'

'Well, I used to want to go to New York and design shoes.'

'Yeah? What happened to that idea?'

'Idea? More like a crazy fantasy. I never studied anything to do with fashion, and it's a bit late now.'

'It's never too late for what's important to you.'

'Well, you say that. But I'm 25, and I don't have the money to go back to college and study fashion. I don't even know if I'd be any good at it. And I'm not even in America.'

'London isn't a bad place to be for fashion you know. Or making shoes.'

'That's true. But I've changed tack now anyway. I'd like to organise fashion events. You know, be an event planner.'

The waiter brought them some complimentary salads to go with their dishes. Sliced cucumbers in soured cream, steamed and shredded beetroot, sauerkraut. Piotr chewed some large mouthfuls of pork as Beata told him about a friend who planned events. She was helping her to write her CV and giving her some tips for interviews.

Piotr offered the grated cucumbers in soured cream to Beata.

'A little bit, please,' she said.

'So your English must be good then?' said Piotr, putting two spoonfuls on her plate.

'It's not bad. I went to classes back at home.'

'How long for?'

'About three years.'

'Where?'

'At home, at a private language school. We had some teachers from here and America. I worked part-time at a shopping mall to pay for it.

'In a shoe shop?'

'How did you guess?'

'Did you take any exams?'

'I got to take one exam, the FCE. Have you heard of it?'

'I didn't study English. Not formally anyway. My Dad spoke it fluently and he taught me at home.'

'Lucky you.'

When they were finished, Piotr paid the bill. He asked the waiter if he could share the recipe they used for the pierogi.

'They're brought in,' he said.

'You don't make them fresh?' said Piotr.

'Nope. It's impossible to do everything from scratch back there.'

Piotr suggested that they go for another drink to a pub nearby. Beata agreed.

The pub was quiet. Piotr asked the barman what a beer was like from a London brewery that he had never seen before. 'I'm not sure to be honest,' said the barman, in an Eastern European accent that Piotr couldn't place. 'Do you want to try a bit?'

Piotr took a sip from a sample and offered it to Beata. 'It's quite nice,' she said. They each got a pint of the beer and went to play pool. Beata asked him how she should hold the cue. He showed her by standing behind her and placing his hand over hers.

Piotr won all the games they played, but he took it easy, missing some shots he could have made. After one of them, Beata went to the jukebox and put some songs on. She danced lightly to the music in between shots.

When they finished the fifth game, he went to get some more beers. Beata asked if she could pay.

'No, I've got it,' he said.

'But you've paid for everything tonight.'

'That's OK. It's my shout.'

When he brought the beers back Beata had sat down at a table.

'So why don't you tell me about your family history. I'm curious,' she said, leaning forwards.

'What do you want to know?'

'Like about your family back home. How you got here.'

'Well, my Dad came to Poland in the 1980s to study. From Uganda. There was some programme going on at the time. The communists were trying to encourage people to come over from all sorts of places, to spread the word about how great their system was. He met my Mum and they settled down after he completed his engineering degree.'

'So he's smart.'

'He was. He died suddenly. Heart attack, ten years ago.'

'I'm sorry.'

'It's OK. It seems like a very long time ago now. But yeah, he was smart. He learnt Polish really quickly. And he was fluent in French as well as English. He had lived near the border with Congo and had a Congolese friend he practised his French with.'

'And you said the other day that you lived with your Aunt?'

'Yeah, bit unusual, I know. My Uncle passed on a while back, and they could never have children, so when I decided to come over, she asked me if I wanted to live with her. I know her really well, she's like a second mother to me. She used to visit me in Poland every summer with my Uncle. I wanted to help her out too. Especially since she's had cancer twice. Plus she's got a nice house, and she's a great cook.'

'So the beetroots will go to good use then.'

'Definitely.'

Beata gazed at her beer.

'You think it's a bit weird, don't you?' said Piotr. 'Me living with my Aunt.'

'What? No, not at all. I think it's sweet.'

They stayed in the pub until it closed. Piotr walked Beata back to the station.

'Will you be OK getting home?' he said.

'I'm a big girl.' She gave him a kiss on his cheek before passing through the barriers.

When Piotr got home it was almost midnight. His Aunt was in her bedroom. He wasn't sure if she was asleep. He could hear the soft sound of hushed voices coming from her bedside radio.

He washed his face and brushed his teeth before switching on his computer in his bedroom. He checked his emails and the local news.

Lying in bed, he thought about Beata and then his father. He remembered a time when he was walking with him in a park, throwing a stick for their dog. The dog fell into a pond and struggled to get out. Piotr and his Dad jumped in to rescue her. When they got out of the pond their clothes were soaked and the dog was shaking her wet fur all over them. It was cold so his father gave him his coat to wear, rubbing his chest and arms to help him warm up. When they got home his father wrapped him in a blanket and they drank hot tea and ate biscuits. They laughed about having the only dog in Poland that couldn't swim.

Before long, he was asleep.

THE DOC ASKED ALL THE WORKERS to step into his cabin.

He sat on the edge of his desk, watching them walk in, one by one. They lined up in expectant silence, either looking at the Doc, or at some photos on the wall behind him, where the Doc was posing next to vehicles that had been cleaned at the car wash.

When they were all in, the Doc said, 'There's no easy way to tell you this, so I'm going to have to come straight out with it.

'I've been doing some calculations. And today is the day when I have to tell you that we have been screwed by the banks. Those blood-sucking greedy bastards have led the economy to the edge of the cliff and dropped it like a used condom. And so people don't want to have their cars washed any more. They only want to wash them at home. With crap soap and even crapper wax.'

He cleared his throat and before picking up an envelope off the desk. He opened it and took a sheet of paper out of it. It was a bank statement.

'So I have no choice now. I have to shut down this surgery. This update from the bank shows that the business is in serious debt and we cannot operate like this any more. I've tried to make it work, believe me, I have. But we've reached the limit. The money's not coming in. I suppose most of you already knew that this day would come soon.'

He looked out of the window, briefly remembering better days. 'There might be some part-time work at the other two surgeries. All of you will have first choice for those jobs – in the order of when you joined, of course. I'm sorry boys. I really am. There's nothing else that I can do.'

They drifted out of the cabin and packed away all the cleaning equipment into the Doc's van. When they were done, they all trudged off towards the bus stop, apart from Dennis. Piotr asked him where he was going.

'Thought I'd check out the other car wash down the road,' he said. 'Do you really believe that this is all down to the economy? They're doing a roaring business. Sometimes on a Saturday it looks like they have to turn cars away. They're got all our customers, so maybe they'll have some spare shifts.'

'Sounds like a plan.'

'That's what I thought. Hey, you want to come with me?'

'I don't know,' said Piotr. 'I feel like a change. I think I've had enough of polishing wheels. I'll see what else is out there. Let me know how you get on.'

'You too. Good luck,' said Dennis.

They shook hands.

When Piotr got home, the house was empty. There was a note on the kitchen counter from his Aunt.

Eric has given me a lift to see my consultant. He's got Gapczo. Back by dinner time.

He opened the fridge and examined its contents. There was a can of beer on one shelf and a bottle of milk in the door. He took out the milk, opened it, and drank half of it in one go.

Sitting down in the front room, he opened his wallet and took the piece of paper with Mr. Stablinski's number out of it. He stared at it for a while and then rang the number. A receptionist answered at the other end.

'I'm afraid Mr. Stablinski is unavailable at the moment,' she said. 'Can I leave a message?'

'It's OK,' said Piotr. 'I'll call back later.'

He sat gazing out of the window for a couple of minutes and then went back into the kitchen to get the beer. He opened it and took a long drink. Back in the front room, he scrolled through his contacts list on his phone until he reached 'H'. He pressed the call option.

'Henio, it's Piotr.'

'Piotrusz! How's it going?'

'Not bad, not bad.'

'Yeah? How's the dojang? All OK?'

'It's going fine at the moment. Still early days, you know how it is.'

'Sure. But you're settling in?'

'I think so.'

'I need to pop along for a few sessions. But you know how it is, with work and the kids. I've got my hands full.'

'It'd be good to see you there. Anyway, how was your holiday?'

'Great. Really warm. And the Egyptians are nice people, very welcoming. Not too many mujahideen either.'

'So you had a good time.'

'Yeah, we did. Only downer was that the place was full of Russians. Never seen anything like it. Our hotel was like some sort of KGB gathering. So what's up, you got today off?'

'Not exactly. I've been let go from the car wash.'

'Damn. Sorry to hear that man. That's tough.'

'Well, wasn't the first time, probably won't be the last.'

'Was it something you did?'

'No, we weren't making enough. The boss had to let a load of us go.'

'Right. Tough times. Got anything else lined up?'

'Actually that's why I was calling. I was wondering if you'd heard of any openings. Or if I could even help you out with the phone cards for a bit.'

'The phone cards? That's dying. It's all the internet or just dialling straight numbers now. I'm not getting good vibes, so I've upped my hours with Pizza Village.'

'How's that going?'

'Not too bad. I'm actually picking up some knowledge from the kitchen guys about how the business works. And don't worry – I'm noting it all down for Porski's.'

'Anything there?'

'Maxed out with delivery guys. Don't think there's a kitchen vacancy at the moment, but I'll keep my eyes open for you. Hey, but you know what? There might be some work.'

'Really?'

'Yeah, I know a guy who's started working as a foreman for a building company, he's running two sites. But they're both over the river. Rebuilding houses into flats. There could be something there.'

'Have you got the guy's number?'

'No, but I'll get it for you.'

'Thanks. So what other stuff have you got going on?'

'Me? Ah, not that much, you know, business is slow.'

'Come on man, you've always got something going on,' said Piotr, taking a sip of his beer.

'I'm being serious. I've been mostly thinking about Porski's and that idea you had. You know, the one about selling pieorgi from a van at first, before trying to get permanent premises. It's a great idea. It's big in the centre of London, near the City, selling food from vans. Street food is what they call it. All the cool kids are into it. They sell all sorts near Old Street, you know where it is?'

'Not really.'

'It's not far from Liverpool Street. Anyway, they have everything there. You name it. Curries, sausages, pies, stews, pizzas. But no pierogi.'

'No pierogi?'

'Nope. The German stall has the sausages covered. And then there's some Hungarian goulash girls. But there's no pierogi. There's no one selling the South American copycat version either.'

'So there's a gap in the market.'

'Could be.'

'How are your savings?'

'Not great. You?'

'I've saved a bit.'

'So why don't we just do that then? Buy a van, get some ingredients and get going?'

Piotr drank some more beer. 'We're not ready yet though are we? We have to keep practising the recipes for starters. And I don't have enough money to fall back on if I need it for a few months.'

'Hey man, where's your indomitable spirit? Sometimes you've got to go for it.'

'Maybe. But I'd like to save up a bit more.'

'The longer we leave it, the more chance there is that someone else comes in and does it.'

'I'll be ready soon. So you'll let me know that number, right?'

'Of course.'

When Piotr finished his beer he went upstairs and checked his email. Then he had a long shower and read through some of his training notes before dozing off. He woke up to the sound of the front door opening.

From the top of the staircase, he watched his Aunt slowly take her coat off and adjust her headscarf in the corridor mirror.

Gaphco ran up the stairs to greet him.

'I didn't realise you were going to the hospital today,' said Piotr, making his way down.

'I rang up this morning. The consultant suggested I come in.'

'What did he say?'

'He got me to do some tests, so I did. Blood, scans. They got me straight in. He said it was a priority that I get checked out. Just to make sure.'

'Anything back?'

'Not yet, they'll let me know as soon as they can.'

Piotr sat at the bottom of the stairs and stroked Gapczo. 'He was concerned then.'

'I suppose so.' His Aunt smoothed her coat and put on a hook by the mirror. A few tears trickled down her cheeks. Piotr stood up and hugged her.

That night Piotr dreamt about being followed from the car wash all the way home by two men. He tried to shake them off by switching buses and then walking into a clothes shop and changing his outfit, but they kept tailing him. When he got into the house, they stayed on the street, staring into the house behind the bush in the front garden.

He woke up sweating. He got up to look out of the window, but there was no one there. He crept downstairs and drank the rest of the bottle of milk that he had opened earlier. Before going back to his room he peered through the front window curtains. The street was quiet.

The next morning Piotr woke up to the sound of his phone buzzing on the floor. It was Henio. 'What's happening?' he said.

'Not much. I was sleeping.'

'Sleeping? It's 7 in the morning man. You should be up and about. Anyway, listen. I've got some news on the job front. If you're still looking.'

Piotr got out of bed and looked out onto the street. 'Well, nobody came over and handed me a job over night.'

'Alright wise ass. Well check this one out. You know I told you about those sites over the river?'

'U-huh.'

'Well, I did some legwork for you. Turns out one of them is definitely looking for help. I know the foreman's cousin, second removed or something. He gave me the heads up last night. You want to go check it out this morning? I need to go there anyway to deliver some phonecards. It's in South London. Balham way.'

'That's miles away isn't it?'

'You can do it in an hour on the Tube. What do you say?'

'It's worth checking out I guess,' said Piotr.

'OK. I've got to drop the kids off at school first. I'll see you at 9:30 outside yours.'

Henio turned up at 10. He hit the horn as he parked outside.

Piotr was ready for him. As he walked down the front garden path, he stopped for a moment to speak to Eric, who was washing one of his cars. He was kneeling down by one of the wheels and scrubbing it with a brush. It was an old French car from the early 1980s. Piotr had never seen a car like it before coming to London. It had silver tubes that ran along the edges of its curved roof and small red brake lights that popped out of them above the rear window. The car's body was low to the ground, as if it was weighed down with too much luggage. Piotr thought that the chassis would sit right down on the road if Eric got it in, with the tyres disappearing inside it.

'Looks brand new,' said Piotr.

Eric stood up. 'Should do, the amount of scrubbing I've done on it this morning. Bet you don't get them this clean at your car wash, eh?'

'Definitely not,' said Piotr. 'Especially now that I've lost my job there.'

Eric wiped his brow. 'Oh, sorry to hear that son.'

'It's alright. Something will come up. I'm off to see if I can find another job that my friend knows about right now.' He pointed at Henio, sitting in his car.

'That's the spirit. I'll keep my fingers crossed for you.'

'Thanks,' said Piotr.

They drove into the centre of the city, towards the Thames, heading past the large new shopping centre near the BBC television studios in Shepherd's Bush. Henio started speaking to someone on his Bluetooth earpiece about selling some phone cards. Piotr looked out of his window. Every time he travelled into the centre he was fascinated by how big and diverse the city was; how neighbourhoods that were so different managed to sit side-by-side and somehow merge together seamlessly into one big mess thanks to a few Underground signs, black cabs and red buses.

Piotr supposed that if you drove for long enough in the city then you would catch a glimpse of someone from every part of the world, toiling through its leaden road system. Many would be doleful and resigned, others angry, a few confused. Some would be plain lost.

When they passed the road down to Stamford Bridge, Henio pointed out the football stadium to Piotr.

'That's crazy that there's a stadium just down there,' said Piotr. 'It seems so out of place here.'

'That's this city for you,' said Henio. 'Things are hidden behind other things everywhere here.'

They got stuck in a tailback on Battersea Bridge.

'What have you been up to the last couple of weeks then?' Henio said. 'Apart from the dojang.'

'Not that much. Had a date last night.'

'Yeah? You dirty dog. How did it go?'

'Good. I'm seeing her again at the weekend, I think.'

'Who took training then?'

'Krzsytof. Jacek was tied up with his gym work.'

'So you trust him now?' Henio said, lighting a cigarette.

'Not really. But sometimes I have no choice.'

'Well, you could have re-arranged the date,' said Henio, rolling down the window and blowing smoke out of the car.

'I suppose. But he can't do any harm taking a session here or there.'

When the traffic had cleared a little, Piotr received a text message from Adam. He read it. *Hey Sabum. Lesson good last nite. Lots of sparring, no tuls, but good workout. Kris was a bit late but got the cleaning done in time after Father L opened up.*

'This place is miles away,' said Piotr, reading the text again.

'Don't worry,' said Henio. 'Think about it this way. If you get it, it'll only be for a few months. We'll have the pierogi wagon going before long. Everyone has to travel for work at the moment. It's scarce.'

Henio tried to park near the building site but there were no free spaces. He circled the block a couple of times, until Piotr told him not to bother any more.

'I don't need you to hold my hand,' he said. 'If you keep circling the block, I'll catch you up when I'm done.'

The foreman was standing outside the building site talking on his mobile in English, ordering some material. When he was finished he put his phone into a pouch tied to his belt and stroked his moustache.

'Morning,' said Piotr. 'I heard there might be some work for a labourer here. He extended his hand. 'I'm Piotr. I'd like to put myself forward for it.'

The foreman stared at him for a moment before shaking Piotr's hand. 'Grzegorz,' he said. 'There might be. Where did you hear about it?'

'My friend told me. He knows your cousin.'

'What's his name?'

'Henryk. Henryk Stalewski.'

'Stalewski? What's he up to these days?'

'Sells phone cards, delivers pizzas too.'

'So he's legit now?'

'Legit? I didn't know he was anything else.'

'Maybe I'm thinking of the wrong guy. Have you worked on sites before?'

'I did some general labouring last year, for about four months.'

The foreman examined Piotr for a moment. 'So you can carry bricks and fill skips?'

'Sure.'

'No injuries?'

'Nope.'

'£290 a week to start. That's for a trial period. Then it goes up to £350.'

'Sounds good,' said Piotr.

The foreman took a small notebook out of his top pocket and wrote something in it with a thick rectangular pencil. 'You can start tomorrow. 8 o'clock.'

Piotr found Henio driving slowly on an adjacent street. He thanked him for finding the job.

'Don't be stupid Piotrek,' he said. 'You'd do the same for me.'

'Well, it's appreciated.'

'No worries. Now you just have to sit tight while I drop off some phone cards.'

They drove for a while before Piotr said, 'That foreman said something weird back there. He asked me if you were still legit.'

'Legit?'

'That's what he said. Legit.'

Henio chuckled to himself. 'He's probably talking about the bootleg stuff I used to sell.'

'Like what?'

'Fake luxury brands. Some clothes, handbags, that kind of stuff. I sold them on a hush hush agreement. Loads of guys brought them over from back home, Ukraine, Latvia, Lithuania. Hardly anyone checked the boys who did the mini bus and coach runs. They did it a lot. They can stash a few boxes each time for dirt cheap and then sell them to market stalls here.'

'Who took them?'

'Loads of guys. It used to be big business.'

'But the market sellers could get done for that couldn't they?'

'No chance. If they're caught they play innocent. Say they bought the stuff in good faith. Nobody cares anyway, apart from the luxury brands. It's not like the police storm market stalls all the time for some knock off Gucci belts.'

'So it made you some money?'

'Made me a bit, nothing major. Heck, maybe I should look into it again the way it's going with these phone cards. Everyone used to want them. Indians, Somalians, us lot, South Americans. The guy I get them from was making big money out of it at one point. But everyone's got Skype now. Damn internet's ruined everything.'

They took until midday to go through all Henio's drop offs. On the way home, Henio tuned the car radio into London's Polish radio station. It was playing a classic song by a popular band from back home.

Henio kept his window down and turned up the volume. He slapped his hands on the steering wheel to the music, while Piotr tapped his foot.

When they got back to Sudbury Hill, Henio asked Piotr if he wanted to come to his wife's birthday drinks.

'Where?'

'Over the hill, in a pub in Harrow. They've got a band playing too. I know the singer. Dorota, good friend of Ania's. Gives you a chance to celebrate your new job. What do you reckon?'

'Sounds good. When?'

'Next Friday. You can sleep the drink off on the tube ride to work the next morning.'

'Mind if I ask Beata if she'd want to come?'

'Course not. It'd be good to meet her.'

AS THEY WALKED INTO THE PUB, the band was playing a song that Piotr recognised. He started moving his head to the music. Beata, with her arm slipped under his, pouted and moved her shoulders from side to side.

Almost everyone in the pub looked Polish to Piotr, even the staff behind the bar, apart from one older man with a comb over that had enough grease to fry up a thousand pierogi. Piotr guessed that he was the landlord. Nobody gave him a second look and the crowd was heavy on couples. Piotr let his guard down a little.

Henio was with Ania and some other people in a corner of the pub. They were all laughing at one of his jokes. Henio spotted Piotr and waved them over.

Hugging Piotr, he said, 'Great you could make it. And you must be Beata.' He took her hand and kissed it lightly.

'He's a real gentleman,' said Piotr, rolling his eyes at Beata.

'Let me introduce you to everyone.'

Henio stood between them and put his arms around them. 'Hey everyone, Piotr and Beata are here.'

He pointed to each person in turn. 'So that's Ania, my darling wife. Next to her is Paweł, Ania's brother. He lives in Slough. Agnieszka over here is a friend of Ania's, Bartek and Małgosia live on the same street as us. Robert is Dorota's boyfriend. Dorota's up on stage with the band and the guy coming back now from the gents is Kamil, Robert's cousin.'

'Pleased to meet you all,' said Piotr. 'Can I get anyone a drink?'

'Hang on,' said Robert. 'I'm about to buy a round. We're all on beers,' he said, raising a bottle. 'That OK for you?'

When Robert came back with the drinks, Beata started chatting to Ania and Agnieszka. Henio stood by Piotr.

'She's a looker,' he said in his ear. 'Nice work.'

'Thanks.'

'So. We never got a chance the other day to properly talk about the dojang. You know, how's it all going and everything.'

'It's all good. So far,' said Piotr. 'I'm thinking about promoting a couple of the guys actually, get some fresh black belts on board. I'm struggling to come up with a good test for them though.

Nothing's come to mind yet.'

'It will, don't worry. Man, I remember how long I had to wait to get my belt. It killed me. I thought Sabum would never ask me. It turned out that he wasn't delaying deliberately. He was waiting for the right opportunity.'

Henio raised a hand to a man across the pub floor. Piotr checked to see if he recognised the man, but he didn't. He was wearing a black shirt and a big silver necklace. 'Who's that?' said Piotr.

'Some guy I know,' said Henio. 'So how about the job, how's that working out with training? Are you going to be able to still run all the sessions with all that travelling?'

'It's worked OK this week. Longer-term, I'm not sure. I might need to negotiate my hours a bit. Still, I've got Jacek to help when he can. And Krszystof.'

'Only for as long as Kris wants to be there though, eh?' said Henio.

'What do you mean?'

'I thought he would have set up his own thing by now. You know, after you were made Sabum. That was always his dream, wasn't it? He always talked about doing things a bit differently when he was in charge. New rules, entering bouts. I thought you knew that.'

'Yeah I do. But he hasn't gone anywhere has he? Maybe he's changed his mind.'

Henio took a long gulp of his beer and wiped his mouth as he put the bottle down. 'I would keep an eye on him. Maybe he sees a vacuum there without Sabum. Have you not noticed anything?

'Not really. The only weird thing has been a couple of students asking about underground bouts. Don't know why they suddenly think they can enter those.'

'They're just testing the water. Seeing if you're a soft touch or not.'

They both raised their hands and applauded the band as it finished a song. Piotr said, 'If you're so worried about Kris, why don't you come back and help me keep tabs on him?'

'I would if I could. But I need a little time to get my act together. Plus I need to get into shape,' he said, patting his stomach. He tapped his bottle. 'Too many of these.'

'You don't look that out of shape to me. Anyway, we'll get you into condition in no time.'

The guitarist struck the opening chords to another song that Piotr knew. As Henio finished his beer, Piotr said, 'I'll get these.' He went to the bar. Beata followed him.

'Need some help?' she said.

'Well, if it's from you, then yes,' said Piotr turning to look at her. 'Are you having a good time?'

'Absolutely. Your friends are really nice. So what were you and Henio in such an intense conversation about?'

'We were just talking about a guy we know. Nothing major.'

They ordered drinks off one of the barmaids who was young enough to still be at school. Beata asked her how long she had worked there. 'A month,' she said. 'I've only got another one to go. I'm going back home to Gdansk, I'm a student there.'

'How often do you have these Polish nights?' asked Beata.

'Every Friday,' she said. 'The pub was losing money as the locals have stopped coming as often. But this has revived it. We have a late licence and can do disco nights on Saturdays too. They're even more popular than band nights at the moment.'

They went back to the table and carried on drinking and talking with everyone. Towards the end of the night, Robert asked Piotr what song he wanted the band to play. He had a piece of paper with some songs jotted down on it.

'I don't know. I'm not too bothered. They're playing some good stuff as it is.'

'Oh come on, what's your favourite song? I've asked everyone so far. Write it down here. They'll play the request they like the most. If they know it, of course.'

Robert handed Piotr a pen. Piotr wrote down the name of the song and the band that had written it.

When the band finished playing, Robert went up to the stage. Dorota crouched down to catch what he was saying. She stood up and the band huddled together. She showed them some chords. After some nods of approval, she turned to Robert and stuck her thumb up.

'So what are they going to play?' said Kamil when Robert got back.

'You'll see. They're well up for the one they've chosen.' He held his beer aloft. 'Good luck with your song choices everyone,' he said, emptying his beer down his throat.

Dorota addressed the crowd.

'This one's been chosen by Piotrusz,' she said. 'Thanks for coming out to hear us play and have a safe journey home.'

The guitarist strummed the opening chords to the song. The whole table turned to face the band, clapping and whistling in acknowledgement. Robert picked up another bottle and clinked it with Piotr's.

Henio played air guitar and Paweł started headbanging. The girls danced with each other. When the band reached the chorus, the men put their arms over their shoulders and sang it together, at the top of their voices.

The lead guitarist finished the song with a flashy solo. Everyone at the table roared their approval and raised their beers high up in the air as the band hit the last note in perfect time.

Afterwards Piotr walked Beata to the Tube station at Harrow-on-the-hill.

'I had a good time tonight,' she said. 'Thanks for inviting me.'

'I'm really glad you could make it.'

'So now it's my turn to invite you somewhere.'

'Oh yeah?' said Piotr, raising an eyebrow.

'No, not what you're thinking,' she said gently pushing him in the chest.

'Next Friday is Aga's birthday party. You know, my flatmate. She really wants us to go. I told her I'd ask you.'

'Where is it?'

'Hammersmith. At the Polish club.'

'Sounds good. Count me in.'

They got to the station and stopped at the ticket barriers. 'You don't have to walk me into the train you know. But it's very sweet of you.'

She kissed him on the lips. 'I'll call you about Friday.'

Smiling, Piotr walked out of the station and down a side street that was parallel to the platforms. He could see Beata standing in the middle of one of the platforms through the wire fencing. To her right, some teenagers were laughing at something one of them had on their phone. Further down from them a couple of Asian guys were sitting on a bench. To the left of her three girls were shuffling impatiently.

Beata's train arrived and she got on it. Piotr went back to the end of the side street. The main road was quiet, apart from a car outside a kebab shop. Piotr stepped back into the shadows. After a minute, a man jumped into the passenger seat with a plastic bag full of food and the car pulled away. When it was out of sight, Piotr moved, heading for the bus station. When he got there, the electronic board said that his bus was 20 minutes late. He left the bright lights of the bus station and pulled his hoodie over his head, looking over his shoulder as he walked into the night.

Piotr turned up early for work the next day. One of the workers, Buszek, had opened up the site as the foreman had gone to pick up some material. Buszek was sitting on a stool and had his head in his hands. There was an open can of beer by his feet.

Piotr got changed into his work gear. 'Late one?'

'You could say that. Any chance you could cover for me this morning? I need a couple of hours sleep to shake this off.'

'Sure. What time's the boss here?'

'About 11.'

'Alright, I'll give you a shout at ten to, if he's not here by then.'

Piotr went outside. He had to dismantle a shed in the back garden and then scoop up some earth in preparation for a digger. As he started, another worker came to fill a bucket with some water from the outside tap.

'Morning,' he said. 'I'm Michał, but everyone calls me Uncle.' He was short and had a grey moustache. He was wearing a baseball cap, back to front. It had a Detroit Lions emblem on it. 'You must be the new boy.'

'That's right. I'm Piotr.' They shook hands.

'Have you seen Buszek?'

'He's having to sleep off his hangover,' said Piotr. 'He must be in the basement.'

'What is it with that pisshead? He's always pulling this stunt. He owes the rest of us big time.'

During the morning break, Uncle sat outside on a wall in the back garden. Piotr asked him if he could sit with him. 'Be my guest,' said Uncle.

Piotr had a ham sandwich. Uncle ate some cold sausage and bread. He dipped the sausage in a pot of mustard before each bite. They both drank dark coffee. Uncle talked a bit about how he had got to London.

'I was never meant to stay here,' he said. 'I was stopping off on my way back from Detroit just after the Wall had fallen. Then I met my wife and got stuck here. How about you?'

'Came here a couple of years ago. I messed up at uni and there weren't many prospects for me back home. Plus I had family here already.'

'You like it here?'

'Yeah, I think I do.'

Before they finished eating, Buszek emerged from the basement. He went over to some sand bags that were neatly stacked by the fence and bent over to retch. He waited until all the sick had left his stomach before he went to the tap and filled a bucket full of water. He tried to wash away the vomit as best he could.

Towards the end of the day Piotr and Uncle swept up outside where Piotr had dumped all the remains of the shed into a skip. They cleaned themselves up before getting changed. Piotr welcomed the relief from the layer of dirt and dust that had enveloped his hands and forearms. When Piotr took his shirt off, Uncle saw two scars beneath his right rib cage.

They walked to the Tube station together and took the same route into the centre before changing onto a different train out West. Uncle fell asleep on the second train while Piotr read a book about being an entrepreneur he had bought from a second hand bookstore. It was in English so he had to read it slowly.

His Aunt was home when he got in.

'You're early,' she said.

'We finish at 2 on a Saturday,' he said. 'I thought I'd told you that, sorry.'

'You probably did,' said his Aunt. 'My memory's getting worse by the day. It's all this diabolical medication.'

'How are you feeling today?'

'Not great dear.'

Piotr nodded at her medicine cabinet. 'Well, you need to keep taking that stuff until you do. When did you say you get your results back again?'

She looked out of the kitchen window, with her back to him. 'Early next week.'

Piotr touched his Aunt's shoulder. 'I'm sure they'll come back OK. You're doing too much, that's all.'

She put her hand on his. 'Maybe you're right. I'll go and have a rest.'

Piotr went to the fridge. 'Is there anything I can eat before I go to training?'

'There's kabanos in the fridge,' said his Aunt, sitting down on the sofa in the dining room.

Piotr found some of the thin smoked sausage. He spooned some mustard onto a plate and scooped it up with the kabanos.

'It's such a shame you have to travel so far for this job. You wouldn't be in a rush if you were more local. Are you sure you want to spend so long going to work?'

Piotr checked his watch. 'Ah, it's not that bad Auntie. It's good physical work. It's not forever and it keeps me fit. Don't forget, no cooking today. I'm making pierogi, so you can sit back and take it steady.'

Piotr met Kris at the door of the church hall.

'I was about to ring for Father Leopold,' said Kris. 'I wanted to get in some *tul* practice beforehand.

'Sorry, the bus was delayed,' said Piotr, unlocking the front door.

'You need to get a car.'

'Tell me about it.'

'Maybe we should get some keys cut, for me the other black belts, you know, when you're away.'

'Probably a good idea. I'll check that it's OK with Father Leopold and get them done.'

When they were getting changed Piotr said, 'So how was training on Thursday?'

'Good.'

'How many tuls did you get through?'

'Not that many. We got into a lot of sparring in the end. I could feel their energy, they were up for it, so I went with it.'

'I thought I'd asked you to drill their tuls?'

'I didn't think it would do any harm. They were agitated, I could sense it.'

'Agitated?'

'Yeah, you know, restless. I wanted to use that.'

'What does that mean?'

'They weren't in the mood for it, you know how it is. Sometimes you have to go with it.'

'You don't need to feed me some hippy explanation. I told you what needed doing and you went and did something else. It wasn't a session that could be changed. Next time you lead training, you need to run it how I want it run. Is that a problem for you?'

With his back to Piotr, Kris pulled hard at the ends of his belt as he tightened its knot. 'Sorry. Like I said, they wanted to spar. No harm done.' He walked out into the hall, without looking back at Piotr.

Piotr showered for a long time, leaning against the wall and letting the hot water almost scald him. He checked his emails as he got changed and then called Jacek.

'You want to grab a couple of beers? Up at Horsenden Hill?'

'Don't tell me you want to go up and count planes again.'

'We can just sit down and look in the other direction at the golfers.'

'Golf? Seriously? If you want I suppose. I could do with an afternoon nap. I'll get some beers.'

They met outside an off licence. On the way it started raining, so they stopped outside a derelict snooker hall and sheltered in the hall's doorway. They stood underneath its old broken neon sign and drank a beer. Piotr eyed the street. Jacek took a cigarette out of his jacket pocket.

'Don't say a word to Monika, ' he said, as he lit it. 'I've told her I was giving up.'

Piotr kept his eyes on the street. 'Don't worry, my lips are sealed. But shouldn't you be giving those up?'

'Why?'

'I didn't think your MMA mates would approve.'

'I don't smoke in front of them. Anyway, as long as they're happy with my kickboxing class, then what harm can it do?'

'Tell your lungs that 20 years from now,' said Piotr, examining the view behind Jacek.

'What are you scoping the street out for?' Jacek said.

'That car down there. The black saloon. I swear I've seen that car before.'

'So what?'

'It makes me nervous. What would it be doing here? I didn't see it here earlier. And I saw it somewhere else. I just can't remember where.'

'Same number plate?'

'I forgot to check the first time.'

Jacek looked at the car. 'You're acting weird.'

'I can't help it,' said Piotr. He took a large swig of his beer.

Once the rain eased off they walked up to Horsenden Hill. There were some golfers on one of the greens near where they wanted to sit. They were wearing waterproofs and their hair was wet through. One of them was crouching down and looking at the line his ball needed to take to the hole.

'How can anyone play such a boring game,' said Jacek. 'I mean, seriously. How can it be any fun? It must take all day to play.'

He handed Piotr a beer. 'Anything you wanted to talk about in particular? You're not going to ask me if I can get you any work are you?

'No, I'm OK on that front at the moment. I'll be working at a building site for a few weeks at least. Which is why I wanted to talk to you. I need you to be at the dojang more often. You might have been right about Kris. He's up to something. I won't be able to always make it to training, travelling from this job. I need someone to keep an eye on him when I'm away.'

'So give it up. Do something else.'

'It's pretty good money for what it is. And there's not that much else going at the moment. It's only temporary anyway, until I get things going with Henio.'

'That's been your line for – how long now – a year? At least.'

'You can't rush these things,' said Piotr.

All of the golfers had missed their putts and seen their balls roll off the green. They were joking with each other, trying to work out whose ball was furthest away from the hole.

'Well surely if something's not happening after a while then it's time to abandon it, or at least look at doing it a different way.'

Piotr took a long sip of beer. 'Like I said, these things don't happen overnight.'

'Well they don't take an eternity either.'

Piotr ignored his last comment. 'So, what do you say? Can you at least get there for Thursdays? That could be the most tricky day for me.'

'I'll try. Really, I will. So what's made you worry about Kris?'

'When I had my date I told him to focus on tuls. Turns out they sparred the whole time instead. Which fits. I've had two of the students going on at me about competing in some underground stuff. They wouldn't be so vocal if they weren't being encouraged. And I don't need to hire some detective to work out who's behind that.'

'What happened to letting Kris do what he wants, and all your talk about it's what I say and do that really matters? Anyway, like you keep saying, everyone knows the rules. They get kicked out if they challenge you. Kris knows that too. You have to show him who's boss.'

One of the golfers found the hole. They all cheered, holding their clubs aloft.

'If you're so worried then give him an ultimatum,' said Jacek. 'Respect the code or go.'

'I wish I could. But we're so low on black belts at the moment. It's not an option.'

'You know what you need to do? Set up a meeting. Clear the air. Thrash a few things out and make sure we're all on the same track.'

'Maybe you're right,' said Piotr, peeling the label off his beer bottle. 'I should have had one before we even started training again.'

'Never mind all that could-have-would-have stuff. Just call it. There's no shame in talking. People need to know that you're running the show.'

They had another beer before making their way back down the hill. On the way, Jacek asked Piotr if he could come to his house for some extra training.

'Of course,' said Piotr. 'What sort of training?'

'I need your take on a couple of moves I've been working on.'

When Piotr got home he cooked some pierogi for himself and his Aunt. He put some garlic and onions in the food processor and added them to a mixture of beef and pork, along with some herbs and a few chilli flakes.

He gave his Aunt three pierogi as she said she wasn't that hungry.

'What do you think?' he said. 'They've got a little garlic and chilli in there. I've read that they help fight cancer.'

She sliced into one of the dumplings and took a mouthful. She chewed slowly. 'They're nice. But a little dry.'

While they were eating he opened up his notebook. He jotted down what he had made, taking care to remember the exact ingredients and timings he had used. He chewed the end of his pen. 'Do you think the dryness could be solved by serving lots of sauce?'

'Possibly. But they should be a bit moist themselves.'

'Next week I'll do them with a sauce.' He wagged his finger at her. 'You'll like them eventually.'

He washed up the dishes and made some coffee for them both before going upstairs to check his email. There were no messages that caught his attention. He scanned the Polish sports papers for a while.

One headline made him pause. POLICE CHIEF ISSUES HOOLIGAN WARNING. The reporter had interviewed a senior policeman who was concerned about organised hooligan gangs meeting up to fight at the European football championships. He said there could also be trouble when Poland met England at Wembley in a few weeks. Piotr saved the webpage and stored it in a folder on his desktop.

PIOTR WOKE UP WITH A START. He grabbed an armrest as the train jolted its way out of the Tube station. He rubbed his eyes and checked out the other passengers on his carriage. They were all buried in their own worlds. The train passed by Wembley Stadium. Shots of sunlight gleamed on and off its arch in the late spring sky, as if it was sending out a message in Morse Code.

When he got home he heard his Aunt talking on the phone in the living room. He walked inside to wave a hello. She looked up at him and smiled, holding the receiver with one hand and clutching a crumpled tissue in the other.

Piotr sat down on a couch opposite her.

'I've got to go dear,' said his Aunt. 'Piotrusz is home. I'll call you again at the weekend.'

She put the phone down slowly, not catching her nephew's eye.

Piotr leaned forward. 'Everything OK?'

'That was Maciek. It's about Ewa, my cousin in Acton. She died last night. God rest her soul.'

Piotr got up and hugged her.

'It's not been a good day,' she said.

'What do you mean?'

'The consultant called earlier as well. With my results.'

'And?'

She took a deep breath and cleared her throat. 'And the cancer has come back.'

Piotr stood motionless. His Aunt dabbed one of her eyes. 'I'm going to see him tomorrow to see what the next step should be.'

'Why did it come back? I thought that it had all gone.'

'So did I.'

'Well then you'll have to have some more treatment.'

'I don't know.'

'What do you mean?'

'It's spread a lot.'

'What do you mean by a lot?'

'To my bones. That's why I've been feeling so weak.'

Piotr took her hand. 'I'm sure they can help you Auntie,' he said. 'They can work miracles these days.'

'Only God can work miracles,' she said.

His Aunt didn't eat much at dinner. Piotr told her to relax while he did the dishes, so she went upstairs to her bedroom. He scrubbed the plates and pots hard. He nicked himself on one the knives and cursed, throwing it onto the draining board. Resisting the urge to punch the wall, he crouched down and let out a quiet scream.

He went into the garage and punched the heavy bag until he felt like he was going to vomit up his dinner.

Later, when he went upstairs, he peeked round his Aunt's bedroom door. She was lying on her bed and had her eyes closed. He wasn't sure if she was asleep or not. He backed out and carefully shut the door.

PIOTR WENT TO THE BAR and got himself a beer and one for Beata with a bit of raspberry syrup in it. They walked through the basement club trying to find Beata's friends. The silhouettes on the dance floor moved to the music in a jagged motion, while the occasional strobe light exposed the expressions on the dancers' faces.

When they found them Beata introduced Piotr to Agnisezka's boyfriend, a guy from Katowice, called Karol. He had studs in both ears and had turned up the collar on his polo shirt. It had a GKS Katowice emblem on it.

'You a football man?' said Karol.

'I don't mind it,' said Piotr.

Two hours later, he was drinking vodka shots at the bar with Karol and two of his friends. They washed the vodka down with strong beer.

'So you're a Radomiak fan?' said Karol.

'I keep an eye out for their results, but never really went to the games,' said Piotr. 'They don't have the best reputation as fans.'

'I know what you mean,' said Karol. 'They've had some fearsome crews over the years. Small, but really tough. When we dropped down the divisions after that financial scandal – which was all bullshit by the way – we bumped into your boys now and again.' He whistled. 'That was some serious action. Serious.'

'You were involved with a crew?'

'More like on the fringes. I had to stop in the end. I got cold feet after a couple of mates got badly busted up after one game in Warsaw. Nasty. One of them still has problems from a brain injury he got.'

'Sounds vicious,' said Piotr, drinking another shot of vodka. He caught the attention of one of the bar staff and circled his finger, indicating that they wanted another round.

'I didn't have the stomach for it in the end. You think you're invincible when you're 22. But the truth is that you're just a moment away from losing everything. And I'm older and trying to live a bit cleaner. I wouldn't want to do anything that pissed Aga off either, you know what I mean?'

'Although the hools have come over as well,' said one of Karol's friends. 'You see their stickers on bus stops and lamp posts all over the place. Legia lot mostly. Whoring Varsovians. You can't get away from them.'

'You think there are crews here?' said Piotr. 'I've never heard of them causing any trouble.'

'It's mainly kids trying to make some noise,' said Karol. 'But no doubt there are a few hardcore guys who are knocking around here now. But they don't get into any scraps. Not that I know of, anyway.'

'I've heard a few of them are gearing up for the England match,' said Karol's friend. 'There's been talk on the forums and all that.'

'Oh yeah? What forums?' said Piotr.

'You know, the usual ones. Don't you know them?'

'No,' said Piotr.

'Do you want to check them out? They're good for a laugh if nothing else.' Karol's friend asked the barman for a pen. He wrote two web addresses and two passwords on a paper napkin and handed it over to Piotr.

'There. But they're not on the regular web. If you catch my drift.'

'So you used to bang a bit?' said Karol. 'You look like you could handle yourself.'

'Me? No. I'm nosey, that's all.'

They drank another round and then joined the girls on the dance floor after one of them kept pestering them to get up and dance. The DJ played a slow song and the couples came together. Piotr leaned on Beata and nuzzled her neck.

'How much have you been drinking?' said Beata. 'You're acting drunk.'

'That's because I am drunk,' he said, pulling her in closer. 'Your friend Karol keeps buying me vodka. It's rude to turn it down.'

She spoke into his ear. 'Well, maybe after this dance you should go to the bar, get me a Diet Cola and get yourself some water, will you do that?'

'Sure. I need to go to the toilet first.'

When the DJ starting playing a new song, Piotr kissed Beata on the lips. She gave him a gentle push when he tried to do so again. 'Go on,' she said. He stumbled through the bodies on the crammed dance floor and went to the toilet.

The urinals were all being used, so he went into a cubicle. He managed to negotiate a pool of urine and stood with his legs far apart, trying to keep his shoes dry.

Karol and his friend walked in. 'So what do you think?' Karol said.

'What, of chimney sweep? Yeah, he's OK, you know, for a banana muncher.' They both laughed.

'Yeah, he's good fun,' said Karol. 'Bit of a mystery though don't you think? I wonder where he and Beata met.'

Piotr pressed the flush handle with his foot and exited the cubicle. He glanced at them in the mirror as he washed his hands, but neither of them had noticed him. Another two men walked in and Piotr left, shaking his hands to dry them as there were no paper towels left, apart from for the pile of used ones that had spilled out of a bin to the side of the sinks.

He bought the cola for Beata and drank a pint of tap water at the bar before getting another one. He and Beata stayed on the dance floor for the rest of the evening. They left before the club closed, to catch the last Tube home. As they said their goodbyes Piotr shook hands with Karol and his friends.

'Good to have met you,' said Karol.

'It was a good evening,' said Piotr.

When they were outside, Piotr took Beata by the hand and he kissed her on the mouth up against a wall, stepping in to press himself against her. He tried to touch one of her breasts. She let him, briefly, before gently guiding his hand away.

The next morning, Jacek knocked on the main garage door. Piotr was inside, trying to sweat out his hangover by throwing kicks at the punch bag.

'Come through the gate,' Piotr shouted.

'Sorry, I slept in,' said Jacek when he walked into the garage. Piotr stopped kicking.

'No problem,' he said. 'I'm in no rush.'

'I was watching some boxing, late one. Cruiserweight fight. Did you see it?'

'I was out,' said Piotr.

'Good night?'

'It was a party for one of Beata's friends.'

'Oh right. How's it all going?'

'Not bad.'

'Been to her place yet?'

'Nope.'

'She been here?'

'No. And there's no way I would bring her here anyway. It would break my Aunt's heart.' Piotr started punching the bag. 'So what sort of training do you want to do?'

Jacek stood behind the bag to stop it from swinging back too far. 'Listen, have I come at a bad time or something?'

Piotr stepped back and wiped his head with his forearm. 'I'm sorry. My Aunt got some bad news this week. The cancer's come back.'

'Oh man, Piotr. I'm sorry.'

'She's going to get some more treatment.'

'They can do all sorts nowadays.'

'That's what I keep telling myself. Anyway, it's good you came over. Honestly. I need some distractions. So what did you want to test?'

'A couple of moves to break a front choke. I've based them on *Po-Eun*. It's something that Sabum Zieliński showed us once. But I've never seen them used since then. And when I tried them out the other week in the gym the guys ripped into me for it.'

'Let's warm up first,' said Piotr.

Jacek swapped places with Piotr and shifted around the punch bag, throwing elbows, knifehands, punches and kicks. Piotr went through a *tul* as he was doing so.

After a few minutes, Piotr said, 'OK, show me what you've got.'

Piotr grabbed Jacek's neck with both hands. Jacek showed him the move in slow motion. A high elbow strike to the face, and then a double elbow strike towards the collarbones, to push the aggressor away.

'I thought it would work nicely in close quarters. What do you reckon?

'I'm not sure,' Piotr said, repeating the moves at half pace. 'Maybe if you drilled it to death. It wouldn't be my first choice in a situation like that. Let's road test it.'

They put their head guards and padded gloves on. Piotr chewed down on his gum shield as they went into the garden barefooted. They took turns putting a front choke on each other and using the defence. Piotr caught Jacek full on the cheek with one elbow strike. Jacek spat some blood out. Piotr held up a hand in apology. 'Good shot,' said Jacek.

I'll tell you what the problem is,' said Piotr when they stopped. 'You haven't got enough time to get the next bit in after you either break free or prevent the initial hold.'

'What I am doing wrong?'

'They're not meant to follow each other. You'd be much better off just punching me in the face.'

'I don't get it, they're in the *tul* like that.'

'Are they?'

'Well they follow each other.'

'Yeah, but that doesn't mean that they're meant to follow each other in a real situation. Or that they apply to a front choke. You're making life too difficult for yourself. Just punch after you break the hold.'

'I wish I knew what to do with every bit of a *tul*. I'd feel like a fighting machine. I could run a programme of moves when I needed them.'

'I know what you mean,' said Piotr. 'But you'd get bored pretty soon if you didn't have anything new to learn.'

'You really believe it, don't you?'

'What do you mean?'

'That the forms have hidden moves. Secrets that you have to unlock.'

'Of course. Don't you?'

'Sometimes. Some days I have my doubts.'

Piotr fetched a bucket of warm soapy water with an old sponge in it. He started to wash a slab of concrete on the pathway where Jacek had spilt his blood.

'Let me do it,' said Jacek.

'No, you're OK,' said Piotr.

Jacek took his gear off and pulled his shirt up to wipe his bloody lip.

'So what were the MMA guys ripping into you about?' Piotr

said, scrubbing the floor where the blood had landed.

'Ah you know, they say the tuls are useless, old tales from the Orient, dead training, that kind of thing.'

'And what do you say?'

'The usual. That they're the alphabet of the art, the building blocks. That kind of thing.'

'And?'

'And nothing. It's always the same with those guys. They call me Mr. Choi and pull the skin around their eyes. Try to talk in a Korean accent.'

'They sound like great guys,' said Piotr, squeezing the sponge into the bucket.

They walked back to the house. Piotr poured the contents of the bucket down the drain and put the sponge back in it and left it out to dry.

'Don't worry, their jokes will run out soon enough,' said Piotr.

'I suppose. Cheers for helping me out anyway,' said Jacek.

'You off already?'

'I've got a busy day ahead.'

'OK, well I'll be in touch soon about a black belt meeting.'

'When do you want it?'

'As soon as possible. We need to clear the air, like you said.'

When Jacek left, Piotr opened his emails. He copied two links into a draft email. One was the web address of the forum that Karol's friend had written on a beer mat for him. The other clicked through to a news story about Poland's upcoming game against England. He typed an address into the email and pressed send.

GAPCZO RAN ACROSS THE PARK. Piotr chased after him, shouting out his name. The dog stopped at a bush near the road and sniffed it.

Piotr knelt down on one knee when he got to him. He cupped Gapczo's face and leant in close. 'What was all that about, hey? Are you allowed to run away from me like that? Are you?'

Gapczo stared at him, his tongue out, panting.

'No, you're not. Do you run away from Auntie like that? I bet you don't.'

He clipped his lead back onto his collar and left the park. They walked along a main road for a bit until they reached a semi-detached house that was split into two flats. Piotr rang the doorbell to the flat upstairs. A minute later, Henio opened the door.

'Is it OK if I bring Gapczo in?' said Piotr.

'What? Don't be ridiculous.' Henio stooped down and ruffled the dog's hair. 'Come on in. I haven't seen the crazy mutt in ages.'

They sat down in the front room. Gapczo jumped up onto a sofa, staying close to Piotr.

'Where are the kids?' said Piotr.

'They're out. Playing with their cousins.'

Ania walked into the room. She was wearing an apron and had flour on her hands.

Piotr hugged her. 'So he's got you doing all the work?'

'He said he needed some help rolling out the dough. If you two want to employ me then it's going to cost you money you know.' She winked at Piotr. 'Do you want a drink Piotrusz?'

'We'll have beers,' said Henio. 'I'll get them.' He stepped out of the room for a few seconds, coming back with two cold cans.

'So you're using the recipes I emailed you?' said Piotr.

'Yeah, of course, what else? I tasted the fillings already. They're great. We're onto a winner.' He raised his beer. 'Good work.'

'What about the sauces?'

'What about them?'

'I thought we were going to try the sauces too.'

'We were? Sorry, I forgot. I didn't get the ingredients.'

'I thought that the point of today.'

103

'Well what do we need?'

'Sour cream, parsley, mushrooms. Tomatoes, chillies.' Piotr took his notebook out of his back pocket. 'I'll have to check my notes for the rest.'

Henio picked up some car keys from the coffee table and took the beers back into the kitchen. 'Ania, look after the mutt will you? We've got to pop out to get some stuff.'

When they were driving to the supermarket, Piotr said, 'It's good that we're out anyway, I wanted to talk to you about something out of Ania's earshot.'

'Oh yeah? What about?'

'The next black belt test. I've had an idea. It's a bit different though.'

'Go on.'

'There's a friendly coming up between England and Poland, at Wembley. Some Polish crews are travelling to it to get into a scrap. I'm monitoring the situation and waiting to hear back from a source.'

'Where did you get this info from?'

'The dark web.'

'The what?'

'It's a hidden part of the internet that hosts loads of illegal stuff. I've been checking out forums where hooligans speak to each other.'

'They do that?'

'Totally. Anyway, that's not important. What I want to do is stop the hools from hurting each other too much, by disrupting the fighting and dispersing the crews. It probably won't last more than three minutes because we'll be calling the police after two. But it would be a great test for anyone. And it means we get to stop some of these knuckleheads from smashing their teeth in.'

'Sounds like a serious step up to me.'

'Is it? We've all had hard tests.'

'Still, those football hools. They're an ugly breed.'

'Ugly, yes. But skilled? Not so much. And probably not that sober either. Plus we'll go there in numbers. Every black belt.'

'Which is why you're telling me.'

'Hey, it's not like you've officially left or anything. Technically you're still with us. Plus, you should come back. You'll help the dojang massively. And it could do you some good.'

Henio stroked his goatee. 'When's the match again?'

'In a month's time.'

'I won't say no, but I won't say yes yet either. Give me some more details when you can and I'll think about it for a couple of days.'

'If you won't help then I don't know if we can go ahead.'

'Understood. I won't keep you hanging.' He turned into the supermarket car park and drove into a parking space reserved for parents and children.

'Can we park here?' said Piotr.

'I've got the car seats in the back.'

They split up. Piotr went to get mushrooms, chillies, chives, parsley and sour cream. He sent Henio to pick up some brown sugar, onions, Worcestershire sauce, canned tomatoes and tomato puree.

They met up at the tills.

Piotr glanced down at Henio's basket. 'You got the supermarket branded tomatoes?'

'So?'

'We should get some better ones.'

'Tomatoes are tomatoes,' said Henio.

'There's no point getting poor quality ingredients.'

Piotr left the tills and came back with some more expensive tomatoes. 'Italian,' he said, waving the tins at Henio. 'The best.'

They split the cost of the shopping.

Back at Henio's flat, Ania had formed 40 pierogi and left them on a floured surface in the kitchen. When they came in she was sitting on the floor rubbing Gapczo's belly. Henio grabbed the two beers back out of the fridge and Piotr started lining up the ingredients they needed for the sauces. It took them under an hour to get them ready and to cook the pierogi.

They drank beer while they waited, talking about the table layout and what drinks they would serve in the restaurant. Henio said that they should serve different Polish beers in bottles. Piotr said he was leaning more towards serving one draught beer, as that would get them a better deal from the supplier. They wondered how difficult it would be to get a licence to sell alcohol.

'If it's too much of a ball ache we can always serve up my grandmother's compote,' said Henio. 'She used to put a splash of vodka in it to give it a little kick. The food authorities would never know.'

THE BLACK BELTS MET at the dojang at the time they had agreed. They all gripped hands before Piotr opened the doors.

They scrubbed and polished the floorboards, got changed together in silence, and lined up in the hall, facing the flag.

They performed their tuls, from *Chon-Ji* onwards, until they reached the last one they knew, *Ul-Ji*, half an hour after they had begun.

Sitting down in a circle to catch their breath, they stretched their legs. They then sat cross-legged with their hands on their knees for a couple of minutes, saying nothing.

Jacek broke the silence. 'It's a bit weird that we're doing this,' he said. 'I mean, you know, just us three.'

'It does feel a bit strange,' said Kris.

'Strange or not, we'd best get on with it,' said Piotr. 'The agenda is our two proposed black belt promotions, keeping dojang discipline, when to teach new tuls. We've also been invited to step in to help out with a new situation, which is a bit unusual. But it could work well with the black belt test. I'll come to that in a bit.'

They talked about the potential creation of the two black belts – Jan and Adam. The three of them agreed that they were ready to be tested and that they had a good chance of passing. Piotr raised one objection. Jan had been one of those pushing for competitive fighting. 'I'm not sure if his head in the right place,' he said.

'How about we talk to him before he gets promoted?' said Jacek. 'If he passes the test, I mean. Tell him he'll have to drop all talk of organised bouts if he wants the belt.'

'Now that we're actually talking about it, rather than just dismissing it, can I have my say?' said Kris.

'Go ahead,' said Piotr.

'Some students have been talking about getting involved in underground stuff. But they've been scared of being ejected from the dojang. So they've approached me about it.

'I think participating in them could be a valuable training tool. We know that other dojangs have begun competing in open tournaments. They help control adrenaline, teach focus. Give students something to aim for. It also helps with learning from other styles. And it doesn't have to be done through the underground scene. There are good MMA tournaments you can enter now where you can test yourself.'

'How many of them want to get into that scene?' said Jacek. 'I've not had anyone come to me. And they know that I work at the gym.'

'Four of them that I know of,' said Kris. 'And Jan has spoken to Piotr about it. So that makes it five.'

Piotr waved his words away. 'We all the know the Kwan's rules on this. Let other dojangs do what they want. We'll do what we've always done.'

'So how will we test students then?' said Kris. 'It's not like we're flush with requests. Hardly anyone comes to us for anything these days. It's like we're almost not needed anymore, or even relevant. And no wonder, when you look at our numbers. We don't have the manpower. People have lost confidence in us. If members get to compete, then maybe we'd get a lot more recruits. I don't see why we can't consider it.'

'Hang on Krszystof,' said Piotr. 'Do you realise what you're saying? Do you really want to break with tradition?'

'It's not a break,' said Kris. 'That's the wrong way of looking at it. It's more like an evolution, something that improves what we do. How can that hurt us?

'This discussion is closed,' said Piotr. 'This dojang will stay true to the Kwan's original ways. And since you've mentioned not being needed anymore, let me tell you about the new request for help that has come in.'

He told them about the hooligan meeting.

'We got a request on that?' said Jacek.

'Well, we were invited. I made the initial suggestion. The idea is that we target two crews that are set to meet and stop them from clashing.'

'Come off it Piotrek. We're in no shape for something like that,' said Kris.

'I admit it's risky. But we can do it. Henio may help out. And don't forget we'll have Jan and Adam there, and they'll be desperate to do well.'

'Look, I mean no disrespect Piotr, but this is madness,' said Kris. 'Some of these crews are big. And a lot of their guys are no slouches. I've seen them in action, remember? Especially back when I used to cover matches at home. And Henio hasn't bruised a knuckle in years. He'd probably pop a hamstring trying to throw a kick at someone's shin.'

'I respect what you know and where you're coming from with this Krysztof,' said Piotr.

'But I've had a good think about this. It could help us a lot, and plus, it's the right thing to do. Back in the day, even if there was only one guy in a dojang they wouldn't stand for this happening on their patch. We've got to stick to our principles.

'This'll be a test for all of us. I get that. But it'll also show people that the Kwan is prepared to do what's right when it needs to. We can't stand by and let these gangs drag our reputation down further in this country. Heck, who knows, we might even get some of them to actually think about what they're doing.'

'What about Henio?' said Jacek.

'He's solid. He's covered my back enough times, believe me. I trust him.'

'I suppose we could do it,' said Jacek. 'I know the dojang in Nottingham recruited a couple of guys who used to get involved in that sort of stuff. They were converted after meeting their boys at a fight before a match. Similar to what you're proposing.'

'Yeah, back in the day we could do this sort of stuff. We had the men,' said Kris. 'But today? I'd say it's better to leave it to the police.'

'If we work out a plan and stick together then we'll be alright,' said Piotr. He jabbed his finger into the wooden floor. 'All it needs good planning and commitment. Plus, we're going to get the police involved, as soon as we've done our bit. If things get out of hand and we can't handle it, then we retreat and leave it to the coppers.'

After Piotr closed the meeting they got changed without speaking to each other. Kris was the first to leave.

'See you guys later,' he said, with his back to them as he walked out of the changing room door.

When he was sure he was gone, Jacek said, 'What are you going to do? He doesn't sound like he's up for it.'

Piotr inspected his dobok, looking at a mark on one of the sleeves. He tried rubbing it off with his thumb.

'It'll be OK. He'll come around.'

'I'll drive you all the way,' said Eric. 'You shouldn't have to wait for a tube on an occasion like this. You both look like you could do with a nice relaxing car ride as well.'

'Eric. Do not be stupid, otherwise we will simply walk to the station,' said Piotr's Aunt, standing outside the house. 'We are getting the tube as we always do, there's no need to get over dramatic.'

'Have it your way then,' he said. Piotr and his Aunt got into the car and Eric drove them to Sudbury Hill station. 'You both look very elegant,' said Eric, looking at Piotr in the rear-view mirror. 'How does the tie fit?'

'It's good thanks,' said Piotr, smoothing it down.

'You know, I didn't even have a black tie – or a black suit for that matter – until I was 64,' said Eric. 'That's when people close to me started to die on a regular basis.'

They both got seats on the train when it arrived. Piotr yawned and rubbed his eyes as it pulled out of the station.

'Bad night's sleep love?' his Aunt said.

'You could say that.'

'Anything wrong?'

'I've got a few issues with the dojang,' said Piotr, stifling another yawn.

'Care to tell me about them?'

'I didn't think it was anything up until recently but it's been playing on my mind the last couple of days,' said Piotr. 'It's Krszystof. I get the feeling that he's working behind my back, talking to the guys a lot. Challenging my authority.'

'Talking about what?'

'Changing things, mainly. He's always been a bit like that. But since Sabum's gone, it's like he's revealed his true colours. I realised last night that I may have trouble holding things together.'

'Can't you expel him?'

'It's not that easy. Not with the low number of black belts we've got.'

When they got to Hammersmith station they changed tube lines and travelled for one stop before getting off at Ravenscourt Park.

Outside the station, Piotr waved for a taxi.

'What are you doing?' said his Aunt.

'Getting a taxi'

'I can walk.'

'I know you can. But you need to rest as much as possible.'

They got to the church early and sat near the back. Piotr's Aunt was near the aisle. She knelt down and prayed two decades of the rosary before she kept getting disturbed by people coming into the church, tapping her arm or stopping to whisper something in her ear. She eventually put her beads away and waited with the rest of the congregation for the coffin of her cousin, Ewa, to be slowly processed into the church.

One of the readers was the cousin's son. He seemed upset and nervous as he approached the lectern, but when he read from the Bible his voice was steady and commanding.

'Then I saw a new heaven and a new earth,' he read. 'For the first heaven and the first earth had passed away, and the sea was no more.'

After the service he stayed with his Aunt for a little while in the church as she lit a candle in front of a painting of the Black Madonna of Częstochowa. She had not cried during the Mass, but when she stood back up to leave Piotr could see that her make-up had run a little. He put his arm around her shoulder and she put her hand over his and squeezed it tightly.

Ewa was buried in a graveyard not far from the church, next to her husband. Piotr and his Aunt stood near the back of the mourners. His Aunt went through her rosary beads, stoic throughout the burial ceremony.

They went back to Ewa's house for the reception. She had been a widow for over a decade, but had shared her large house with her son, daughter-in-law and two grandchildren.

A long table had been placed up against one the walls in the house's dining room. It was covered with open sandwiches, boiled eggs cut in half topped with mayonnaise, various salads, thinly sliced sausages, hunter's stew, pickled gherkins and mushrooms and stacks of bread. Red and white wine bottles were lined up on another table beside it.

The guests swarmed over the food and the wine flowed. Piotr and his Aunt spoke to some second-removed cousins and family friends. They all asked after his Aunt's health and told them that they would come to visit them before too long. They reminisced about life in London in the Fifties and Sixties. Later on, Ewa's son made a short speech, thanking everyone for coming.

As the evening drew in, people started to filter out and Piotr got talking to some other relatives. One of his Aunt's cousins, who had left London and moved to Bournemouth in the Seventies, remembered visiting Piotr's family home back in Radom when Piotr was a young boy. Piotr barely knew anything about him, but the cousin and his wife seemed to know everything about him.

They were joined by another couple, Aunt Zosia and Uncle Maciek. They were Ewa's cousins too, and were staying at the house for a few days with the family. Piotr wasn't sure which side of the family they were from. They kept joking about how they had played with Ewa just after the war when they had come to England. They said she had been fearless and adventurous, always getting lost or into trouble. Piotr listened and nodded politely.

A friend of the family came over to speak to Aunt Zosia. She started talking to her about how happy she was that Ewa had been buried. 'Too many people are getting cremated these days,' she said.

Uncle Maciek grabbed Piotr by the arm and took him aside. His eyes burned brightly under his huge bushy eyebrows. 'What do you say we go into the other room and have something a bit stronger than this wine, eh?'

Piotr followed him down a long corridor into a room at the back of the house. There was a piano in the corner and a large picture of the Last Supper on the wall.

Maciek opened a drinks cabinet opposite the piano and took a bottle of vodka out of it.

'It's not chilled I'm afraid,' he said. 'There was no room in the fridge or freezer with all the food and I forgot to put it in when we got back. You don't mind do you? I've got whisky too, if you prefer.'

'No, I don't mind at all,' said Piotr.

Maciek went to another glass cabinet and took two shot glasses out of it. 'I thought I'd best bring some booze with me. There hasn't been any decent drink here since Tadek passed on. Andrzej only drinks beer,' he said, thumbing at a picture of Ewa's son at his graduation.

He blew into the glasses to remove any dust before setting them down on a coffee table in front of Piotr. They sat down on sofas opposite each other. Maciek poured out two measures and toasted Ewa before drinking the vodka in one go. He poured another two shots and toasted his wife.

'I almost forgot,' said Maciek, putting down his glass. 'Ewa had some great music. Let's put some on.'

He stood up and went to look through the record collection by the piano. He picked out a vinyl record and placed in onto the record player beside the drinks cabinet.

'Let's have another one, eh?' he said. He poured some more vodka and stopped for a moment. He held the bottle in one hand and stuck his forefinger up with his spare hand. 'It's jazz from 1920s Warsaw,' he said. 'Listen.'

Uncle Maciek sat back, closing his eyes and letting a woman's voice slowly swim over him.

'They just don't make them like that any more,' he said, as the first song ended.

'They don't make great looking record players like that either,' Piotr said.

'You like it? It's fabulous. Ewa must have had it for what, let me think, 47 years? Might even be 48.'

They drank their drinks and listened to the music for a bit longer. Then Maciek filled their glasses again.

'We should have a drink in honour of your Aunt's health. She looks a lot better than I thought she would. No doubt thanks to your help.'

'Nothing to do with me,' said Piotr. 'She keeps herself going. She's a strong woman.'

'That she is.' Uncle Maciek stood up again. 'Let me get some pretzel sticks,' he said. 'And some tea. You want some tea? I'll get Zosia to make us some.'

'Do you want me to go Uncle?' asked Piotr.

'No,' he said, slowly pushing himself up from the sofa's armrests. 'I need to take a leak anyway.'

The large painting of the Last Supper loomed over the room. Piotr wondered if any of the apostles had known that Judas was the traitor in their midst, or if they suspected him. Surely he would have given something away in the way he had acted that night?

Uncle Maciek came back a few minutes later with a tray holding a teapot, two cups and saucers, and a large bag of pretzel sticks. He opened the bag and took some sticks out and put them into a large glass he found in the cabinet. Then he poured some more vodka.

'So tell me. How are things with the dojang?'

Piotr froze, halfway towards the pretzel sticks. 'The dojang?'

'That's right. What, you didn't think I knew? I keep an eye on the Kwan you know. Or used to, anyway. But I still get my ears to the ground when I can.' He winked at Piotr. 'And your Aunt is never shy when it comes to telling us what she knows.'

'Right,' said Piotr.

'So? Are you going to tell me how it's going?'

'It's OK.'

'Just OK?'

'Well, not really. It's a bit tough at the moment.'

'How do you mean?'

'I'm having a few problems with discipline to be honest. White belts wanting different things. Seniors encouraging them.'

'Your Aunt did mention a couple of things.'

'It's the same old stuff. I've heard it all before.'

'Do you think you have it under control?'

'I don't give them an inch. But I can't control what they say behind my back.'

'Have you got allies?'

'Sure.'

'You're a loyal soldier. I'm glad you're not compromising the way of the Kwan. So many dojangs have turned their back on tradition. And then died a slow pathetic death. It's happened everywhere. The Kwan doesn't even exist in some parts of this country where it used to be strong. Even back in Poland, it's dwindling. It's tragic.'

He poured some tea and nibbled on a couple of pretzel sticks.

'I was too old to ever really train. But me and your Uncle, we were big supporters. We helped out your dojang when we could, in our own little way. And all the Sabums, God rest their souls. You keep doing what you're doing.'

He raised his vodka glass. 'To the Kwan,' he said.

'To the Kwan,' said Piotr.

THE MAN KNOCKED ON THE WINDOW BOOTH of the taxi office, where the radio controller was sat. His head was buried in a motorcycle magazine. A blonde girl in a small bikini was pouting up at him, sprawled over a sparkling Harley Davidson.

'Yeah?' said the controller, looking up at him.

'I've got a meeting with the boss.'

The lock on the door next to the booth clicked open with a buzzing sound. The controller stroked his thick moustache and went back to his magazine.

The man passed through into a narrow wood panelled corridor. There was a door at the end of it, slightly ajar. He knocked on it lightly, peering through the crack.

'Come in,' a voice from inside said.

The man walked in. The boss was sitting behind a desk. The man carefully shut the door, and then examined his hand before rubbing it on his jeans. 'I think you might have some oil or something on that door handle,' he said.

'We need a new cleaner, I've been meaning to sort it out for weeks now.' The boss put out a cigarette into a large white ashtray that was full of butts and ran his hand through his thinning grey hair. 'You want some coffee?'

'No, I'm fine thanks.'

The boss got up and walked to a filing cabinet which was backed up against a wall opposite his desk. 'Sit down,' he said to his younger guest, gesturing at a chair on the other side of the desk. He unhooked a set of keys attached to one of his trouser belt loops, selected a key and opened the cabinet. He took a thick loose file folder out of it, slammed the cabinet shut and walked back to his desk. The file dropped onto his desk with a thud.

The younger man cleared his throat. The boss lit another cigarette, sitting down on his revolving chair and running his hands through his hair once more. He flicked something off his left shoulder. 'Whoring dandruff. You can't shift it, no matter what shampoo you use. You ever get dandruff?'

'Not really,' said the younger man, trying to read the writing on the side of the folder. 'I've heard it could be stress-related.'

'Stress-related? That would make sense. My wife thinks her credit card is limitless. And my kids? Don't even get me started on them.' He started flicking through the papers in the file, turning them over backwards and forwards.

'Anyway,' he said, taking a long drag on his cigarette. 'The dojang. What's happening? I heard they cracked some meatheads over the head outside Greenford station.'

'Yeah, that's right.'

'So it's still operational.'

'Sort of.'

'It either is or it isn't. And it obviously is. So, update me.'

'Well, it's a slow process,' said the younger man, sitting back and crossing his legs. 'For starters you have to get the ideas to spread among the dojang. They take time to settle in. But it's working. The new Sabum isn't always there and the younger guys want to see some changes.'

'What changes?'

'They want to compete. In organised fights. And they want less stress on some training methods. They're starting to think of them as old hat. They like the idea of shedding some traditions – ready to leave all that whoring crime fighting crap behind.'

'Is that right?' said the older man, looking down at his file again. 'Well let me tell you something. I don't care what half the whoring members think. It's what they do that matters.'

'I know what you're saying, but it takes time to get these things going. It can't change overnight.'

'Well it needs to speed up. I've had this headache for too long. I want to get on with business quietly. Hardly anyone gets hurt and everyone's happy. But that can't happen when there's some whoring Sabum walking about who thinks he's Batman.'

'Sure,' said the younger man. 'But I haven't heard anything about them dealing with us recently. Unless they're keeping things from me. Have they crossed us again?'

'That's not the issue. It doesn't matter what they've done, it's what they could do. How long has it been since the old Sabum snuffed it?'

'Well, more than six months now.'

'And you're satisfied with the headway that's been made since then?'

'We've always been independent and had our traditions. Like I said, it takes time.'

'You sound like one of them,' said the older man, leaning back in his leather armchair. 'You need to shake something up, make people think about things. Re-evaluate. How traditional are these two guys that are being tested?'

'They're 50/50, as far as I know. They both agree with a lot of the ideas for change.'

'So what's holding you back from getting some changes in then? When they're promoted you'll be in the majority.'

'I don't know, it's a question of time. Piotr's an idealist. Faithful to tradition. It's hard to break with that.'

The boss lent back and smoothed his hair back again. His black tracksuit top lifted up above the lower half of his hairy stomach. The younger man glimpsed the end of a scar, poking above his trousers.

'Here, let me show you something,' said the boss.

He opened the ring binder and took out a piece of paper. 'You know what this is? He held up a photocopy of a typed letter. The younger man shrugged his shoulders. 'No,' he said.

'It's a letter from an insurance company informing me that we're entitled to £3,450 for one of the accidents that one of my cabs was involved in.' He put the letter down and lifted his cigarette off his ash tray and took a short drag on it.

'Thing is,' he said, his smile breaking through a cloud of smoke, 'is that it was no accident. You understand?'

'I think so. I mean, I've heard that you do that kind of stuff.'

'Hearing is different from seeing,' said the boss, putting the sheet back into the folder and snapping it shut.

'What I'm saying to you is that sometimes you have to make things happen. That bit of money is very useful to me from that insurance company, who really couldn't give a whore's ass as to whether the accident was real or not. And I can't wait around on the off chance that some van is going to rear end one of my drivers. The solution is to manufacture a scenario that works to your advantage.'

He checked his watch. 'I haven't got a lot of time right now, but you need to think of something. Something like an accident. To jolt people. Make them wonder if they have the right leader. Maybe even to force him to wonder if he's the right man for the job. That creates an atmosphere into which a more, shall we say, enlightened leader can step in. You see what I mean?'

The boss stood up.

'I'll have a think,' said the younger man, following his lead.

'You do that,' said the boss, showing him to the door.

As the younger man walked out of the cab office another man entered it. He had a shaved head and was wearing a brown leather jacket.

'Taxi man in?' he asked.

'Just been in with him.'

'Is he in a good mood?'

'He's been better.'

The radio controller buzzed the man with the shaved head through.

When he walked into the Taxi man's office, he said, 'What did he want?'

'Gave me an update on the vigilantes.'

The man took his leather jacket off and hung it up on a peg on the back of the door. 'What are we still bothering with those whoring clowns for? They're small time these days. You know how many go to that dojang? Only about 15 guys, max. And only about four of them get involved on the street.'

The Taxi man put the folder back in the cabinet and locked it. They're headed by that whoring half-caste as well. Nobody respects him. They're a joke. Plus they've still got that retarded firearms ban in place. They're like some bad cartoon sketch.'

The Taxi man stubbed out his cigarette. 'Firstly, get your facts right,' he said. 'There are three on the street at the moment. Soon to be five, possibly. And they could still be a threat. I get a sense that they're getting more popular for some reason. Secondly, you of all people should know to never underestimate them. They've managed to screw up plenty of our operations. I want them neutralised on our patch. And he's helping me. We need to stop them while they're still vulnerable.'

'So why not just send them a message?'

'We're done with messages. It's time for Last Rites now.'

IT HAD BEEN RAINING FOR THREE DAYS STRAIGHT before the foreman told them to take the covers off the top of the building. He inspected the open attic to make sure that it had not been damaged by the rain.

'We got lucky boys,' he said, wiping the floor with one hand and then rubbing his fingers together to test them for moisture. 'Now we can get on and get this done before the next inspection from the housing association.'

Later, when the foreman was out of earshot, Uncle said to Piotr, 'I don't see what's so lucky about having to work over the weekend.'

'Me neither,' said Piotr.

After the morning break Piotr went to the foreman and asked him if he could have Saturday afternoon off. 'I'll work all day Sunday with the rest of the guys,' he said. 'It's just that I really need to be somewhere Saturday.'

'Maybe what you really need is a different job,' said the foreman, looking down at his plans.

'What do you mean?'

'We need to meet a deadline. And without everyone here then the deadline is going to run away.' Using the table he had spread the plans out on, the foreman used his fingers to mimic a pair of legs running to the edge of the table and then jumping off it. 'And leave us in a big hole.'

He lifted his head up. 'Your choice.'

'OK,' said Piotr. 'I get it.'

He went for a walk during the lunch break. He sat by a tree in a small park off the main road and watched the traffic flow by. The sun was beating down. He rolled up the sleeves of his T-shirt and pinched the front, pulling it a few times to get some air to his chest. He found Kris' number in his contacts list and pressed Dial.

When he got back he found Uncle on his own, sitting on the front garden wall. He was holding his phone on his lap.

'Everything alright?'

'It's my brainless cousin,' said Uncle. 'He's been in hospital.'

'What's happened to him?'

'He was found in some park. Stumbling all over the place, bleeding from his head.'

'Is he going to be OK?'

'Apparently so. But he'll only get back on it when he's let out. We don't know what to do with him. He's an alcoholic.'

Piotr sat down next to him. 'How long's he been drinking?'

'As long as I can remember.'

'So he needs help then.'

'Forget it. He's too stubborn. He's like my father was, he's from that side of the family. Wojtek's his name. Doesn't live too far from you actually. He's a funny-looking guy. Like an overgrown clown. He's really tall and has big bushy hair and a huge moustache. And huge feet. I mean huge. He talks with a lisp too.'

Uncle shook his head. 'He's almost on his knees now, but still manages to get cheap vodka from somewhere. He's only 43 but he looks 83 some days, I swear to God.'

The foreman stepped outside and opened the passenger door to his van. 'Piotrek,' he said. 'Get in. You can help me get some material. Oh, and go and get Buszek will you? We need him too.'

When they got to the builder's yard the foreman said, 'I'll only be a minute.' He got out of the van and grabbed his clutch bag. 'I'll check if they have the right wood. If they do, I'll wave over to you. You'll need to swing the van around the back. We can load it from inside the warehouse.'

The foreman disappeared into a store at the back of the yard. Buszek's phone rang. It was his wife. 'I best answer it,' he said.

He started talking to his wife. Piotr opened up a newspaper and read a story about the England game. The Polish centre forward, their star player, was struggling to be fit enough in time. Piotr's mind drifted as he read the article. He thought about the black belt test. He would work on a plan that night, he decided.

Outside, a yard worker driving a small forklift had to brake sharply as a blue van pulled up in front of him. It broke Piotr and Buszek's concentration. The yard worker waved his hands up, as if in disgust at the van driver. As he started to reverse, the driver of the van jumped out and approached the forklift. He pointed a finger at the yard worker and said something. The yard worker started gesticulating back at him.

The van driver got closer to the yard worker and had his arms down by his side. His neck was stretching his head forward, like a peacock. The yard worker stepped off his forklift and pointed at the driver and then at his van. The van driver pushed his forehead up against the yard worker's nose and then shoved him in the chest, goading him to fight. Piotr folded the paper up, placed it on the dashboard, and got out of the van.

'Where are you going?' said Buszek.

'To see what's going on.' Piotr walked over to the forklift and tapped the van driver on the shoulder.

'What do you want?' said the van driver, in bad English.

Piotr recognised the accent. 'I was wondering if I could help you with anything,' he said in Polish.

'Help me with what?' the driver spat back in Polish.

'With your problem.'

'My problem?'

'Yes, your problem,' said Piotr.

'You're my whoring problem, you monkey,' he said. His left shoulder twitched. Piotr recognised the signal. He stepped into his personal space, thrusting a ridgehand into his neck and keeping a high forearm block out in case the van driver's punch came through.

The van driver fell back against the forklift and slumped to the floor, holding his throat.

'How's your problem now?' said Piotr, his fists clenched and his jaw shut tight.

The van driver tried to steady himself by planting his hands on the ground, but said nothing. Piotr saw the foreman coming out of the store, waving. He made his way back to the van.

'The boss wants us to drive over to him,' said Piotr.

Buszek stared at Piotr, as if he was in a trance.

'Well what are you waiting for?'

'Right,' said Buszek, snapping out of his daze and getting the van in gear.

Later that evening, Uncle, Piotr, Buszek and another worker, Marcin, went to a pub close to the building site for a beer.

'I'm only having the one,' said Uncle as they walked in.

Five hours later the barmaid rang the bell, signalling last orders.

Uncle stood up slowly and sauntered unsteadily to the bar. He came back with four beers.

He placed the pint glasses beers in front of everyone, spilling a bit from each pint. Buszek said, 'So Piotrek, let me get this right. Your father was a Protestant missionary. From Africa. Who came over to Poland after the fall of Communism. To preach?'

'That's right,' said Piotr. He drank from his pint and wiped off some beer that had dripped onto his jeans. 'And to study.'

'What did he come preaching for, to a Catholic country?' said Marcin, holding back a belch.

'I guess he thought there were a lot of atheists there,' said Uncle, counting his change before stuffing it into his pocket. 'Anyway, never mind what he was doing in Poland. I didn't even know Africans came over to us,' he said. 'I never saw any in my time. And I travelled a lot back then.'

'Travelled where? From the village hall to the church?' said Buszek, smiling. 'Hey, you probably never even saw a woman with straight teeth in your village, let alone any foreign people.'

'You'd be surprised at what I've seen in my time,' said Uncle. He lifted up his pint. 'Anyway, here's to your Dad's memory. He sounded like a good man.'

They all drank from their pints.

'What was it like to grow up with your Dad?' said Uncle. 'You know, with him being from Africa and everything?'

'You mean being black,' said Buszek.

'Well, it wasn't always easy. It was hard sometimes. But it was fun too, he was great. We'd get some abuse on the street in broad daylight somewhere and he'd shrug it off and start joking about something.'

'I guess that's why you're so tough then,' said Buszek. 'You should have seen the way he handled that chief at the yard. He was what, a whole half a metre taller than you?'

Piotr shrugged his shoulders. 'He wasn't that tall.'

'Where did you learn to fight like that anyway?' said Buszek.

'Here and there. I learnt a lot about fighting at school.'

'Like what?'

'Like that I could take a beating. And get up out of bed the next day and come into class with my head up, even though it hurt to walk and I couldn't speak properly because I was missing a tooth and my face was swollen. And that I could control my fear and face my attackers, I guess. They couldn't stop me going to school and I didn't want to stop. Then one day I won a scrap with one of the ringleaders.'

'And no one touched you after that,' said Marcin.

'Not at school, no.'

Before they left, Uncle and Marcin went to the toilet. Buszek put his hand on Piotr's shoulder. 'Don't worry,' he said. 'Your secret's safe with me.'

Piotr was about to reply, when Uncle returned to the table.

Piotr and Uncle walked to the Tube station together after saying good night to Buszek and Marcin at a bus stop. As they waited on the platform, Henio rang Piotr.

'I haven't woken you up have I?' he said.

'No, I'm still out,' said Piotr.

'Right. Well I've been thinking. About the test.'

'OK.'

'And I'm up for it. I'll help you out.'

'That's the first piece of good news I've had in a while. So what's convinced you?'

'What do you mean?'

'You seemed hesitant before. Like you were unsure. Or chicken. Bwak, bwak.'

'Have you been drinking?'

'I've had a couple. It's been a tough day.'

'Well I figured I'm still part of the dojang, like you said. And maybe it's time I pulled my weight a bit more. This is my first step towards redemption, put it that way.'

'Consider yourself redeemed. But you've got to come to the next training session. Well, the next one that I can make. I'll let you know.'

Piotr and Uncle took a train into central London and changed lines, heading out west. The carriage, nearest to the driver, was rammed full of people.

A few stops later they got a seat each at the end of a row. Uncle fell asleep almost as soon as they sat down. Piotr grabbed a copy of *The Evening Standard* that had been left on the ledge behind him and read about the upcoming football game again.

At Hammersmith, the tube stopped with the doors open and

didn't move for a long time. Piotr looked over at Uncle, who was leaning against him. He was out cold.

Two young men sat opposite them. They were drunk. One of them had a bottle of vodka and was pouring some of it into two plastic glasses, spilling it as he did so. From his tone and inflections, Piotr could tell that he was Russian. The other man was Dutch. His English was good, and it had an American twang to it. After they downed a glass of vodka each, the Dutch man put a cigarette in his mouth and lit it. He then passed it to the Russian and lit another one for himself. One well-dressed woman, who was sitting two seats down from them, got up and walked down to the other end of the carriage.

'You can't smoke in here,' Piotr said.

'What?' said the Dutch man, trying to focus on Piotr. 'Smoking. I said. Smoking isn't allowed on the underground.'

'So what? What are you, the police?'

'No. But seriously, guys, you should put those cigarettes out.'

'Or what?' said the Dutch man. 'What are you gonna do?'

'I really think it's better if you put the cigarettes out.'

'Go home and take your boyfriend up the ass.'

Uncle woke up, squinting. 'Are we in Ealing yet?' he said.

'Ah, you're Poles,' said the Russian. 'They're Polish,' he said, nudging his companion. 'Except he's only 50 per cent Polish. He's like half a gorilla.'

The young men laughed.

The Dutch man flicked his cigarette butt at Piotr. 'There you go 50 per cent. Have a smoke. You probably can't afford this make in Africa.'

Piotr jumped off his seat, brushing the butt away. 'Very clever,' he said. He gestured at Uncle to stand up. 'Come on, let's sit somewhere else before this carriage catches fire.'

Uncle got up, but instead of following Piotr he stopped in front of the Dutch man and threw a punch at him. He missed and fell on top of the Dutch man. The Russian started throwing punches at Uncle, missing with most of them. He dropped the bottle of vodka and it leaked onto the carriage floor.

Piotr walked up to Uncle and grabbed him by the back of his shoulders and pushed him down the carriage. He then front-kicked the Russian in the face, twice, hard. Blood started pouring from the

Russian's nose and he fell face forwards into the pool of vodka.

The Dutch man tried grabbing Piotr by the leg, but Piotr lifted his knee quickly, breaking his grip. Piotr tried to deliver a reverse knifehand strike to his neck, but missed, hitting him in the side of the head, behind his temple instead. The Dutch man lifted his hands to his face as he staggered backwards onto an escaping passenger.

The train pulled into Acton Town, a station where the Underground branched off into two different directions. When the doors opened Piotr saw another train on the opposite platform, which had its doors open as well. It was going in the wrong direction for him.

'Come on, let's get out of here,' he said, pulling Uncle and then pushing him into the other train.

As it set off, Piotr said, 'Are you OK?'

'I'm fine, I've got a bit of a busted lip, that's all.'

'You want me to walk home with you?'

'No, I'll be fine. You get yourself home.'

When they got to Uncle's station, Piotr let him go and travelled back to Acton Town after waiting 15 minutes for a train. Coming into the station he pulled his hoodie up over his head and crossed the bridge to get to the other platform where the trains going out West picked up passengers. Before he got to the staircase, he saw some Transport police talking to some people. An ambulance's lights were flashing outside the station. He headed towards the exit and went to the ticket office. The station officer was shuffling through some papers behind the plastic screen.

'When's the next train to Sudbury Hill?' Piotr said.

'Should be here in five minutes.'

A police car was parked behind the ambulance. It was empty.

Piotr made his way through the station's ticket barriers, swiping his Tube card on the reader. He turned right out onto the road and began running.

He got to the next station along the line, Ealing Common, sweating and out of breath, with a minute to spare. On the train home he stayed close to one of the manual doors that connected through to another carriage.

Lying in bed, the memories rushed back. The monkey chants in school corridors; skinheads spitting in his face; hospital visits to get stitches and have X-rays; bricks thrown through his Dad's car;

hugging his Mother at night as she sat crying, perched on the end of her bed, asking God why people could be so cruel.

The sun was beating down on Piotr's bare back as he carried the cement and sand bags over to the mixer on the driveway.

'You look like you've had about 24 hours of uninterrupted sleep,' said Uncle, holding a cold energy drink can to his head.

'Don't worry, I'm suffering as well,' said Piotr, dropping one of the bags down next to the mixer. 'You should help me with these. If you keep working you can sweat it out.'

'Rather you than me,' he said. 'I'm not sure I've got anything left to sweat out.'

They mixed sand, cement and some gravel with water to make concrete.

After they had filled most of the holes in the driveway, Uncle leaned against the mixer. 'I'm whacked,' he said. 'I shouldn't be out drinking at my age.'

'You're not that old,' said Piotr.

'Yes I am. But still as stupid as I've always been. I'm really sorry about last night. I shouldn't have tried to hit that chief. I don't know what I was thinking. I was probably lashing out because of Wojtek. Or that's my excuse, anyway.'

'Don't worry about it. It happens. How's he doing?'

'I got a text from his sister earlier. They're going to let him out tomorrow.'

Piotr emptied the last load of concrete into the wheelbarrow they were using and pushed it to the final hole that needed filling. When he had poured all the concrete into the hole and patted out it down with a spade, he went to get a hosepipe and started cleaning the mixer. He stood behind the mixer and tipped it to make sure he could clean the barrel properly. Scrubbing hard with a brush, he trod on the handle of the spade and lost his balance. Letting go of the mixer, he rolled to the side of it, breaking his fall. The mixer came down hard on his trailing left arm, hitting his wrist. As soon as he felt the impact, he knew he had damaged it.

Arek filled a bucket with warm soapy water and walked back into the hall. Kris stood by the stage at the front of the dojang. 'You don't need to clean the floor today,' he said. 'Father Leopold's cleaner has been in already. And she's done a great job. You can almost see your reflection in it.'

'Should I check my name off the rota?' said Arek.

'No, don't worry about that. I'll do it later.'

At the start of the session he told the students to gather near him.

'OK, listen up. We're going to go straight into some defences to takedowns, without a warm-up. You'll do plenty of sparring later for cardio. Pad up.'

Kris demonstrated some defensive moves, using Jan as a training partner.

They drilled the techniques for an hour before moving on to some sparring, during which they carried on trying to take each other down.

Afterwards, the students talked about the class as they were getting changed.

'What was all that about?' said Sebastian. 'It's like he was prepping us for MMA bouts or something.'

'Maybe we're going to be allowed to do them,' said Szymon.

'I thought Sabum was dead against them,' said Adam.

Szymon rubbed some muscle balm into his thigh. 'Maybe he's changed his mind.'

'What about the rules?' said Sebastian.

'What about them? It's not like they're set in stone or anything.'

Sebastian said, 'Who told you that?'

'Kris. We spoke about it a couple of weeks ago. Anyway, fighting in tournaments is part of the Kwan's history. That's what the Asian guys used to do, way back when. Kris wants us to go back to some of those early ways. They used to want to showcase their skills. Not hide them away.'

Arek sprayed some deodorant on his chest and armpits. 'I guess that makes sense. It might mean we can shut up some of the haters too. I'm sick of arguing on forums with guys who keep saying how Muay Thai or whatever, would destroy us. They think we're just some crackpot vigilante group that uses batons to crack people's heads open. They don't think we've got any skill. But when I argue back they say OK, then, show me your stuff. Why aren't you on Youtube or something? And I can't argue with it. We've got no evidence.'

'Well, I wouldn't get too excited,' said Jan. 'The rules are still the rules right now. And they say no competitive fighting full stop. I'd love to do it, but I've asked Piotr a couple of times now and he's said no way, end of story.'

Sebastian gave Adam a lift home in his car.

'I'm worried there's going to be some sort of rift,' said Sebastian.

'It won't come to that,' said Adam. 'I'm sure Piotr's got it under control.'

That night Piotr lay in bed with his bandaged wrist resting on his chest.

He picked up his mobile phone, which was by the side of him on the bed. It was 1:30 a.m. He threw the phone across the room onto a chair and got up, keeping his injured wrist close to his body.

He heard some late night revellers walking down the street. They were speaking loudly. He peered through the curtains and watched them until they disappeared from view. He picked up a folder that was perched on his laptop and went downstairs.

In the kitchen, he sat down on a stool and drank some water. He opened the folder, taking out some black and white CCTV images, and a printed map of the area surrounding Wembley stadium. Each image was of a man. Under the picture was a name and a short description.

The map was made up of three separate pieces of A4 paper that he had printed out and taped together. It had red circles drawn all over it, indicating security cameras and likely police positions. He scanned the images for a few minutes, drank some more water and then went back upstairs.

Before he got to sleep, he heard a screeching, whining noise. It grew louder and louder. He got up off his bed again and moved the curtains to the side to see where it was coming from. It was a fox, slowly walking down the street, calling out for its younger cubs.

HE WALKED INTO THE DOJANG, ten minutes before the training session was due to start. No one was cleaning the floor. He inspected the cleaning rota. The boxes for the current and last sessions hadn't been ticked off.

Kris was getting changed in the kitchen.

'Hey, what's up?' he said, looking up at Piotr.

'The rota.'

'What about it?'

'Nobody's ticked off the last session – or today's. And there's no one cleaning now.'

'Oh, right, yeah,' said Kris, taking his dobok out of his training bag. 'Well, we didn't need to clean the dojang last week. Father Leopold's cleaner did a pretty good job, so I let the guys off. She was here again earlier today. It's sparkling.'

'You let them off?'

'Yeah. What's the big deal?'

Piotr stood still. Kris held his gaze. 'Oh come on Piotr, don't look at me like that. It was clean. What was the point of scrubbing it again?'

Some of the students drifted into the dojang. Piotr closed the door behind him.

'Whether it's spotless or not, we clean it. We always clean it. Come on Kris, you know that. We can't let things like that slip.' He opened the door again and looked out onto the dojang hall. 'Sebastian.'

'Yes Sabum?'

'Is Arek in the changing room?'

'I think so.'

'Tell him he's on cleaning duty. And that he's got five minutes. So you may as well help him.'

Piotr closed the door again. Kris said, 'Listen, Piotr, I'm sorry, I didn't mean anything by it. But if someone else is cleaning the facilities for us now, then why waste time with something like that? The guys want to train, not clean the floor.'

'It's a tradition,' said Piotr, pulling a wrist support over his hand. 'We don't neglect it. And you need to discuss anything like that with me first. Not that it would be up for discussion,' he said, feeling his wrist.

'Yeah, well, we could discuss if you were here,' said Kris.

'I'm always available. You know that.'

'But that's different from actually being here. Me and Jacek have been carrying the weight for a few weeks now you know. Filling in for you here and there. You could cut us some slack.'

'Come on Krszystof. You know that we clean the floor – even if it hasn't got a speck of dust on it. Whether I'm here or not doesn't matter.'

Henio walked into the kitchen. 'Surprise,' he said. He gripped hands with Kris.

'So you're back training?' said Kris.

'I've had my arm twisted,' he said. 'What's happened to your wrist Piotrek?'

'Hurt it on the building site. It looks worse than it is.'

'Not the best timing eh?' said Henio.

'I guess not.'

Piotr took a couple of minutes at the start of the lesson to introduce Henio as a returning bousabum to the students who had never met him.

He ran a hard session for the white belts, but allowed himself, the bousabums, as well as Jan and Adam, an easier one. They all supervised sparring and drills, and didn't get involved.

At the end of the class he addressed the group.

'OK, as you all probably know by now, we have an assignment coming up on Saturday and Adam and Jan are being tested. So wish them luck when you get a chance. Because of the assignment there's no class on Saturday, but try and train at home if you can. Oh yeah, and there's also a film night on tomorrow at Sebastian's place. Isn't that right Sebastian?'

Sebastian put his thumb up.

'Bruce Lee marathon this time apparently. So if some of you want to come along then talk to him after class. I'll be there for a bit of it.'

After the lesson Jan and Adam stayed behind with the black belts. Piotr went over to his kit bag and took his folder out of it.

'OK, Saturday,' he said, taking out the CCTV images and handing them over to everyone. 'Try and memorise these faces.

They're the main guys. If we neutralise them, then we'll be in a good position. We should know where it's going to take place by Friday night. We're only going to the main fight. If it splits, we'll go where they expect the most numbers.

'We meet at the station at 10:30. I've been told that the fight should not happen any further away than a one-mile radius of the stadium, probably to the west of it, in a industrial estate car park.

'We stick close together at all times. All we're doing is stopping our lot from fighting. We're not trying to engage with the English unless we absolutely have to. We're there to keep the peace, always remember that.

'Any questions?' Nobody replied. 'OK, good,' said Piotr, shutting the folder. 'You two,' he said, pointing at Adam and Jan, 'stay back for a bit will you.'

The bousabums went to get changed.

'How are you feeling?' Piotr asked.

'OK,' said Adam.

'Yeah, not bad,' said Jan.

Piotr put his hands on their shoulders. 'You'll both be fine. Just remember —always stick with someone. The five-metre rule – that's the most important thing. Then if you're in trouble we know and can do something about it. If it all kicks off, drop someone and move. Some of the guys in these crews are tough old bears. They can take quite a lot of punishment and they'll no doubt have had a drink or something stronger. If we have to get into a fight it will be absolute chaos at some points, but if you're always in eye sight and close by, then we'll all be alright.

'Don't forget, we're all watching each other's backs. And Henio's in on this one too. You know how experienced he is. If we have to engage, I know you can handle it. You wouldn't be up for testing if you couldn't. Trust your instincts and let your combinations flow. OK?'

They both nodded.

'Good. Get a good night's sleep tomorrow. If you can't sleep then do all your tuls before you go to bed. Twice.'

Piotr was the last to arrive. Sebastian showed him to an armchair that was positioned in the middle of the room. 'You can sit here,' he said.

Piotr shook hands with the five other dojang members who were there before sitting down. 'The royal treatment,' he said, crossing his legs. 'I like it.'

'We're going to watch *Way of the Dragon* and *Enter the Dragon*,' said Sebastian.

'I've never seen *Way of the Dragon*,' said Arek.

'Me neither,' said Piotr.

'Seriously?' Sebastian said. 'Oh man. You'll love it, it's great. A little under-rated by the critics.' He handed Piotr a beer. 'You complete the party so we can start watching soon.'

'I can't stay for both movies,' said Piotr. 'I need a clear head and clean eyes for tomorrow.'

'Well, it's a good job it's *Way of the Dragon* you haven't seen then. That's the first one we're watching. It's got Chuck Norris in it.'

'Hey, you know the real reason why Hitler killed himself, right?' said Szymon. 'He found out that Chuck Norris is Jewish.'

He clinked his bottle with Arek as everyone laughed.

After the film they ordered some pizza. Piotr said he didn't want any. 'I don't want to eat late tonight,' he said.

Szymon said, 'How do you think the guys will do tomorrow?'

'I'm not sure. It depends on how they handle it,' said Piotr. 'They've got the skills. If they've got the nerve as well then they'll be fine.'

'Were you nervous when you took yours Sabum?' said Ziggy.

'I guess so, but not as much as I could have been. It all happened pretty quickly.'

'What did you have to do?' said Sebastian.

'I'm not sure I'm even supposed to tell you that.'

'Kris told us how he got his,' said Szymon.

Piotr took a slug of beer. 'He did, huh? I guess it won't do any harm telling you. I was set up without even knowing it. I was jumped outside a bar after having one too many by four guys. My Sabum took me out in Warsaw. He knew a few people there and we went out in a shadier part of town. During the evening he'd tipped off some local small-time thieves that I was an American tourist who had loads of cash on me. When we were leaving the bar he told me to wait round the corner while he went for a piss. I was standing there and these four guys followed me out and pounced on me.'

'And?' said Sebastian.

'And I put them all down. My Sabum had got out through the back entrance with one of his bousabums to watch.'

'That was a weird way to do it,' said Ziggy.

'It was to do with how I had joined the Kwan in the first place. I had to relive a bad memory.'

The students all sat still, waiting. Piotr chuckled. 'You all want to know what that was now too, right?'

'Hang on, I'll just get some more beer,' said Sebastian.

'Just a water for me,' said Piotr.

Sebastian came back in from the kitchen with some beers and a glass of water. Piotr finished his beer and had a sip of the water.

'OK. So back then you still had to be asked to join the Kwan. You couldn't turn up and train and then get invited to officially join. You needed an invitation to step into a dojang.

'I was invited after me and three friends got jumped coming out of a bar. We were seventeen. We'd been drinking quite late as we knew the barman – he was one of my friend's older cousins. He had let us stay for a lock-in after the owner had left. The owner knew we were under age, so it was the only way we could get a drink there.

'We were having our last drink when there was a loud bang on the door. The bar was based on a sort of Wild West American theme. It was called the *Country & Western*, or something like that. The front door was solid oak and had a grilled metal gate in front of it, but behind that, to get to the bar, you had to go through two salon-type swing doors. You know the ones I mean? Anyway, the banging was so strong that it made the swing doors rattle.

'At first we ignored it, thinking it was a couple of drunks who would give up and go away, but the knocking continued. It sounded like they were kicking the door too.

'After a minute or so my friend's cousin went to one of the windows to see who it was. It turned out that it was a bunch of guys that he knew and letting them in might have been less of a problem for him than leaving them to keep banging on the door would be, if you see what I mean. So he opened the door.'

'Tracksuits?' said Szymon.

'Not quite. But sort of affiliated with gangs I guess. We stayed at the bar and kept talking, while the barman got drinks for them. There were seven of them. We didn't say anything to them and they didn't say anything to us, but you could feel some tension. A couple of the guys started looking over at us and they were clearly talking about us from a corner in the bar where they had sat down.

'So we finished up our drinks and got the hell out of there in case it turned out that they decided to start something with us. I asked the barman if he'd be OK if we left. He said not to worry and to head home, as they'd come in late like that a number of times. So we left. Problem was, they didn't stay to finish their drinks.'

Piotr took a sip of water. 'They followed us out and asked us to empty our pockets.'

'Did they show you a blade?' said Arek.

'No, it wasn't like that. They just walked up behind us and barged into us. We were taken by surprise. You have to remember that we couldn't hold our beer at that age. Plus we were naïve. We should have switched our burners on and got out of there. But we just stood there.'

'Did you say anything?' said Sebastian.

'Well, we were frozen on the spot, like I said. But then one of my buddies spoke up. He said we'd spent everything in the bar. One of the guys then grabbed one of my friend's, Bogdan, by the throat. Or he tried to anyway. Bogdan managed to grab his hands and hold them, so that they were placed somewhere between his chest and his throat. He then got hold of Bogdan's shirt and started pulling him towards him, shouting at him to empty his pockets. Bogdan kept shouting at him to let go of his shirt. I had no idea what was going on, my brain wouldn't click into place. Then this fat chief comes around the back of Bogdan and his attacker and smacks Kazik, my other friend, flush in the chops, sending him straight down. As Kazik falls, he dives on him and starts trying to go through his pockets. So I did the first thing that came into my head, which was to throw a roundhouse kick at him, straight in the jaw. I heard this loud cracking sort of noise and saw him slump on top of Kazik – he was out cold. I was really lucky.'

'So you were training already by then?' said Sebastian.

'I'd done some kick boxing for a couple of years, but that was it.'

'And then what?' said Arek.

'Well, then I was about to pick up Kazik and try to see if he was

OK, when we were rushed by the rest of them, or so it seemed. One of them ran towards me and planted me with a nice knee to my face, giving me this nose,' said Piotr, pinching his two nostrils.

'From then on, it's a blur. What I do remember is blinking like mad due to the tears and blood in my eyes and crawling up to Kazik and then getting kicked hard in my ribs. I covered up and rolled up into a foetal position. For some reason he didn't follow up with his kicking.

'Anyway, Bogdan told me what had happened once I'd got kneed. After he saw what had happened to me and Kazik, he lost the plot and threw as many punches as he could at the guy who had grabbed him. He fell on top of the guy and somehow knocked him out. I guess he must have struck him enough times or he hit the ground and was sparked out that way.

'I got up, not really knowing what was going on and saw that my other two friends were on the floor and in trouble. So I ran at one of them and tackled him down to the ground and started hitting out again. And that's when I could feel that someone else had joined the fight. I was pulled off and pushed back a bit and I heard someone tell me to sit down on some grass nearby. The way he spoke, there was something in his voice. It made me obey him even though I was so disorientated.

'Sitting down, I could see what had happened. The guys who'd come into the bar were all sitting or lying on the ground. At first I couldn't work it out. Then the man who'd told me to sit down dragged the guy I had tackled by his collar and threw him to the ground. He told them to never come back to the bar. They all stood up and limped away. Then the man who'd spoken came over to check if I was OK.'

'He was Kwan,' said Bartek.

Piotr nodded. 'He was with three black belts from his dojang. They'd known about this gang prying on drinkers at a few bars in the area. And they'd decided to deal with them that night. We'd got seriously lucky. Afterwards they told me and Bogdan that we had balls. They liked the way that we fought back.'

'So they invited you to join their dojang?' said Arek.

'Well, not there and then. We went to get checked out at hospital by a couple of doctors they knew and took us home. I had an adrenaline dump and was shaking afterwards on the way back. Kazik had to stay in hospital for a couple of days and I'd had to go to his place, wake his mother up and confess what we'd been up to.

'A week or so later, one of them, who was the highest ranked bousabum, came to see me outside our block of flats. He caught me on the way to school and told me that his Sabum would like to talk to me.

'I was curious so I went to see him. I never thought a dojang would want someone like me. I didn't know anyone involved with the Kwan. So I went along and trained with them one night. It was an eye opener. I vowed to join them. Right there and then.'

The door buzzer to the flat rang.

Sebastian got up. 'That'll be the pizzas.'

Piotr stood up as well and put his jacket on while Sebastian paid for the pizzas. He shook everyone's hands.

'Hope it goes well tomorrow Sabum,' said Sebastian at the door. 'Good luck.'

'Thanks,' said Piotr. 'By the way. If anyone round here ever delivered pierogi, would you order those? Instead of pizza sometimes?'

'Pierogi? I don't know. They don't sound like a takeaway food to me. Why do you ask?'

Piotr patted his arm. 'Just curious. Have a good night.'

PIOTR WOKE UP EARLY the next morning and let Gapczo out into the garden while he drank a glass of milk and read the hooligan file again. Once he'd finished the milk, he put on his running shoes and left the house.

He ran faster than he normally would. Before long he was struggling for breath. He slowed down when he reached an uphill stretch of his route. His thighs burned, but he pushed on until he reached the top. After regulating his breathing he got back into his stride and climbed the side of Horsenden Hill, through the wooded area, where he and Jacek liked to go and drink beer.

When he got through into the clearing near the top, where the hill mingled with the golf course, he stopped and tried to do some press ups, but his wrist wouldn't hold up to the pressure. He jogged back home thinking about the hooligans.

After he showered he strapped up his wrist again as tightly as he could and looked over the map. He checked his emails one more time and then made some scrambled eggs and sausages for himself and his Aunt. The day was already warming up so they sat in the garden drinking coffee after they ate.

'You were out early,' said his Aunt.

'I didn't sleep too great,' he said.

They all met at Wembley Central station as planned. Jan couldn't keep his feet still, Adam's mouth was dry. He kept sipping from a bottle of water. Piotr briefly thought about getting them a can of beer.

Jacek and Kris both said that they were hungry. 'I could do with another coffee,' said Henio, finishing the one he had in his hand.

'McDonalds still serve breakfast up until 11,' said Kris.

'OK, let's go there then,' said Piotr. 'But get these around you first,' he said, taking some Poland scarves out of his rucksack.

'What do we need these for?' said Jacek.

'Hools don't wear team colours. If we're stopped by the police then we have some cover.'

136

They chose a table in a corner of the restaurant and spoke quietly. Henio, Jacek and Kris ate some food. All of them drank black coffee. Henio poured four sachets of sugar into his. 'I need it for the energy,' he said, winking at Jan and Adam.

Four England fans sat down on a table a few rows down from them. They were all wearing replica shirts. One of them placed a rolled up flag on the table.

'Alright lads?' he said, looking at the dojang's hierarchy.

'Good luck today, may the best team win and all that,' said one of the other England fans.

'Thanks,' said Henio. 'It should be a great game.'

'What's with the friendliness?' said Kris, in Polish.

'Not all football fans are rabid dogs you know,' said Henio.

When they had finished eating, Piotr said, 'OK, listen up. Here's the plan. The three Polish crews have agreed to join forces to fight four English crews. It's all to do with some beef from a European club game that took place years ago.'

Piotr took out the folded map from his back pocket and spread it out on the table. He pointed to a section he had circled with a blue pen. 'They're meeting here,' he said. 'As our source expected them to.'

'Isn't that a car park?' said Jacek. 'They'll be loads of cars there.'

'No it's a big industrial estate, closed off to public parking. You need a pass to get in there, so it's got barriers at the entrance and an exit point. It's not far from a pub that some of the English fans like to drink at.'

'How many?'

'A few members from each crew. Could be up to 20 guys on each side.'

Adam stared at the map, Jan looked wan.

'All we need to do is break it up enough to make them all step away. We just stand our ground. Get in the way. If it all kicks off, we start pulling the main guys off, and we make sure they can't fight on. Nobody does anything but follow my lead. Remember, Sebastian is on stand by to call the police a minute after we arrive. So hopefully it'll be over before we realise it's even started.'

'After which we're going to have to run,' said Jacek.

'Possibly. They've picked a good spot, quite far from where the police will be patrolling. It's not easy to get to with horses and wagons because of the traffic. We might be able to just walk away.'

'What time?' said Henio.

'12:30. But we need to be there a bit earlier than that.'

Jan shot up. 'You OK chief?' said Henio.

'I need a piss,' he said, walking off to the toilets. Piotr nudged Jacek and nodded in Jan's direction. Jacek got up and followed him into the toilets.

Kris turned to Adam and said, 'How are you feeling?

'I'm OK,' he said, forming a half smile. 'Want to get it over and done with.'

'We all do,' said Piotr. 'It'll be OK, trust me. We'll be right there with you both.'

'All you have to do is concentrate on what you do every time you train,' said Henio. 'Be decisive and vicious. You're a predator, remember that.'

'That's some good advice right there,' said Piotr. 'But if we're lucky, then we won't have to do much at all. Hopefully we can delay them for long enough before the police clear them away.'

Jacek came back to the table.

Piotr said. 'All OK?'

'He's puked up a bit.'

When Jan got back, Piotr went through the plan again. When he was done, he stood up. 'OK, let's go stop a bunch of meatheads smashing the hell out of each other.'

Outside, they split into two groups. Some of them put baseball caps on. The second group left a 20-metre gap between the first one as they walked down the high road towards the stadium. The traffic was building up with coaches and cars full of fans. As they got closer towards the stadium, Piotr led them down a side street, breaking away from the stream of fans.

On the way, they passed a narrow side road. Further down it, some England fans were drinking outside a small pub. Piotr stopped the first group, letting the second one go on. 'Jan, take a pic of those guys will you?'

Jan walked back to side road and took two quick pictures with his phone. When he got back he said, 'There were two of the guys outside that pub.'

'Are you sure?' said Kris.

'Definitely. I was looking at their photos this morning.' He showed the group one of the pictures on his phone.

'Well spotted,' said Piotr. 'That was two of them for sure.'

When they got to the industrial estate, they climbed up onto the flat roof of a building by the vacant parking lot where the hooligans had planned to meet. Piotr gave them a short overview of the roads nearby and showed them three possible escape routes. The dojang men who had baseballs caps on took them off and gave them to those who weren't wearing any.

'As soon as we split, caps come off,' said Piotr. 'Jacek, you stay up here and lay low to keep a look out. When you see the first group on its way climb down and we'll get ready. We're going to stay here behind the building where they can't see us.

'If we get split up, we meet back at the station at 1 and then separate again. We don't even acknowledge each other. Pretend to be on your phones or looking at a shop window. All I need to know is that you've all made it out safely.'

He pinched his watch. 'We've got about 20 minutes. Gather round.'

They huddled together in a circle. Piotr said, 'Right, are we all clear on the plan?' They all nodded.

'No questions? Adam? Jan?

Jan clenched his jaw. 'No, all good Sabum.'

'Good. Remember, stay close to one of us at all times,' he said, pointing at Jan and Adam. 'If we have to engage, and you're in a tight situation, then don't be a hero. Use your heads. Get away if you have to and grab one of us.'

They climbed down the metal ladder at the side of the building, leaving Jacek on the roof.

Down at ground level they made sure they were out of view. Henio put a cigarette in his mouth and was about to light it when Piotr pulled it out and threw it behind him. 'What are you trying to do, get us found out?' he said.

Henio put his hands up in the air. 'Sorry.'

'Low voices only from now on.'

Jacek climbed down the ladder about ten minutes later. 'They're coming,' he said.

'How many?' said Piotr.

'35 Poles. The English aren't on the march yet.'

'35? Are you sure?' said Kris.

'Yeah, I'm sure,' said Jacek. 'What, are you worried?'

'That's a big number.'

Piotr checked the time again. 'OK, the English must be late,' he said.

Jacek climbed back onto the roof before climbing down a few seconds later. 'They're coming now.'

'How many?' said Piotr.

'No idea. Didn't have time to count. More than 30 though. Maybe 40, I'd guess, at a stretch.'

'What the hell's with that information Piotr?' said Kris. 'Are we sure we want to carry on with those numbers?'

'We carry on as normal,' said Piotr. 'It's a little over what we expected, but that's OK.'

'OK? How is it OK?'

'You want to walk away?'

Kris was silent.

'Right, then sort yourself out. This is happening. We can cope.'

Jan was looking down at the ground and blowing hard out of his mouth. Henio put his hand on Jan's shoulder, rubbing it.

'Breathe,' said Henio. He looked at Kris. 'Those numbers don't change a thing. We still target the lions of the pack. Everything follows from there.'

'Exactly,' said Piotr. 'Most of them will run when their leaders fall.' He peered around the corner of the building. 'What do you reckon Jacek, two minutes?'

'30 seconds for our lot. English two minutes later.'

'OK,' said Piotr, looking at Jacek. 'Text Sebastian. Tell him to call the police in exactly four minutes.'

They all gripped hands. '*Baekjul Boolgol,*' said Piotr, looking Jan and Adam in the eye.

Piotr made a fist with his left hand and punched his right palm a couple of times. He ignored the sharp pain in his wrist. 'Let's go,' he said.

The Polish hooligans were gathered in three groups. They were finishing cans of Polish beer and crushing them in their hands before dropping them or kicking them away. Some of the men were barechested. Their torsos were covered in tattoos. They were prowling in small circles, focussed on the road ahead where the

English would come from.

One of the ringleaders saw the dojang men walking towards them.

'Hey, what's happening?' Piotr said.

'Who the hell are you?' he said. 'You with a crew?'

'No, we're not with a crew,' said Piotr, getting the attention of the rest of the hooligans.

'Then what are you whores' sons doing here?'

'When did they teach monkeys to speak Polish?' said another ringleader. He had a tattoo of a five-pointed star on his neck. 'You best get out of here unless you want to get a kicking.'

'Why don't you all walk away and let us deal with the English,' said Piotr, leading the dojang men in between two of the groups to position themselves between them and the incoming English hooligans.

'What, are you out of your whoring mind?' said the first ringleader. 'This is our fight.'

Piotr recognised the men from the file. Between them, they had 14 years of prison time behind them.

'The English have lied to you. They've brought more numbers. Let us deal with it and you can walk away without getting smashed up. You can live to fight another day,' said Piotr.

'What are you? Cops?' said the hooligan with the star tattoo.

'No. We just don't want to see you get hurt.'

The English came into view. They swaggered towards the industrial estate, pointing at the Poles and baiting them.

'Get ready boys,' said the first ringleader.

Piotr put his arms up and spoke to the English crews. 'There's no need for this guys.'

They ignored him. A bottle flew over his head. A moment later, the English charged.

Piotr reached behind his back and took out his baton. The rest of the dojang men mirrored him.

With the first hooligan almost upon him, Piotr flicked his baton open, dropped to one knee and struck the hooligan in the solar plexus before smashing his jaw with the end of the baton's handle as he stood back up.

The two sides rushed at each other.

'Step away,' said Piotr. His men obeyed, splitting into two and moving to each side.

A fractured beat of smashed bottles accompanied the collision of bodies. Men were thrown to the ground, others had their T-shirts pulled over their heads as their opponents hammerfisted them. Frantic punches and kicks sliced through thin air.

Piotr gave a signal. Henio and Jan started helping him pull hooligans away from the rumble, targeting the ringleaders where they could. They aimed kicks at their knees and ankles, to try and incapacitate them.

Across from them, Adam, Jacek and Kris were doing the same.

A breakaway group from the Polish crew drove a small gang of the English to the other end of the car park. They were overwhelming them. One of the English hooligans was on the floor, covering his head as the Poles stamped on him. Another one was retreating with his torn shirt hanging off his stomach and blood streaming down his face.

Kris spotted them and shouted out. 'Leave them,' Piotr shouted back.

Some of the Poles turned on the dojang men and tried to fight back. The brawl became more fragmented and Jan was pushed away from Henio and Piotr. He was up against three attackers. He dropped one of them with a side kick and got rid of another one with a hip throw. He had retreated so far that he was closer to Jacek than he was to Piotr. Jacek tagged his shoulder and motioned him over.

Piotr and Henio were being backed up further into the industrial estate's car park. They were fending off some of the English hooligans. One of them had a long metal bar and was swinging it at them.

'We need to drive forward,' Piotr said. 'We need to get back to the others.'

The hooligan with the metal bar went at Henio, who lost his balance and rolled away from harm. Piotr started to get to Henio, but as he struck one of the English with a punch, he felt a sharp pain in his left wrist. He grimaced and held it, dropping his baton. Three hooligans noticed his vulnerability and advanced.

Piotr stepped back, still holding his wrist. His attackers jumped at him. He went into autopilot, checking off his strikes in Korean. *Najunde ap cha busigi, wi palkup taeragi, yop cha jirugi, sonbadak golcha makgi, doo jirugi, sun sonkut tulgi.* With his last move, he threw one of his assailants over his shoulder, summoning a *kiup* from deep within his diaphragm as he watched the hooligan twitch on the ground.

Henio kept rolling his body, narrowly avoiding the metal bar as it crashed down onto the ground. Piotr picked up his baton and struck Henio's hunter at the back of the head. The hooligan fell forwards, like a toppled communist statue with one arm up in the air, raised in premature celebration.

Sirens broke up the fighting. The crews split in different directions, throwing a few last blows as way of a farewell.

Piotr and Henio scrambled to Jacek, who was holding his back and lying on the floor.

'Where are Adam and Jan?' said Henio, wiping blood from his nose.

'They went around the corner,' said Jacek.

'On their own?' said Piotr.

He ran towards them.

Piotr watched the ambulance set off from a safe distance and then ran back towards Wembley High Street. He jumped on a bus towards Central Middlesex hospital.

When he got there, he spoke to a man at the reception desk.

'I'm trying to find my friend. He's been stabbed. He came in here a few minutes ago I think. He's almost two metres tall, fair-haired. He was wearing a white T-shirt.'

'What's his name?'

'Adam Kowalewski.'

The man picked up the phone. 'Hi Bridgette. I've got a guy here asking about an A&E entrant. Adam Kolaksi?'

'Kowalewski.'

'Kolawksi. That's right. He's in theatre? OK. Thanks.' The man put the phone down.

'He's being operated on right now. You'll have to wait in A&E. Are you family?'

'A friend. I'm his friend.'

'Right. Well, you'll have to wait.'

'What's his situation?'

'If you go to the A&E desk they may be able to tell you. You're lucky as it's still early so they might be able to talk to you.'

'Where do I go?'

'Down the corridor, turn left, then it's on your right.'

The receptionist in A&E told Piotr that he would have to wait until a doctor came to speak to him. He sat down, near a stand of leaflets. His mind blank, he read their titles. *How to stop smoking. Spotting drug abuse. Signs you're having a stroke.* His phone rang. It was Henio.

'Where are you?' Piotr said.

'In a pub. Don't worry, it's miles away. What's the situation?'

'He's in theatre. How's Jan?'

'Shaky. He's on his fourth vodka shot.'

'Maybe you should all go home after the next drink. What about the others?'

'Not too much damage. Jacek got a cut to his head, but it's minor. It's stopped bleeding now. You'll let us know as soon as you can right?'

'Of course.'

Piotr thought about the fight for a while until he realised that he was hungry. He stood up holding his left arm and walked to some dispenser machines and slowly punched in the code for a chocolate bar. He put some coins in the machine, noticing that the skin on his right hand was torn over the knuckles. After getting a soft drink, he sat back down and drank it all in go before inhaling the chocolate.

Then he called his Aunt.

It was late when he got back home. The muffled voices on his Aunt's favourite radio station drifted through the house from her bedroom. He went into the kitchen, switched the light on and poured himself a glass of water.

He heard the creaking staircase as his Aunt walked down it to see him. She came into the kitchen in her slippers and dressing gown.

'How is he?' she asked.

'OK. Someone up there must have been looking out for him. They said they'd never seen someone stabbed so many times and not be in a serious condition because of it. They needed to patch him up a bit, and then get a lot of stitches into him. They said there was no serious internal damage. His sister's there now.'

Piotr drank some more water.

'Are you OK?' said his Aunt, touching his arm.

'I hurt my wrist again. Kept my face clean I think.' Piotr touched his chin.

'No, I meant are you OK about what happened?'

'I'm fine.' He paused as if he was about to say something else, but drank a bit more water instead.

'Do you want some soup?'

'It's a bit late for soup,' said Piotr.

'You go and sit down, I'll warm it up for you,' she said, taking a pot out of the fridge.

'No, you relax. I'll do it. I might take a shower first though.'

When Piotr came back downstairs his Aunt had warmed up some chicken broth and dumplings.

'Don't make a fuss,' she said. 'I'm feeling OK today.'

When he was finished he cleaned up his dishes. 'Do you want anything else to eat?' his Aunt said.

'No thanks. I think I need a beer. Do you want a drink?'

'Maybe I'll have a little sherry.'

Piotr went to the drinks cabinet in the front room and poured her a drink. He went into the kitchen, took a can of beer out of the fridge and opened it, taking a gulp as he walked into the back room. He handed his Aunt her sherry and switched on the TV.

His Aunt started knitting. He flicked through the channels and settled on a police documentary. Two police officers were running after some criminals through the back gardens of a row of terraced houses, while a helicopter camera was helping other officers to keep track of where the criminals were heading.

Piotr wondered if the police would be in touch with him before too long.

JACEK, KRIS, HENIO AND JAN waited outside the church hall in silence. Piotr walked up the alley towards them. He felt as if the souls of the dojang's past Sabums were following his every step.

Inside, they congregated by the raised stage at the back of the hall. Henio, Jacek and Jan perched on the edge of it. Kris and Piotr stood facing them.

'I called the hospital on the way here,' Piotr said. 'Adam's awake and talking. You guys can go and see him after 3 if you want. I should be there about then.'

Piotr faced Jacek. 'How's your injury?'

Jacek took off his baseball cap, revealing a large bandage that covered most of his forehead. 'It seems OK. I cleaned it really carefully last night. It's not that deep. Doesn't seem infected.'

'You sure it doesn't need stitches?'

'Don't think so.'

'You best go and get it checked out anyway. It's better to be sure.' Piotr looked at each of them briefly, before saying, 'OK, who wants to offer some first thoughts on what happened?'

'We did the wrong thing,' said Kris. 'The whole thing was wrong. Like I said it would be.'

'That's helpful,' said Piotr.

'Well, it's true. Nobody can deny it. We should have pulled out when we knew the numbers involved. It was reckless.'

'Steady there Krysztof,' said Henio. 'We need to find out the details first.'

'Details?' said Kris. 'I can give you details. One. There were too many of them. Two. Loads of them had weapons. Three. We got separated at crucial points. I said it was a bad idea for us to get involved in that fight, and I was right. Any of us could have been outnumbered and hurt like Adam.'

'You're angry. I get that,' said Piotr. 'We all are. It went wrong. I take full responsibility. But I need to know exactly how it went down. Let me tell you what I know, then you guys see if you can fill in any gaps.

'We know that our intelligence was way off. There were way more than we expected. I'm going to try and find out why that was. I

146

could have handled the stand off a bit better, I admit that. Jan – you and Adam were always with someone up until you got separated and went off without one of us. What happened?'

Jacek cleared his throat. 'I was with Adam before he went to help the English guys,' he said. 'I saw that they were outside the car park, getting a serious kicking. I told him I had to help Jan first and then we'd go in there to help. I didn't tell him to engage them. I turned, gave Jan a hand and before I knew it, Adam had gone.'

'So why didn't you follow him?' said Piotr.

'I wanted to, but then I got jumped again. It was bedlam. This guy was trying to stab me with a bottle. That's how I got this,' he said, touching his head. 'Then I told Jan to go and bring Adam back straight away. Drag him back, I said. Or at least that's what I think happened. Like I said, it was mad, there were so many of them. But it was my fault they were on their own. What can I say? I'm sorry. I'm gutted for Adam.'

'Let's backtrack a second,' said Piotr. 'Jan, how come you split from me and Henio at the start?'

'I didn't mean to split, I swear,' said Jan. 'I was backing off and then before I knew it, I was next to Jacek and Kris, so I thought it best to stay with him.'

'You did right,' said Piotr.

'That was my mistake. I got pulled away for a bit too long there and he got a bit overwhelmed,' said Henio.

Piotr put his hands up. 'OK, and then why didn't you come back to Jacek like he told you to when you went for Adam?'

'I got sucked into fighting,' said Jan. 'And the group had got bigger.'

'Bigger? What do you mean?'

'There were more guys there than when we first spotted the English in trouble.'

'Who were they? Where did they come from?' said Henio.

'Poles. There quite a few of them, they came rushing at us when we went around the corner,' said Jacek. 'As if they were waiting for us or something.'

'So we were dealing with even more than the original ridiculous number that we had to face off against,' said Kris, shaking his head. 'Great.'

'Are you sure about this?' said Piotr.

'Definitely. I guess it was hard to tell. Everyone scrammed when they heard the police, but yeah, the group was bigger. I swear it.'

'Why were we so interested in that group in the first place anyway?' said Henio.

'They were about to get seriously hurt,' said Jacek. 'One of the English had already got stamped on the head.'

'What happened to you Kris?' said Piotr.

'I got stuck fighting the lot that Adam and Jan should have been helping us with. I'm lucky I didn't end up in that ward with Adam.'

Piotr rubbed his temples. 'There's no point going on about this. I have to speak to Adam anyway to get his version of events. We all come to training tomorrow as normal. I'll need you all to send me a written account of how you saw it all go down. I'll text you all to remind you later. None of what we've said or seen goes beyond us six.'

On their way out he stopped Jan and said, 'No matter what comes out of this. You did really well. And you're not to blame for any of this. Remember that.'

'Thanks. I wish I could have done more to help Adam though.'

'I know. But there's no point beating yourself up about it.'

Piotr waited for the rest of them to be out of earshot. 'Listen, tell me. Did you hear what Jacek said to Adam? Before he went off?'

Jan shook his head. 'No Sabum,' he said. 'I didn't.'

Beata stirred the coffee in the percolator.

'Are you sure you're OK?' she said.

'I've got a lot on my mind.'

'That building site is giving you some nasty injuries,' she said looking at his bandaged wrist. He had wrapped tape all the way up to his knuckles to hide the scars from the hooligan fight.

'You sure you don't want any cake? It's a best seller at the shop.'

'No, really, thanks.'

She cut herself a slice of cheesecake, put it on a plate with some raspberries and poured Piotr a cup of coffee. She placed it in front of him on the kitchen table and sat down across from him. Taking a large mouthful, she said, 'Well if you won't talk about your troubles then I may as well bore you with mine.'

'Like what?'

'Well it's more Aga than me. She's in some sort of money trouble. I don't know what exactly. She says it's not a problem, but I had to pay for most of the rent last month. There's no way I can do that more than a couple of times. And now I'm worried that she won't pay me back.'

'Why are you worried? She's still working right?'

'Yeah, but she's keeping something from me.'

'Do you want me to lend you some money? I have some savings.'

'No, that's very sweet of you, but I think we need to work it out between ourselves.'

After they drank their coffee Beata showed him some photos from Aga's birthday on her phone. She started talking about what some of the girls had been saying about Piotr, but his mind drifted.

'Piotrusz?' she said, nudging him. 'Did you hear what I said? They said you were a nice guy.'

'Oh right,' he said. 'That's nice of them.'

'Piotrusz, what is it? I can't have you and Aga keeping things from me.' She reached out for his hand. 'Come on, you can tell me.'

Piotr played with his empty coffee mug. 'One of my friends got stabbed yesterday,' he said.

Beata withdrew her hands and held them over her mouth.

'He's OK,' said Piotr, raising his hand to reassure her. 'He's in hospital but it's not life threatening or anything.'

'How? Why?' she said.

'He was in the wrong place at the wrong time. He's not a troublemaker or anything like that. I'm going to the hospital soon to see him. He's OK. He just needs to rest.'

'But how did it happen?'

'He was trying to break up a fight between some hooligans. He got caught in the middle of it.'

'Dear Lord.'

'He was doing the right thing. Just in the wrong place, like I said. He was unlucky.'

'What was he getting involved for?'

'He wanted to help. People were getting hurt. He wasn't going to stand by and witness that without stepping in.'

'Sounds very brave of him.'

'Yeah, I guess it was.'

Piotr felt like the hospital corridor would never end. He walked under signs and passed doors with names of wards and departments that he did not recognise until he turned a corner and continued down another hallway which looked identical to the one he had just been through. When he reached an intersection that was brightly lit by the sun streaming through some large skylights, he saw the sign for the lifts.

He got off on the fifth floor. Six sets of double doors later, he arrived at the ward that Adam was in. A musky warm smell filled his nostrils. He breathed through his mouth for a bit. He went by a nurse who was surfing the internet on her computer. He expected to have to explain who he was there to see, but she paid him no attention.

The smell got even stronger in the room. There were eight beds, one on each side. The piercing sunlight shone through the wide windows at the end of it. Adam was at the far end, on the left hand side. One of his arms was in a sling. A gap in the blue hospital vest that he was wearing revealed a large bandage on the side of his stomach.

'Hey Sabum,' he said. 'How's it going?'

'Adam,' said Piotr, putting his hand on his shoulder, 'how are you doing?'

'Really well,' he said, looking down at his bandaged arm and lifting it up slightly. 'I'll be ready to get back into training before too long.'

Piotr showed him a clenched fist. 'Good to hear. Can I sit down?'

'Of course.'

'I called up this morning but they said you were out of it.'

'It's the painkillers. I didn't have a great night so they gave me a few more. They knocked me out for a bit.'

'I brought you some pretzels,' said Piotr, holding up a large packet. He put them on a tray that was attached to the side of the bed.

'Thanks. I need them. The food here is terrible. Even I can cook

150

better stuff than some of the crap they serve up.'

Piotr laughed. 'What do they give you?'

'It's varied, meat and potatoes, curry and rice. But it doesn't matter what it is, it all smells and tastes the same. It's really weird.'

'Sounds bad. You need some Maggi or something.'

'I'm desperate for a good Kotlet or some soup,' said Adam.

Piotr pointed at the pretzels and said, 'You want some of those now?'

'Go on then. I'm starving.'

Piotr opened the packet and placed it on Adam's tray, next to a copy of a novel by a Polish crime writer. 'But apart from that they're treating you OK?'

'Definitely. The nurses and the doctors are great.'

Adam took a handful of pretzels and popped them in his mouth. 'You have a few as well.'

'No. I'm good, thanks,' said Piotr.

They talked some more about the hospital. After a while, Piotr leaned forward in his chair. 'Listen. About what happened. It wasn't meant to get anywhere near as bad as it did. I'm sorry I let you down. I should have done a better job in looking after you.' He gazed out of the window.

Adam kept chewing on a pretzel but didn't say anything.

Piotr turned his head, checking to see if anyone was paying them any attention. 'Are you alright to talk about it yet?'

'Sure.'

'Can you remember what happened?'

'Kind of,' said Adam, putting down a handful of pretzels he was about to eat. 'But I should be saying sorry, not you Sabum. I messed up, going around the corner on my own like that. I don't know what I was thinking. I should have waited and stuck to one of you guys, like you'd told us to.'

Piotr leaned in a bit further. 'So why did you leave us then?'

'Jacek told me to. I guess maybe I thought it was part of the test. A test of my character, or bravery or something. I thought I had to show that I had a pair, you know?'

'Jacek told you to? What do you mean? He actually told you to go around the corner?'

'It wasn't quite like that,' said Adam. He pushed the pretzel packet to the side of the tray and used it to re-enact the scene with his hands. 'From what I can remember, two or three of the English lot had got surrounded by quite a few of our guys. At least ten, and one of them was getting a kicking. He was on the floor and they were laying into him. It looked bad. And someone had flashed a blade too. So Jacek told me to go help and said he would be right behind me, I got over there and starting pulling the Poles off the guy, I had to drop two of them. I think I might have broken a third one's arm. It was enough to roll the English guy over. He was bleeding from his head and his mouth but he managed to get up and started stumbling away. I saw that the other two English hools were in trouble as well and were trying to get away, that's when the group moved round the corner. So I followed them. Jan was with me by then.'

Adam stole a glimpse at the rest of the ward and said, in a lower voice. 'But then there were like another dozen or so hools there. They came out of nowhere. That's when one of them pulled a knife on me,' he said.

'Did you not use your baton?' said Piotr.

'That's the thing. It was gone. Somehow I'd lost in it the whole mess. I've got no idea how. I was using my forearms to protect me as much as I could. It was only when he got me in the stomach that I had a window to hit him square. Which I did. When he was on the floor I stamped on him to make sure. Then the police arrived.'

'Well you fought well,' said Piotr. 'By the looks of it,' he said, pointing at Adam's arm. 'How many times were you stabbed in the arm?'

'The doctor said four times, plus six surface slashes.'

'And your stomach?'

'Just the once. Like I said, that's when I could fight back properly.'

'So you can't remember what happened with your baton?'

'I swear I was gripping it when I saw the knife. It must have been the adrenaline. I don't know how I lost it. But someone obviously knocked it out of my hand. It was as if they knew that they had to target it.'

Piotr leaned in a bit closer. 'Given the circumstances you did amazingly well,' he said. 'Worthy of a black belt.'

'I guess I got lucky.'

'You make your own luck.'

Piotr glanced over at the rest of the ward again.

'Police been yet?'

'They were here earlier today.'

'What did you tell them?'

'Standard. I said I was a passer-by, got jumped on the way to the game. I was even using my scarf to cover my wound.'

'Good man.'

'There's one more thing,' said Adam.

'What's that?'

'A couple of them seemed skilled to me. As if they were trained. Not like your normal hooligan types.'

'How skilled?'

'They were like us.'

'Are you sure about that?'

'100%.'

PIOTR PUT HIS HAM SANDWICH down on the carpenter's bench and lifted up the bottom of his T-shirt to wipe the sweat off his brow.

'You OK?' said Uncle. 'You've been quiet all day.'

'I've got a bit on my mind,' said Piotr.

'Is it your Aunt?'

'Sort of. There's some other stuff I need to deal with as well.'

Uncle broke a sausage in half and dipped one end in his jar of mustard. He took one bite before tearing off some bread from his small loaf and chewing on it. 'Sometimes helps to talk about it,' he said.

Piotr drank some water from a large bottle. 'I'm worried that someone close to me has maybe lied about something.'

'About something important?' said Uncle, taking another bite of his sausage.

'You could say that. I need to figure out how to deal with it.'

'I had something like that before. It was with my brother. Why don't you ask them why they lied? Maybe they had a reason to. Things aren't always straightforward you know.'

Piotr picked up his sandwich and examined it from different angles.

'What did your brother do?' he said, taking a large bite out of it.

'He lied to me about some land that we had inherited back home. But the reason he did it was because there was a legal dispute and he didn't want me to get involved. It was when my wife was ill. He didn't want me to have the extra stress.'

'I don't think anyone's trying to protect me like that,' Piotr said. 'If anything, it's the other way. They're doing it to hurt me.'

'Still, asking them may not be a bad idea.' Uncle stood up. 'Come on, we'd best get back to work.'

'OK,' said Piotr. 'Let me make a quick phone call first.'

He dialled Jacek's number. When he answered it, Piotr said, 'We need to meet up.'

Piotr met Jacek in a pub in Wembley that served Polish food.

They sat at the bar.

'You hungry?' said Piotr.

'Starving.'

Jacek asked for some potato pancakes and Piotr ordered pierogi. They got beers to go with their meals.

'You're still checking out the competition eh?' Jacek said.

'Something like that.'

A television screen in the corner of the bar was showing a Polish sitcom that they both recognised. Jacek chuckled at one of the punch lines delivered by the main character, played by a fat balding actor wearing a white sleeveless vest. They both took a long drink from their beers as soon as the barman served them up.

'This guy's mental,' said Jacek, laughing at another joke.

'My grandad used to love this show,' said Piotr, drinking some more beer. 'We used to watch it together.'

Their food arrived after the episode had finished. They ate quickly. The barman switched channels to a sports show.

'Good pancakes?' Piotr said.

'Not bad at all. You?'

'Really good,' he said. 'I need to steal the recipe.'

'So why did you want to meet up without the other guys?' said Jacek in between mouthfuls.

'I saw Adam yesterday,' said Piotr, picking some food out of his teeth.

'How is he?'

'In good spirits. He told me his side of the story.'

Jacek put down his cutlery and wiped his mouth with a napkin. 'And?'

'He told me something that didn't make sense.'

'Like what?'

Piotr took a gulp of beer before speaking. He kept looking at the television. The host and his guest were dissecting Poland's loss to England.

'Well, he reckons that you told him to break off and go and help the hools that were in trouble. And that Jan went over to help him.'

'He said that?'

'That's right. I know there was a lot going on and he's been traumatised. He may have misheard, or forgotten exactly what you said.'

155

'But you believe him,' said Jacek.

'I didn't say that. I'm trying to piece things together. It's hard to get the whole picture, so I'm asking you again. I'll ask him again too. And everyone else. Don't you worry about that.'

'So you don't trust me?'

'When did I say that?'

'I can hear it in your voice.'

Piotr sprinkled some pepper on his pierogi. 'This isn't about trust. It's about knowing what happened. It's hard for people to recollect things accurately. I'm not blaming anyone. I'm only trying to get the right story. Can't you put yourself in my shoes? I've got a potential full on rebellion going on here with Kris. I need to know what happened. That's my responsibility. I already messed up getting us in this situation. And I don't want to get anything else wrong.'

'I didn't put them in trouble,' said Jacek. 'Not intentionally, anyway. What I remember is telling them that we would go and help the English guys together. In the heat of the battle, Piotr. You know how it is. There was so much going on. He must have misheard, because he shot off towards them straight away.'

'Or maybe you gave them instructions that could be misinterpreted?'

'OK, maybe it's my fault. I'll hold my hands up. I shouldn't have said anything, as it obviously got misinterpreted. And you know what? We were doing really well on our side. We'd separated most of the hooligans on our flank and they were stepping back. Maybe Adam got over-confident. But I told Jan to get him and get right back. There was no one else there and I was under attack. I had no choice. It was either Adam on his own or Jan and Adam on their own for a few seconds. Well, that was the theory. Maybe both of them thought they could deal with it without me there. It happened in a split second. I'm sorry, I really I am.'

The barman asked them if they wanted any desserts.

'No, just another beer,' said Piotr, holding up his empty glass.

'Talking about being in other people's shoes, maybe Adam is saying what he's saying because he doesn't want to lose face and admit that he broke the rules,' said Jacek.

'I guess that's possible,' said Piotr. 'Is there anything else you can recall? Even the smallest detail?'

'Not really, well, apart from you and Henio. What was all that about? You guys kept backing away from us. Every time I looked you were a few more metres away.'

'I don't know to be honest. That hasn't been my main concern. But it was worrying at the time. He's slowed down. Become hesitant. He used to be a lot quicker, more decisive. He would drop guys without a moment's thought. It was like he wasn't able to let his strikes go.'

'Well whatever it was, it didn't help us. We could have done with being tighter.'

'I know. But I couldn't leave him the way he was fighting.'

When they had paid, Piotr said, 'Listen. I don't want any of this to drive a wedge between any of us. What's happened is bad enough already. I don't want anyone blaming anyone else. This could all just be one big mix-up. If anyone should take the blame it should be me for getting us into that hole in the first place. But if we can know the truth then we should push to find it. If we can't, we say it was one of those things and draw a line under it.'

'Hey, I'm with you on that one,' said Jacek. 'Maybe we should have another meeting, to clear the air,' he said. 'Away from the dojang.'

'Might be a good idea,' said Piotr.

Piotr opened his laptop. As he waited for it to start up, he took a notepad off his shelf and drew five columns in it, underneath a large question mark. He wrote down five names at the top of each column: Jacek, Kris, Henio, Adam and Jan. He jotted down some thoughts in each column. He checked his email and wrote a long message to a contact, checking the notepad to make sure he was passing on the right information. When he was finished, he sent a text to the black belts, calling for a meeting. He picked up a book off a shelf in his bedroom and lay on his bed. He read *The Assassination of General Choi Hong Hi* for a few minutes before his phone rang. It was Beata.

'Can you come over?' she said.

'Sure, if you want. Are you OK?'

'Not really.'

'What's happened?' said Piotr.

'Aga is in a bit of trouble.'

'What do you mean?'

'Some men came here earlier. They threatened her.' She started crying. 'I'm scared Piotrusz.'

'I'm coming now,' said Piotr. 'I'll be there as soon as I can.'

He ran downstairs and put his jacket on.

'Auntie?' he said, standing in the corridor.

His Aunt was sat in the front room, doing some knitting. 'Yes dear?'

'I've got to go out and see Beata.'

'It's a bit late isn't it?'

'Something's happened. She's shaken up. Ring me if you need me.'

'What is it?' she said, waiting for a reply.

But he was gone.

He ran to the Underground station. A train was pulling in as he got to the platform. His carriage was almost empty, but he stood for the journey. He checked his phone. Henio couldn't make the meeting, but Kris and Jacek said they could. He texted them all back, reminding them that he wanted them to write an account of what they remembered from the hooligan fight. From start to finish. He said he wanted their reports within 24 hours.

Beata opened the door to him and hugged him. 'I'm so happy you're here,' she said, not letting him go.

'Come on, let's go inside,' said Piotr, gently pulling himself free.

They sat down on a sofa and Piotr held her hand. 'Tell me what happened.'

'You know I told you about Aga having some money trouble?'

'Yeah.'

'Well it turns out that she borrowed some cash from some guy.'

'What guy?'

'You know, the ones who can give you cash without asking questions.'

'A loan shark?'

'Looks like it. She said she did it so that she could pay the rent a couple of months ago. She said she had to do it. But she can't keep up with the payments now. And they keep going up. She's lost control of it. And now I don't know what's going to happen.' Beata held back her tears.

'Hey, hey,' said Piotr cradling her head on his shoulder.

Beata wiped her eyes, trying not to smudge her mascara, 'And then these two guys turned up at the flat tonight, and-'

'What two guys?'

'Two of the loan sharks.'

'Did they hurt you?'

'No. They came to scare us I think.'

Beata started crying. Piotr stood up and grabbed some tissues from a box on a bookshelf.

'Hey, come on, it's OK,' he said, letting her bury her face in his chest.

'Here,' he said, sitting back down next to her. 'Take these.' She wiped her eyes with a tissue and held it tightly in her fist.

'Do you want a drink?'

'No, I'm OK thanks,' she said.

'Tell me what happened. Can you do that?'

'Yes,' she said, sitting upright.

'Take it steady.'

'They turned up at about 8 I think. We were going to sit down to eat and then there was a knock at the door. Aga looked through the keyhole and saw a neighbour from downstairs. She's called Mrs. De Costa. She's lovely, she's from the Caribbean. So Aga opened the door. But then these two guys pushed past her. They'd got her to knock on the door after they found her walking back inside the building. She was so shocked, bless her.'

'They forced their way inside?'

'Yes, they pushed past her but pulled Mrs. De Costa in as well. I guess they didn't want her to raise the alarm.' She blew her nose. 'And then they shoved us down onto the sofa. Aga screamed at them to get out of the flat but one of them slapped her really hard. Mrs. De Costa told them to leave us alone, but they said that she'd be next if she didn't shut up.

'They told Aga that they needed some money there and then and that if she didn't give them something then they would take something as a replacement. Aga said she didn't have any cash, so they forced her into her bedroom. They took almost all her jewellery. Then they slapped her again and said they would be back in a week to collect the money.'

'Did they touch you?'

'One of them stroked my hair and smelt it. It made me feel sick.'

'Have you called the police?'

'No. They said that if we called the police then they'd do more than just slap Aga next time.'

'Where's Aga?'

'She's in her room. She won't leave. Do you want me to get her?'

'No, let her be. What did they look like?'

'One of them had a scar on his forehead. It went from his temple to his eyebrow almost. His left one.'

'Are you sure?'

'Yes.'

'Tattoo on his wrist?'

'Yes, like some sort of doves, or birds flying in a line.'

'Crew cut? Nose looks like it's broken?'

'How did you–'

'I know the guy,' said Piotr.

'You know him?'

'For my sins. So what does she owe him?'

'Thousands now, by the sounds of it.'

KRIS AND JACEK WERE ALREADY SITTING AT A TABLE in a booth, nursing two large bottles of beer, when Piotr walked in. Kris stood up. 'I'll get you a beer,' he said. 'We've almost finished these.'

Piotr shook Jacek's hand.

'No Henio?' Jacek said.

'He's busy.'

There were only a few old men inside, either talking to each other or reading newspapers. One of them was sitting on his own at a table near a fake fireplace, facing the rest of the pub. He wasn't looking at anything in particular. He had two full pints of stout in front of him.

Kris came back with three beers and sat down. 'So Jacek's told me about what Adam said. Sounds like someone's not got their story right.'

'Actually, it sounds like six people haven't got their stories right,' Piotr said. 'I've read through everyone's accounts, apart from Adam's. I'm going on what he said to me for now.'

'Different how?' said Kris.

'In details,' said Piotr.

'Well only one of us can be right,' said Jacek.

'Or none of us are,' said Kris. 'We can't all have the full picture.'

'Exactly my thinking,' said Piotr. He pushed his beer to one side and placed his elbows on the table. He ran his hand over his face.

'There was a lot of adrenaline flowing and the whole thing was a total mess. People do and say things they maybe wouldn't normally do. And they remember things incorrectly.

'We may find out what happened, but it's also possible that we'll never know for sure. I'm still waiting to hear from our source on why we got the numbers so wrong. But for now, the important thing is to put this behind us, as soon as we can, and to move on.

'And as for blame. If anything, I'm to blame here. I didn't keep a decent eye on what was going on, and this all happened on my watch. We did an OK job all in all, it could have been a lot worse. Nowhere near as many got hurt as would have if we weren't there.

And I think Jan and Adam did well. They proved their worth.'

'I'm all for moving on,' said Jacek.

'I knew it would end up like this,' said Kris.

'What do you mean?' said Piotr.

'I said the hooligan thing was a bad idea. Why did we have to get involved in that? The odds were always stacked against us. Something like this was bound to happen eventually. And you just want to brush it away, like it was nothing.'

'No I'm not,' said Piotr. 'I'm trying to get to the bottom of it. But we need to start looking ahead again. Sure, mistakes were made, but we've always made them. And we'll make them again probably.'

'And then another one of us will get an early funeral,' said Kris. 'The mistakes happen because we're doing the wrong thing.'

'What do you mean?' said Piotr.

'You know what I mean. Taking it to the street all the time for testing. Putting the dojang in danger. Unnecessarily. There's other ways to test you know.'

'Like how?' said Piotr.

'You know how,' said Kris.

'What? Getting dirty money for busting up someone's skull?'

'Come on Piotrek,' said Kris. 'Competition, sparring, whatever you want to call it. It's controlled, safer. And you go up against decent fighters who can test you, one-on-one.'

'You talk as if you know a lot about it,' said Piotr.

'Yeah, well I've heard stuff,' said Kris. 'I keep my ears and eyes open.'

'I'm sure you do,' said Piotr.

'Guys, seriously,' said Jacek. 'There's no need for this now.'

'No,' said Piotr, looking at Kris and lifting his hand up in Jacek's direction. 'We all know that Kris has his ideas about the dojang and where it should go. Relaxing rules, mixing with other arts, tournaments and all the rest of it. So why don't you tell us exactly what you're planning Kris? Eh? You want the dojang to change, don't you? And now you've seen your chance. To take advantage of Adam's injury. I didn't think you'd stoop so low.'

'I'm not getting into this now,' said Kris.

'Why not?' said Piotr, raising his voice. 'Hey? You're the one who brought it up. Do you even believe in what the dojang stands for? In what the Kwan was created for? Our pledge? Does any of that even mean anything to you anymore?'

Some of the old men in the pub turned to look at their table.

'Times are changing Piotr,' said Kris, leaning back in his chair. 'And we need to change with the times. This incident with the hools proved it, that's all. If we don't change then we'll fade away.'

'We've got more students then we've had for about ten years,' said Piotr. 'That doesn't sound to me like we're fading away.' Piotr reached for his beer and put it to his lips, when Kris said, 'Well Jacek agrees with me.'

Piotr put his bottle down and looked at his friend.

'Hang on,' said Jacek, holding his hands up. 'I never said I agreed with everything you're saying. I've said that I sympathise. Big difference.'

'You sympathise?' said Piotr.

'It's complicated,' said Jacek. 'With what's happened, well, maybe it is time to re-evaluate a few things. I'm not talking about making big changes, no way. But maybe we should look at how we approach testing and real life engagement. Fighting in a controlled environment could be a way to keep sharp. But I'm only saying it's an option. That's all.'

'We can work together on changing things,' said Kris. 'This isn't about taking over from you, or standing in your place. Nobody wants your crown.'

'Well if you don't want my seat, then you should be instructors of your own dojangs then, if you don't agree with what I'm doing,' said Piotr.

His bousabums were silent.

'We can't have conflicting messages coming from the black belts. The message has to be the same. And mine is the same it's always been. I'm passing down what I've been taught. I don't know why you're saying what you are, but it's not something I recognise. And it's not a message that I can stand by and allow to spread.'

'Things are changing Piotr,' said Kris. 'Sometimes you have to change with the times to survive.'

'If we change then we don't survive anyway. We won't be Kwan anymore. We'll be something else. An imitation,' said Piotr.

'At least hear me out,' said Jacek. 'We can still be what we've always been. But sometimes it doesn't hurt to adapt a little, you know, to your circumstances, your environment. Isn't that what we've always done on the street anyway? I've seen how the MMA guys change their game. How something new comes up and they learn from it. It makes sense in a way. We don't have to drop our traditions. But we can make them fit with today's world. With where we are.'

'There could be advantages to it as well,' said Kris. 'This is a chance for us to do something. This is a ticket.'

'A ticket,' said Piotr.

'Yeah, a ticket to opportunity,' said Kris, spreading his arms out wide. 'To do something good. For us, for the dojang, for the Kwan.'

'What opportunity? Are you talking about making money?'

'Money's part of it. But I'm talking about all the new guys we could attract. We can help them improve their lives and teach them proper values. Who knows, we may get loads of guys to join us, once they see us in action.'

Piotr stood up. 'I've got to go,' he said.

'Don't you want to talk about this a bit more?' said Jacek. 'Come on, I'll get you another one.'

'No thanks. This beer's left a nasty taste in my mouth.'

Piotr got back home and found his Aunt in the kitchen. She was staring at one of doors kitchen cupboard doors. It was hanging off its bottom hinge.

'What's happened?' he said.

'I was in the middle of cooking dinner and the door came loose when I opened it to get some herbs,' she said. Her cheeks were red and her breathing was shallow. 'Stupid thing.'

Piotr took her hand. 'Sit down, Auntie, I'll make you some tea.'

'I haven't finished making dinner.'

'I can finish it off. What else needs doing? Do I need to peel those potatoes?' he said, pointing at a pile of them on a chopping board.

'Yes, then boil and mash them.'

'No problem, I can do that. Now what about that tea?'

'OK. I'll have a peppermint. I don't want any caffeine getting my blood pressure up.'

His Aunt went into the dining room and sat down at the table.

Piotr watched her take her DIY blood pressure kit down from a bookshelf and strap it onto her forearm. He switched on the kettle and rummaged in the cupboard for the peppermint tea.

'Shouldn't you let the doctor do that?' he said, standing in the doorway.

'It gives me peace of mind.'

When the peppermint tea was ready Piotr's Aunt said, 'Pass me some of the holy water.'

He opened a drawer in the dining room and took a plastic bottle out of it. A handwritten label had been stuck onto the bottle. It read, *Lourdes water, 08.08.85.* He unscrewed the top of the bottle and poured some into the mug of tea. He sat down at the table with her. 'Have you taken your tablets today?'

'Yes, I have dear.'

'You shouldn't let a little cupboard door stress you out like that Auntie.'

'I know. I've not patience at the moment.'

He watched her drink her tea for a bit and then went into the kitchen to finish getting the meal ready.

He served up a breaded pork chop with mashed potatoes sprinkled with fresh dill, some wilted cabbage and runner beans. He poured breadcrumbs that had been lightly fried in butter over the vegetables before he sat down to eat.

'Smacznego,' said Piotr's Aunt, after making the Sign of the Cross. They ate slowly and said little.

After he'd cleared up and washed the dishes, Piotr took Gapczo for a walk and called Henio.

'The meeting didn't go well,' said Piotr.

'What do you mean?

'Kris and Jacek want us to go in a different direction.'

'Jacek said that?'

'He said we should think about it at least. Or something like that. I tuned out when he started explaining himself.'

'You think he's on Kris' side?'

'Sounded like it.'

'I can't believe it.'

'You and me both. I don't know what to do.'

'You're in a tough spot.'

'I don't get it. I thought Jacek would never have stood for what

Kris is saying. Now he's siding with him? Where did that come from?'

'Maybe you've taken your eye off things.'

'Maybe. I kept thinking that the real threat was external. But it's always been under my nose. A conspiracy, inside the dojang itself.'

'You want me to talk to Jacek?'

'I don't know what good it would do right now.'

'You just said that you stopped listening to him. I could get his side of the story. Try and convince him that he's wrong.'

'I don't know. I need some space to think about all this. It's like it's all happened overnight.'

'OK, well, remember, I'm here if you need me.'

Piotr ended the call. He took Gapczo to a park and threw a stick for him a few times, but the dog wasn't interested in chasing it. Piotr sat down with him instead and they both watched the sun set on the city.

PIOTR WAS THE ONLY BLACK BELT at the next training session. He asked Jan to help him supervise. He worked the white belts hard, running them through a tough conditioning session. When they were done he told them to get ready to do some breaking. 'Now that your knuckles and feet are numb breaking should be easy,' he said.

The students split into three sets, based on their breaking ability and length of training. In each set, one of the white belts kept a plastic board in place on the breaking holder while another one tried to break the board in half. The rest practiced their breaking techniques as they waited for their turn.

The boards wouldn't break for Szymon. He was trying to break three of them, stacked up one behind the other. He had tried to break them more than three times with a side kick.

He swore under his breath after another failed attempt.

'You're getting frustrated,' said Piotr. 'And you're breaking dojang rules by cursing. 20 burpees and then you can carry on.'

He shook his head.

'Well, what are you waiting for?' said Piotr.

'Nothing,' he said. He wiped the sweat off his forehead with his dobok sleeve and accepted his punishment. When he was finished Piotr asked him, 'Are you aiming behind them?'

'Yes. Or at least I think I am.'

'Measure up again and let me see your position,' Piotr said.

Szymon slowly lifted his knee up, turned his body sideways and carefully placed his foot on the boards, where the line separating the two pieces of hard plastic was.

'Your footsword position looks fine,' said Piotr. 'Do it again after some of the others have a go. Maybe you're not generating enough power with your hip.

'These boards haven't been worn in properly,' said Szymon. 'They're harder to break.'

'They've been split enough times, don't worry about that.'

Szymon tried again. The board at the front broke in two, but the ones behind it remained intact. 'They're too hard,' he said.

'Everything's too hard if you have an attitude like that.'

When he called an end to the breaking practice he lined up the students in pairs, matching them in height. They went onto the mats in their protective gear. He instructed them to take turns putting a chokehold on each other, applying 70% of their strength. He gave each white belt being strangled four seconds to escape from it.

Most of them failed after a few attempts.

Piotr called them to a halt. 'What happens when someone chokes you?'

Sebastian raised his hand. 'You start to lose your air and blood supply to your brain.'

'Right,' said Piotr. 'And?'

'And you lose consciousness and could get brain damage if it's left for too long,' said Arek.

'Correct,' said Piotr. 'And how many seconds do you have to play with?'

'Not many,' said Arek.

'That's right. Hardly any time at all. You have to react as soon as the choke comes on. Now I saw you all trying variations of the three escape routes you've been taught, but I can see you're all rusty. So let's go through them.'

He asked Jan to put him in a choke and then told the students to watch him. He showed them the three techniques, twice each, from different angles. For the first defence he kicked Jan below the knee, hard enough for Jan to react to it. He bent his legs, stepped back slightly and grabbed Jan's arm before bucking his hip into his, before throwing him onto one of the mats. For the second defence he kicked to the leg again, twisted sharply and struck near the groin with a knifehand, finishing with two punches to the head. Showing the students the final escape technique, he crouched down, grabbed his attacker's arm again, twisted to butt his nose and then rotated Jan's shoulder through 180 degrees until he lost his balance.

When he had finished he asked them if they had any questions. No one did.

'Alright then. Have some fun with it. Do the defences as fast as you can, but keep it light. But remember, when you really have to do it, you have to mean it. You have to be vicious.'

Jan approached Piotr after the session.

'Do you mind if I ask you something Sabum?'

'Fire away.'

'Why didn't you say something back there? About what happened with Adam and stuff.'

'I want to wait until Adam is back. Things still haven't settled down yet. You haven't said anything have you?'

'Me? No way. You said to keep it between us for now, so I have. But the guys have been talking, you know how it is.'

'I know, I'll say something soon,' said Piotr. 'Are you going to be here for the next session?'

'I'm planning to be.'

'OK, make sure you are.'

'Why? What's happening?'

'I need you to be there, that's all,' said Piotr.

Jan left and Piotr locked up the hall. As he was checking that the door was shut properly, his phone started ringing. It was Kris.

'Kryzstof,' he said. 'I didn't expect to hear from you so soon.'

'Well, I didn't expect to call you so soon either. But it's important.'

'OK.'

'I think we need to have a formal council meeting.'

'We had one the other day.'

'Well, given the circumstances, we need another one. And the other black belts agree.'

'Is that right?'

'Yes. We spoke about it,' Kris paused. 'After you left the pub the night before. And we called Henio and he thought it was a good idea.'

'He said that?'

'Yes.'

Piotr thought for a moment.

'Are you still there?' said Kris.

'So you've organised a meeting. Above my head.'

'Well, you have to agree to be there obviously, without you there won't be a meeting.'

'But you haven't left me with much choice have you?'

'It's not like that. It's like you're not listening to us. We're crying out here for a voice.'

'What the hell does that mean? What sort of a voice do you need? We have one voice already.'

'Well maybe that's up for us to decide,' said Kris. There was another pause before he said, 'There'll be someone else there too.'

'What are talking about?'

'I've asked Father Leopold. He needs to hear what we have to say.'

'What? Why?'

'It's a bit complicated. But it's to do with the police. And training on church grounds.'

'The police? Are you even being serious? Who brought the police into it?'

'We'll explain it. I'll text you the best times this weekend for Father Leopold. And don't worry about the agenda, we'll bring it,' said Kris, ending the call.

Piotr threw his training bag to the floor and punched the wall, four times, with his damaged arm. His hand bleeding, he picked up his bag and marched to a house attached to the church.

He pressed the doorbell for longer than was polite. No one came to the door so he rang it again. He noticed that his hand was covered in blood. He reached into his bag and quickly wrapped some fresh bandage over it before Father Leopold came to the door. Through a small window to the side, Piotr could see that he was re-arranging his dog collar.

'Piotrusz,' said the priest, after he opened the door. 'Sorry about the delay. What a nice surprise. Do come in.'

They went into a living room on the ground floor of the house. There was a large photograph of Benedict XVI on the wall above a large, overflowing bookcase.

'Coffee?' asked Father Leopold. 'I've got some on the go. Or maybe a biscuit?'

'No, thanks,' said Piotr.

'Please, sit down,' said the priest, pointing at two sofa chairs. 'What have you done to your hand?'

'I hurt it at work. It's nothing.'

He sat down opposite Piotr, carefully pulling up his black trousers as he did so. He placed both his hands on his knees and said, 'So, what can I help you with?'

'Well, it's a bit of a spur of the moment thing, but I just got off the phone to Krysztof. He said that he had asked you to a dojang meeting. I was curious to find out why. He wouldn't tell me much.'

'Ah. Yes,' said Father Leopold. 'This would be in regards to some worrying information that I have received.'

'Such as?'

He put his hands together as if he was praying and touched his nose with the tips of his fingers. 'Something about an incident with some hooligans.'

'Who told you?'

'Well, I'm not sure that's important now.'

'It's important to me.'

'OK. One of your members told me.'

'Kris?'

'You can find out for yourself perhaps. Are you sure you don't want some coffee?'

'No thanks. I'm fine. So, what happened? Did he tell you in the confessional box or something?'

'No, nothing like that. But I did promise that I would keep his identity safe for the time being. This is a very delicate situation for me. As I understand it, the police may be interested in what happened in relation to the stabbing.'

'What would they know about it?'

'Well, they would have spoken to Adam wouldn't they? They saw him get into the ambulance, I presume.'

'You seem to know a lot about what happened.'

'Yes. But in any case, this would put me – or rather, the parish – in a precarious position. We cannot be seen to be playing host to violent vigilantes who break the law.'

'We don't break the law. We uphold it as much as we can.'

'Do you?'

'Natural law, and the law of the land, as far as we possibly can, yes. We were trying to stop two groups from hurting each other.'

'By hurting them and almost getting one of your own killed?'

'The operation ran into difficulties.'

'I see. But my point remains. If I were to be questioned by the police then I would have to be honest and tell them what you are and what you do.'

'You'd do that?'

'I cannot lie to them.'

The priest stood up. 'Excuse me, let me get some coffee before it gets cold. Are you absolutely sure you don't want some?'

Piotr shook his head. 'No, thank you.'

Father Leopold came back with the coffee and a plate of biscuits. 'My worry is that you are overstepping the mark. You are supposed to be protectors of the peace in disputes within the community. A last resort for the vulnerable or oppressed. Correct?'

'Sure.'

'So how do hooligans represent that group?'

'Well they are vulnerable. They're misled. It's hard to talk people out of some of the stuff they do. Sometimes you have to get rough, within reason.'

The priest sipped some coffee. 'Well, this, getting rough, as you put it, isn't something I, or indeed the Church can approve of. We have the State to administer justice. I was under the impression that the Kwan had, shall we say, modified its methods and its behaviour since coming to these shores.'

'What gave you that impression Father?'

'Well, after all, we are in a very different environment here in London, and indeed in the whole of Britain. This country does not have major corruption problems. And our communities do not need help from outside to fight criminals. The police can do that. In fact, the police should, and must, be left to be able to do it. Without the added complication of over-eager vigilante groups.'

'What are you saying?'

'I will no doubt repeat this at the dojang meeting when it is held. But what I am saying Piotrusz, is that your dojang must change with the times and take a step back from this unnecessary violence. Otherwise we cannot host you on the parish's grounds. From a simple ethical standpoint, but also from a practical one. I cannot be found to be on the wrong side of the law.'

'Father Leszek never had a problem with us.'

The priest bit into a biscuit. 'I am not Father Leszek, though. Am I?'

BEATA POURED OUT A GLASS OF WHITE WINE for Piotr and herself. He sat down on the sofa in her living room and took a sip.

'I got it from work,' said Beata, placing her glass on the carpet and re-arranging her ponytail as she sat down next to him. 'It's Romanian. We've started stocking it last week.'

Piotr swirled the wine and tipped his glass at an angle. 'It's pretty good.'

'So how's your Auntie?'

'She's OK. Taking it in her stride. She explains parts of it all to me and then says it'll all work itself out. Whatever that means. I sometimes wonder if she's getting delusional with all those tablets she takes. She's talked about a hospice though. Apparently that's the best place for her.'

'When would she go there?'

'When she gets worse I guess. Whenever that happens. Or the doctors tell her that it's time.'

'So they don't know how long she's got?'

'Not really. Right now she looks like she could live to a 100. In a month's time, she might feel completely different.'

'Do you have a hospice in mind?'

'There are some options for her, not too far from us. I don't want her to go though. I know it would be the best place for her, but I just can't imagine it. Her not being at home, I mean.'

Beata took Piotr's hand. 'If you need me for anything you let me know, won't you? I know we haven't known each other for very long, but I'm here if you need me. I mean that.'

Piotr drained his glass. 'Thanks.'

'Do you want some more wine?'

'I think I need some,' he said, holding his glass out for her. She picked up the bottle and poured the wine quickly. Some of it splashed onto his bandaged wrist.

'Sorry,' she said, wiping the wine away with her hand. 'Hang on, let me get a tissue.'

She pulled some tissues out of the box on the coffee table in front of her and used them to dab his wrist and hand.

'This injury looks as if it's getting worse, not better,' she said.

'I damaged it again. By accident. It'll heal soon enough.'

She held his hand and placed the tissue on it and pressed gently.

'You need to look after yourself a bit more.'

'I'll try.'

Piotr moved in a bit closer towards her. They kissed and he put his hand on her face as she held his forearm. He tried to touch her breasts, but she pushed him away gently.

'What's wrong?' he said.

'Nothing's wrong. I mean, there's nothing wrong with you.'

'You sure?'

'Yes.'

He drank some more of the wine and checked his watch. 'Look, it's getting on and I don't want to miss the last tube. Maybe I should head home.'

'Are you upset with me?' said Beata.

'What? No. Not at all.'

She looked down at the floor briefly. 'OK.'

'I had a nice time this evening, I really did. And the meal was great. I'm a convert. I might even try and do some Thai flavoured pierogi for Porski's.'

Beata touched his arm. 'I had a great time too.'

At the door, he said, 'I almost forgot. You know you mentioned at dinner that you thought the loan sharks would be back soon? Do you know when that might be?'

'I'm pretty sure Aga said they will come every Wednesday night until they're paid in full. If she gives them a big chunk of money then they come back in a fortnight or something like that.'

'Every Wednesday?'

'That's right.'

'I'd like to ask her some questions about them. Could I call in when you're both in some time?'

'Sure, if you want to. What do you want to ask her?'

'About how they work and where they're based, that kind of thing. I might be able to help a little.'

'Really?'

'I can't promise anything, but I can try.'

'What would you do?'

'I'm not sure. But remember I know one of them. I could maybe talk them out of it, or get them to ease off. I don't want to see her suffer like this. It's not right.'

'Well, we're in on Monday evening,' said Beata. 'Do you want to come over then? We can have something to eat.'

'Sounds good.'

He kissed her on the forehead and left.

The traffic wouldn't move.

'Got any idea how you're going to play it then?' said Henio.

'Not really,' said Piotr. 'It sounds like one of those cases were you get tried by a bunch of Commies even though there's no evidence against you. You know what I mean?'

'Yeah. Like a kangaroo court.'

'A what?'

'Kangaroo court. That's what they call it.'

'Right. One of them.'

Henio strained his head over Piotr's side of the dashboard. 'Can you read that sign down there?'

'The bus lane one?'

'Yeah.'

'It says no cars between 7–10 a.m. and 4–7 p.m.'

'So what the hell are we doing in this traffic?' said Henio. He pulled into the bus lane and sped down it, jumping in front of a car further down the road. 'These bus lanes are mental,' he said. 'People see that picture of the camera on those signs and act like little obedient sheep.'

He turned off the main road and drove down an empty residential street.

'You want my advice?' he said.

'Shoot.'

'Alright. Hear my out. This might sound wrong to you, but I reckon you should grit your teeth and let it happen. Say you've thought about what Leopold's said, that he was right, spoke words of wisdom, blah, blah and that you've accepted it.'

'And how does that help anything?'

'Think about it. You knock the wind out of Kris. He's expecting you to just abdicate right there and then. He thinks he's got you in a checkmate. This way, you stop him from taking full control. Without full control, he can't do anywhere near the damage he wants to. And you can plan what to do after that. We don't get involved in anything for a bit, stay low, wait until things have blown over. Then work out what to do later on.'

Piotr stared out of the window. 'Is that what you'd do?'

'Definitely. Anything else is suicide.'

Father Leopold was the last to turn up.

'We usually start these with some forms,' said Piotr. 'But since you don't know any Father, maybe we should sit down and get on with it.'

'I'd appreciate that,' said the priest. 'I haven't done any exercise since I played football at the seminary.'

They pulled out some plastic chairs that were stacked in a corner of the hall and arranged them in a circle and sat down, facing each other.

'So Kris,' said Piotr. 'Do you want to explain what this is about?'

Kris said, 'I know this isn't an official dojang meeting because it hasn't been called by Piotr, but we all know that we've had a bad experience that needs dealing with. And Father Leopold is here because he's been informed of the situation with Adam. And he has some concerns he wants to share with us. Father, do you want to explain?'

The priest sat with his hands folded on his lap. 'Yes, of course. Well, I have already talked to Piotrusz about this, so he may have filled you in on my position, but I will reiterate it to avoid any confusion.

'Essentially, the unfortunate attack on one of your students has led to rumours that the parish is acting as some sort of a safe haven for vigilante activities. And since I spoke to you Piotrusz, I have had a visit from the police. They asked me some questions, but I didn't name any of you. I did tell them that some men train here in a martial arts club and have done for years. They didn't ask me anything about the stabbing, or the hooligan fight, or about any vigilante activities at all. Which was surprising. But if they had, then I would have had to tell them what I know.'

'Who told you about the stabbing Father?' said Henio.

'I told Father Leopold about it,' said Kris. 'We got talking the other day outside the hall. He asked me how things were going and I came out with it.'

'And the police?' said Piotr.

'They didn't tell me,' said Father Leopold. 'They said they couldn't put informants in danger. But that's not important. The point is that I can't have this hanging over the parish. I was under the impression that you had modernised and changed your ways somewhat, what with us living in a very different environment here in London. So this came as a bit of a shock.'

'We've always held to the true tradition and mission of the Kwan,' said Piotr. 'So I don't know where you got that picture from.'

'I know plenty of parishes in England which have close ties to dojangs,' said the priest. 'Many of them have modified their ways, to various degrees.'

'We aren't doing you any harm,' said Jacek. 'Are we?'

'As I said, the rumours are there. And no doubt the bishop will know before too long. How he reacts to the news is anyone's guess. If you persist down this path and do not change, while using the church facilities, then I will simply report you to the police. You either demonstrate change, or you can go somewhere else.'

The priest opened his arms. 'Gentlemen, I'm giving you a chance to reform.'

'Is there no way you can reconsider?' said Piotr. 'Think of all the help we've provided for parishioners who have been in trouble in the past. We've helped so many people. And they still support us. Have you thought about that?'

'Sympathy for your cause is dwindling I'm afraid,' said Father Leopold. 'And has been for some time.'

Kris said, 'None of us can deny that. We're not needed anymore. We live in a different country, with a different mentality. This isn't like the old days back at home. They have proper police here and a proper justice system. We need to adapt to the times. Loads of dojangs have reached the same conclusion.'

'You can't call it a dojang, or a part of the Kwan if it doesn't do what the Kwan is supposed to do,' said Piotr.

'Well, most of the students want change,' said Kris. 'They want a new era for the dojang. Can't you see that?'

Piotr said, 'You know the deal, if people don't want to train here, be part of the Kwan, then they can go elsewhere.'

'You keep saying that. As if you're the only one who is real Kwan. But you're swimming against the tide, you're resisting the changes that are going on everywhere.'

Piotr stood up, sending his chair flying. 'Resisting what?' he said, with his arms outstretched.

Henio put his hand up. 'Hang on Piotr, you're getting emotional.'

'That's because I am emotional. Like I was saying. You say I'm resisting. I'm not resisting. I'm ignoring. Ignoring false authority. You understand? All these Sabums imposing new ideas and rules on dojangs – they don't realise it, but they've given up their own authority as Sabums in the Kwan. The Kwan has condemned what they do already. It's legislated them out of existence. Or don't you remember taking the oath when you were given your black belt?'

Piotr stepped out of the circle and cut the air with both his hands. 'This meeting is over,' he said. 'We will go elsewhere if that is how it is to be Father. I'll keep you all in the loop on what happens next.'

Henio got up. 'Piotr, come on, we need to think this through.'

'I've done my thinking,' said Piotr, walking out.

The punch bag swayed back and forth. Piotr stood with his hands on his thighs. Sweat poured from his forehead. He checked his left hand. There was fresh blood seeping through the bandage.

He left the garage and went back inside the house where he washed his wound and put a fresh bandage on it when it was dry. He clenched his fist a few times before putting a wrist support over his hand and lower arm. Covering his hand with a small freezer bag, he went upstairs to shower.

When he got out of the bathroom he checked his phone. Jacek had tried calling him. He dried himself and loosened the bandage a bit to rub some ointment onto his wrist. When the ointment had dried, he called Jacek back.

'How are you doing?' said Jacek.

'I'm OK.'

'Listen. We should talk. I mean, we haven't really discussed this properly, you know, since everything that's happened. You just walked out this morning. We could have talked a bit more.'

'I've heard enough from Kris. But if you want to meet up, just us two, then let's do that.'

'So when are you free?'

'Tonight.'

'OK. You want to come to mine? 8? Monika's out with some friends.'

'Make it 8:30.'

'No problem, see you then.'

As he walked downstairs his Aunt came through the front door with Gapczo. The dog ran up to him. Piotr dropped down and Gapczo licked his face. 'Hey, I've just had a shower,' he said, picking up Gapczo and stroking his head. 'You trying to make me all mucky again?'

He stood up. 'Shouldn't you be resting Auntie?'

She took her beret off, picking some fluff off it. 'I want to walk with him. While I still can.'

Piotr stood up and helped his Aunt take her coat off.

'I was going to make some toast and ham,' he said. 'Do you want some?'

'I'm not that hungry but I suppose I should eat. Only a little though.'

As they were eating, his Aunt switched on the television to watch a bulletin on a 24-hour Polish news channel.

A politician was criticising a right-wing political party that was climbing in the polls. She tutted, shaking her head and nibbling on her toast.

Piotr said, 'Would you mind if I had some guys come to train over the next few weeks? In the garage and the garden? It'll be small numbers probably. Only until I find some new premises.'

'Of course. But what's happened with the hall?' said his Aunt.

'Father Leopold doesn't want us there anymore.'

'Since when?'

'Today.'

'Why?'

'He got wind of the hooligan fight. And the police have too apparently. It's spooked him. He says he had no idea that we were still involved in things like that. He said the parishioners wanted us out too. Did you hear anything about that?'

'No,' said Piotr's Aunt. 'Nothing.'

'I figured as much.'

Piotr had to squeeze past a stack of cardboard boxes in the narrow corridor of Jacek's flat.

'Monika got some furniture the other day,' he said. 'I haven't had time to sort it all out yet. Come into the kitchen, I've got to watch this soup for Monika. You want a beer?'

'No, I'm OK.'

They sat down on some small stools in Jacek's kitchen.

'What soup is it?' said Piotr.

'Vegetable.'

'Smells good.'

'You want to try a bit?'

'No, thanks.'

Jacek opened a can of beer. 'I went to see Adam earlier. He's up and about at home. He'll be back to work soon he reckons, and then training before too long.'

Piotr said, 'That's good. I feel like I've almost ignored him with what's been going on.'

'I didn't tell him about what's happening. I left that to you.'

'Thanks. Well I'm going to text everyone today. Tell them if they want to carry on with the dojang then they have to come and train at my Aunt's place for a while.'

'That's what you're going to do?'

'What choice do I have?'

'So you're going to let Kris step in and take over?'

'If he wants to run his own sessions at the hall, that's his choice. He can do what he wants. But he won't be doing it in the dojang's name. Not in the real dojang's name, anyway. I'm going to call him after this to expel him.'

Jacek drank a bit more beer, and then fiddled with the tab on the can. 'So I suppose you want to know what I'm thinking?' he said.

'I thought you made yourself pretty clear at the last meeting. Do you want me to repeat what you said to me? Because I can if you want. I remember it very clearly. You held your peace this morning though. Have you had a change of mind?'

'Not exactly. But I had never decided anything anyway. I've listened to both sides of the story. And I can see merits in what you're saying, and in what Kris is saying too. I'm not sure what to think. But I do know that nobody wants to see the dojang torn in two like this. It doesn't have to be this way.'

'What made you even consider what he's had to say anyway?' said Piotr. 'You used to stand shoulder-to-shoulder with me on this. You were even warning me about Kris if I'm not mistaken. And now?'

'To be honest, my faith has been a bit shaken by the hooligan thing.'

'It's affected everyone. But only because it went so wrong.'

'Maybe it was a wake-up call for us.'

'Maybe. But I've got some new info on it.'

'Like what?'

'I think we were set up.'

'What? What do you mean?'

'Someone got tipped off about us being there and sent some people in to sabotage our operation. That's what I mean.'

'What the hell? How do you know?'

'My contact said there's no way there should have been that many hools there. He says it's not possible. And then Adam told me something really strange. He said that there were a couple of them that were Kwan trained.'

'Well who would have done that?'

'I'm not 100% sure. But with the way Kris jumped on this, getting Father Leopold involved and everything, I have my suspicions.'

'You think he'd do that?'

'I don't know, but who else could it be?'

THE TAXI MAN LIT ANOTHER CIGARETTE and closed down the video on his computer screen.

'You think they can handle that sort of contact?' he said to the man sitting across from his desk.

'Definitely. They're trained for it. Remember they know a lot more than just how to hammer people over the head with a baton.'

'No objections?'

'None. The boys are up for it. And everyone's happy to make some money out of it. Plus, you don't even need to be a black belt to fight. The new Sabum has relaxed the rules.'

The Taxi man paused and took a long drag on his cigarette. 'So the changes are going to stick?'

'Absolutely. If you're faced with the possibility of getting stabbed or losing face in some controlled bout with a referee, then it's a no-brainer.'

'No-brainer for most people. Maybe not for those loyal to the Kwan though.'

'That's over. All that whoring Samurai spirit. No one's interested.'

'What about the half-caste?'

'Nothing. A couple of students have stayed loyal to him, but that's it. They're not even black belts. Small fry.'

'You sure about that?'

'He hasn't got any muscle. He's embarrassing himself, clinging on like a stubborn mule. Nothing will come from it. He's got no premises, and no one is going to give him a hall anytime soon. And even if they do, he's not going to know what's hit him. You need insurance these days, everything has to be above board. Nobody's going to insure his training, believe me.'

'But he's still training people?'

'They're nobodies. They weren't even his best students. He'll end up being a one-man job. He trains people too hard. People don't want his old school BS. It's done. Finished.'

The Taxi man checked the time on his mobile phone. 'We'll see. It's too early to be so cocky. We'll have to keep an eye out for him.'

'Give it a few months,' said the man. 'It'll fade. If not then I can deal with him. It's working out exactly how we planned.'

'Maybe. He still makes me nervous though.'

'Everything's on track. We don't need to worry about him anymore.'

The Taxi man took another long drag on his cigarette. 'So you say. But if he suddenly pops up interfering in our business then you and I will be having words. You understand?'

The man put his hands up. 'Sure. But it won't come to that, trust me.'

'When will you have some fighters ready?'

'I can't say for sure. They need to be prepped. They're not used to rules-based fighting.'

'Well, there's no major rush. We can use some time to get the word out and build up some tension,' said the Taxi man. 'But not too long. I have some fights that could be set up soon. Even within the next couple of months.'

'Local?'

'No, not local. Never too local.'

'Where then?'

'Swindon.'

'Swindon? Never heard of it.'

'Don't worry,' said the Taxi Man. 'You give me the fighters, I'll draw you a map.'

They gathered in the garage. Four dojang men sat on garden chairs that Piotr had unfolded for them. Piotr rested on his Uncle's work bench.

'What's this all about Sabum?' said Arek, looking up at Piotr. 'Are we training here now?'

'That's the plan. It's only temporary. I haven't had time to sort anything else out.'

Piotr clasped his hands together and thought for a moment before speaking again.

'OK guys, so I'm not sure how best to tell you this, but I'll get straight to the point and then you can ask me any questions you might have.

'So you all probably know that there's been some tension since

Sabum Zielinski passed on. I suppose you could call it a kind of division. You all don't need to play dumb with me. I know you talk. And despite some efforts, we've not been able to heal it. You also know that there was a major incident in the last initiation test, during which Adam was badly injured. Thankfully, Adam's on the mend now. Right?'

'I'm feeling stronger every day Sabum,' said Adam.

'There you go,' said Piotr, holding up a clenched fist. 'The test brought the division out into the open. And I haven't been able to heal it. Father Leopold heard about what happened and he's told me that we can't have the church hall anymore – unless I change the dojang's ways. And I'm obviously not going to do that, which is why we're all here. So from now on, I teach here. And I'll teach whoever wants to train with me, and wants to preserve the Kwan's original purpose.'

'What are the others doing then?' said Ziggy.

'They're doing their own thing. But they're not part of the Kwan in my eyes, or in the eyes of any of our predecessors. They're forming a fake dojang, joining a fake Kwan.'

They were silent for a few moments before Piotr said, 'Listen guys, I know this is partly my fault. I took my eyes off the dojang a little. I'm sorry about that and I'm sorry for letting you down.'

Arek said, 'So is it just us now?'

'I contacted everyone, but only you four responded. If you want to keep training with me, and helping people as we always have, then we'll have to train here for now.

'What about Henio?'

'Henio's with us,' said Piotr. 'He's too busy to meet up today.'

'Where's Jacek?' said Sebastian, 'I thought he'd be here.'

'He won't be joining us today,' said Piotr. 'He's thinking things over. Any other questions?'

'What changes did Father Leopold demand?' said Sebastian.

'He wants us to stop being a vigilante group.'

'And do what instead?' said Adam.

'What Kris and the others want. Treat it as a club where you learn self-defence, but never use it. Take nothing to the street. Do black belt testing in organised fights.'

'No offence, but we don't have much equipment or space in here,' said Sebastian.

'That's true,' said Piotr. 'But we can train a bit in the garden sometimes. While there's a small group of us, it should be manageable. Thankfully this garage is bigger than average. We'll have to make do for now, until we can find a new venue. On the equipment side, I can start buying some padding and other material that we need. I've got a makiwara, breaking board holder, punching bag. That's a start. Plus, we can train here when we want, and be more flexible about training times. Some weeks we can train more often, or for longer. And there are no hall fees to pay. Until we get bigger again, it might all work to our advantage. None of you have to decide anything right now. Take some time to think about it.'

Sebastian stood up. 'I'm in,' he said. 'There's no way I'm throwing everything away.'

'Me too,' said Adam.

Arek and Ziggy got up as well. 'We wouldn't be here otherwise,' said Arek.

'When do we start training?' said Sebastian.

Piotr smiled for the first time in a while. 'Well, we can do a bit now if you want. But before we do, there's the small matter of a promotion to deal with,' said Piotr, smiling.

He walked to the back of the garage and took a small plastic parcel out of a cardboard box. He ripped it open and took a black belt out of it.

'Shouldn't I be in my dobok for this Sabum?' said Adam.

'It's OK. After everything's that happened you get a pass on that. Line up.'

The students made two rows, with Adam and Sebastian at the front.

'Adam, step forward and hold your right hand up. Can you remember the oath?'

Adam nodded.

'Go ahead then,' said Piotr.

Adam swallowed hard. 'I will observe the tenets of the Kwan. I will uphold the traditions of the Kwan. I will never mis-use my training. I will protect the oppressed and the weak. I will be a champion of freedom and justice.'

He stayed still as Piotr tied the belt around his waist. 'There,' said Piotr, pulling the belt tight and then stepping back.

Adam bowed to his Sabum.

'Congratulations,' said Piotr. He shook Adam's hand. 'You've earned it.'

Adam turned to face the others. They bowed to him as their superior. He returned their respect, then he stepped forward and embraced them, one by one, as brothers.

BEATA PLACED HER FORK BACK ON HER PLATE. She had hardly touched any of her chicken salad.

'Are you OK?' said Piotr.

'I'm nervous.'

Piotr stretched his left hand out and placed it over hers. 'Don't be. It'll be fine.'

'But you're putting yourself in harm's way. They're dangerous people.'

'All I'm going to do is talk to them.'

Beata stood up and went to the sink. She poured herself a glass of water.

'You've got to trust me on this. I've dealt with people like this before back at home. I can strike a deal with them. Get them to lay off a bit.'

He turned to Aga. 'All you have to do is agree to pay back the original amount you were going to give them. Are you happy with that?'

'If it means they don't come here ever again, then of course,' said Aga.

'Good. You'll have to have a think about how much you can pay and in what instalments and then let me know. Can you do that?'

'Sure.'

'So you say they work out of a coffee shop. In Greenford?'

'Almost,' said Aga. 'It's on the Greenford Road. Right before the traffic lights between the shopping mall and the petrol station. It's called Café Koncert. Do you know it?'

'I've been past it.'

Beata sat back down at the table and offered her plate of food to Piotr.

'If you're sure you don't want any,' said Piotr.

'No, you eat it.'

He picked up the fork from his empty plate and started stabbing bits of chicken breast and salad leaves with it.

'Do you know anything more about these guys?' Piotr asked Aga.

'Like what?' she said.

'Who their boss is, or who else they run with. Stuff like that.'

'I don't know that much really. I borrowed the money off one of the guys who came here the other week to scare us. I had to meet him in the coffee shop. All he told me was the terms of the loan and that I had to come to the shop every Thursday evening to pay back the instalments.'

'What was his name?'

'I don't know.'

'How did they know where you live?'

'I had to give them some proof that I was earning and could pay him back, so I showed him a payslip from the shop. It had my address on it.' She put her head in her hands. 'I'm so stupid.'

'You're not stupid. Describe him to me one more time.'

Beata and Aga sat down to watch some television after the meal. Piotr stood at the window, taking in the quiet main street. It was getting dark.

'Where do all the residents here park their cars?' said Piotr.

'At the back,' said Beata. 'It's free after 6. Some people get permits off the council.'

They half-heartedly watched the highlights of a celebrity dancing show on the TV while having some coffee and then Piotr left.

'Please be careful,' Beata said to him.

He hugged her, kissing her forehead. 'I will, don't worry.'

He went to the stairwell and walked up to the top floor of the building. There was an emergency exit door at the end of the corridor. He pushed its lever and stepped out onto an emergency staircase. He checked the lay out of the street below for a few seconds, before closing the door and walking all the way down to the basement. A waste and recycling room automatically lit up when he entered it. There were seven large bins lined up against the walls. He noticed a small space in one corner.

Going back upstairs to ground level, he made his way out through another emergency exit at the back of the building. He walked up and down the street behind the apartment block twice, taking in as many details as he could. Finally, with one last glance at the outside stairwell, he headed off to the Tube station.

On his way home he received a text from Henio. He had seen an old food caravan that he wanted to check out. *We can buy it together,* the text said. *Only £750. Unbelievable bargain. I know you've got a lot on your mind, but we should snap it up. When can you go see it?*

The coffee shop was sandwiched between a halal butchers and a plumbing store.

A black sign above it featured a wavy set of piano keys and a few music note symbols. Some of the piano keys were arranged to form the shop's name.

Piotr crossed the road and walked in.

Its black and white tiled floor resembled a giant chessboard. Photos of famous musicians were positioned in between some dim lights on the wall.

Towards the back, on the left hand side, there was a long bar, with a black marble finished top. Various cakes and sandwiches were on display in a glass cabinet underneath the bar top. The shop smelt of freshly ground coffee beans and burnt toast.

He saw the man with the bald head in the far corner of the shop, as Aga had said he would be, reading a newspaper and nursing a coffee. He raised his head briefly when Piotr walked in, before going back to reading his paper.

When Piotr reached his table, he kept reading, as if Piotr wasn't there.

'Looking for someone?' said the bald man eventually, staring at his paper.

'Guy called Guzik,' said Piotr. 'I need to have a word with him.'

'Guzik?' The bald man drank some coffee. He folded his newspaper and put it to one side, next to the empty plate.

'You can talk to me,' he said, looking at Piotr.

'It's about a loan he's got out with someone.'

'Who told you he gives out loans?'

'Aga Sławska. She lives near Rayners Lane station, in the flats above the shops opposite the station. She says he's hassled her at her place. In fact, she said that you were with him.'

'Did she now. And so what have you got to do with it? Have you brought her money with you?'

'No.'

'So what do you want to talk to me for without any money?'

'I've come to tell you to lay off her.'

'Lay off her? What are you, her bodyguard?

'You need to lay off her.'

'Are you threatening me?'

The bald man held Piotr's glare and then pointed his finger at him. 'You listen to me, hero. You tell that little bitch that I've just added another £200 to it. As of this very moment. And that the interest will double from tomorrow. So she'd better sort it out, because I'm going to collect Thursday night if she doesn't come here and pay me. Personally. You think you can remember that?'

'No deal,' said Piotr. 'She wants to pay you back her original loan, under the original terms. But nothing else. And she'll pay you in four instalments. The first in two weeks, and then the other three every two weeks after that.'

Piotr took a step back. He was about to leave, when he said, 'Oh and one more thing. She doesn't want to see you, or your friend Guzik anywhere near her place anymore.'

The bald man lowered his tone. 'Are you for real? You've got some serious whoring nerve, I'll give you that. But if you think you can come in here and throw orders at me like you're some big-time player then you've got another thing coming. Now get out of my sight.'

As Piotr left the café, he spotted a black estate pull up in front of it. It had a mini cab badge attached to the inside of its windscreen. The Taxi man got out of the driver's side. He watched Piotr until he disappeared out of sight and then walked into the café. When he reached the table where the bald man was sat, he said, 'What was the half-caste doing here?'

'Who? The black kid?'

'Yeah, who do you think I meant? The garden gnome?'

'He was asking about some girl we've loaned some money to.'

'Which girl?'

'Some whore called Aga, near Rayners Lane. We're going to go and get straighten her out tomorrow night.'

'Why, what did he say?'

'Some cheap threats about only paying the minimum.'

'What did he say, exactly. Word for word. Can you remember?'

The bald man put his paper down and leant back. He scratched his head. 'He said she wants to pay us back her original loan, but only under the original terms. And that she'd pay in two weeks. Then he said she didn't want to see me or Guzik round her flat any more. He told us to lay off her. The chief must be off his head on something talking like that.'

'So he basically warned you.'

'He didn't warn me about anything. He made some sort of empty threat. He's got balls, I'll give him that.'

'Yeah, he warned you.'

'Seriously, what's this about? Guzik will take care of it. He'll hassle that bitch until she pays up.'

'What if that monkey is there as well?'

'What about it? Then he breaks his head in half, the whoring dog.'

'Don't be so sure,' said the Taxi man. 'You'd better go together.'

'I can't go, I've got something else on.'

'Maybe you should postpone it. Or at least warn Guzik to not go there empty handed.'

'What do you mean?'

'You don't know him do you?'

'Know him? Why would I know a dog like that?'

'Come in the back with me.'

Beata's phone went to voicemail. Piotr cut the call off and tried again. He was about to leave a message when his phone buzzed.

'Hey,' said Piotr. 'I was wondering where you were.'

'I was in the shower. What's up?'

'I went to see one of the loan sharks today. He wasn't happy about what I told him. You should stay alert. Maybe keep the lights on low, don't have the volume up too high on the TV.'

'Why? What did you say to them?'

'I told him that Aga would pay him back over the next few weeks, but that they needed to lay off. That's all. He told me they would come to pick up some money on Thursday if Aga doesn't go to pay him an instalment. But they might come before that.'

'I'm scared Piotrusz.'

'Don't be. It'll be OK. It'll sort itself out.'

'Surely we should call the police now.'

'No. That could make things a lot worse. And anyway, there's not much that they'll be able to do. What you both need to do is start looking for a new flat. You understand? You can't stay there anymore. You need to disappear from there.'

'What are you going to do now?'

'I'm going to wait outside your flats in case they do come on Thursday.'

'Why?'

'To try and talk some sense into them. This isn't big money for them. But they can't lose face. That's what's it all about for them. Reputation. Keeping people afraid.'

'Piotrusz, please be careful.'

'Don't worry, it's all under control.'

HENIO CALLED PIOTR THE NEXT MORNING.

'Your timing is perfect Henio, you know that,' said Piotr. 'Don't you think we've got other things on our mind at the moment?'

'I know. But this food van has popped up and we can't just let it go, it's a serious bargain.'

'I don't know. I can't concentrate on Porski's right now.'

'I know you're worried. Everything's turned upside down. I'm worried too. How about we go to see the van this evening, just for a few minutes. It's near you as well. Hey, you never know, it might help you take your mind off things a bit.'

'I don't know.'

'Listen, put it this way – are you busy tonight?'

'Not exactly.'

'So you've got nothing to lose then, have you?' Anyway, you've got to take the mutt out for a walk don't you?'

'I guess so.'

'Good. So I'll see you there then. I'll text you the address. Hey, before you hang up, I need to ask you a question.'

'Fire away.'

'What happened at the meeting?'

'What do you mean?'

'Well you walked out. I thought we'd agreed that you were going to play along with it all a bit.'

'I didn't agree to anything. I listened to your advice, but decided against it. Simple. Anyway, why didn't you back me up? Or walk out with me?'

'Well, it kind of happened pretty quickly don't you think Piotrusz? You went off on one and then got up. I was trying to compute it all I guess.'

'Compute it? I thought I could at least rely on you and Jacek over all this.'

'Hey, we're loyal.'

'So you say.'

'Listen, Piotrusz, you're pissed off. I get that. Let's talk later, OK? We'll see the van and then have a beer or something.'

When he got back from work, Piotr ate his dinner quickly and showered. He checked his email and then took Gapczo out with him.

The food van stood in the front garden of a semi-detached house at the end of a street, along with three cars that were rusting away at the edges. Piotr peered over the fence at the back of the house as he walked by it. The garden was a junkyard. Stacks of tyres, car doors, seats and engine parts covered what used to be a normal suburban garden. There was a garage at the end. Its door was half open. It was full of tools and other car parts.

Henio was talking to a man in a blue overall. The man's hands were covered in oil and he had a pencil tucked behind his ear. Gapczo barked at them both.

Piotr pulled him by his lead.

'Hey, what's got into you? Calm down.'

Piotr tied Gapczo's lead to the front garden gate and the man in the blue overall showed them the van.

It was missing two wheels and its faded silver paint was peeling off in places. The shutter for the service opening was stuck halfway down. When they inspected the interior, most of the old kitchen was missing. It smelt damp and was dusty and dirty. The man said that it had belonged to a burger seller who had retired.

'When did this guy retire?' said Piotr, opening up one of the cupboards below the hob. '1960?'

'Hey it needs a bit of work, but, listen, what do you expect for the money?' said Henio. He stuck his head under the shutter. 'We can put a blackboard up on the side here, with the menu on it,' he said. 'I think it's perfect. I can see the potential.'

Piotr tapped the wall and the ceiling. 'It seems like a load of work. It'll probably cost at least treble what it costs to fix it.'

'We're not going to get a chance to pick up something local like this for this price for a long time. And this gives us a chance to make it look the way we want it. Plus, there's hardly any transportation costs.'

'And how are we going to transport it? It's got no wheels.'

'I know a guy who can use a tow truck for this sort of thing. He can stick some tyres on it for us. Won't cost much.'

'And where are we going to keep it?' said Piotr, fiddling with a loose worktop.

'Well I was going to ask you about that,' he said. 'What with you having a driveway and everything.'

'Are you being serious?'

'Sure. Why not? Just for a bit.'

'Well, for starters I can't drop a piece of junk like this at my Aunt's place. And anyway, it's a shared driveway. The neighbours need to be able to get in and out of their garage.'

'OK,' said Henio. 'What about the garage?'

'No chance. You know I need it for training right now. And anyway, it's too wide for the garage.'

Henio thought for a moment. 'Tell you what, don't worry. I know someone else who could store it for us for a while. So, shall we put an offer in?'

'I don't know,' said Piotr. 'It's all a bit too soon. We don't even have our recipes right yet. We can't throw money at this when we're not even ready with the pierogi.'

'You're over-thinking this,' said Henio, as they walked out of the van. 'You don't start a business with perfect conditions or a perfect plan. You just go for it. What does your gut tell you? That's all that matters.'

Piotr glanced at the caravan and then at Henio, who was smiling. 'Hey?' he said, spreading his arms wide open.

Henio drove Piotr and Gapczo back home. On the way, he stopped and bought six beers.

'Thirsty?' said Piotr.

'A couple of them are for you,' said Henio. 'We've got to celebrate our new purchase. Things are going to start moving now, you'll see.'

When they got to Piotr's place, they went into the garage.

'You sure training in here is going to work?' said Henio. 'It's pretty small.'

'Yeah, but think about it,' said Piotr. 'It's June now, right? And so we have at least until mid-September to train in here and out in the garden for a bit in the evenings, when the weather's good. And even if we don't find a new dojang by then, we switch it up a bit and train Saturday and Sunday mornings. We do breaking in the garage, bag work, a bit of conditioning. Sparring in the garden. It's not ideal, but I figured that the Koreans used to train outside a lot, back in the

195

day. So why can't we?'

'How many have said yes?'

'Well, four so far. Plus you're a maybe.'

'And Jacek?'

'Jacek's thinking things over.'

Piotr pulled out a garden chair for Henio and sat down on his Uncle's work bench.

'Here,' said Henio, taking a beer out of a carrier bag and handing it over to Piotr. 'So you're resigned to losing the hall?'

'Well I don't have much choice do I?' said Piotr, opening the can. 'The decision's been made.'

'I guess it has.' Henio drank some of his beer. 'You mind if I have a smoke?' he said.

'No, go ahead,' said Piotr.

Henio lit a cigarette. 'It's all happened pretty quickly hasn't it? I mean since the hooligan fight. Everything's gone crazy.'

'Sounds like Kris had been planning it all along. He was just waiting for his chance. I should have listened to you. And Jacek. Paid more attention.'

'Hey, don't beat yourself up about it. It's one of those things. As long as you're still here training with the guys, then you're still running it all, right? You can still do what the dojang's always done. That's what matters. Not where you train.'

'I guess you're right,' said Piotr.

'Speaking of still running, anybody been in touch about any action?'

'Not so far,' said Piotr, standing up to open the garage window. 'There is one thing that may be happening though.'

'Yeah? What's that?'

'Do you know anything about some loan sharks who operate out of a coffee shop on the way to Greenford, near the petrol station?'

'That's not a good way to pay for the caravan.'

'Jokes aside. Seriously.'

'I know there are a couple operating locally. But I'm not sure about this coffee shop. What's the name of it?'

'Café Koncert.'

'Don't know it. What's got us onto loan sharks?'

Piotr took a long drink of beer.

'Beata's flatmate has run into trouble with some sharks who

base themselves at this café. And we know one of them.'

'We do?'

'Yep. Guzik is one of them.'

'Guzik? There's a name I haven't heard anyone say in a while. You sure about that?'

'Yes. You know anything about what he does these days? Who he runs with?'

'I know that he used to hang with some people who played that game. But I'm not sure if he's on his own now or not.'

'The people he was with, were they all Polaks?'

'I think one of them was Ukrainian. But yeah, the rest were. Listen, you're not going to engage them are you Piotrek? After everything that's happened?'

'Not engage, no. Not if I can help it.'

'You either engage or you don't, there's no in-between is there?'

'There's always an in-between.'

Henio tapped some ash into an empty plant pot by his feet. 'If you say so.'

'There's another thing,' said Piotr. 'I think they're connected to the Taxi Man.'

Henio took a long drag on his cigarette. 'What makes you say that?'

'I saw him outside the place.'

'You sure about that?'

'Certain.'

'Well you know what you need to do then. You need to help Beata's friend, what's her name–'

'Aga.'

'Aga, yeah. You need to tell her to pay him. And never borrow from him again.'

'I've done that. But I need to make sure that she doesn't get hassled anymore.'

'Piotr man, we haven't got the muscle for this. These guys won't think twice about putting a bullet in your back if you provoke them.'

Piotr finished his beer. 'It's a risk I'll have to take. I can't back down now. '

'Now? What do you mean? What have you done?'

'I went to the coffee shop and told them to lay off her. That's how I know about the Taxi Man connection. When I was there the other day I'm pretty certain I saw him going into the café after I left.'

'You did what? Have you lost your head?'

'It's OK. I know what to do.'

'What do you mean, you know what to do?'

'I'm going to speak to them again, that's all.'

'They don't do negotiation Piotrek. If you try to back off they don't just shake hands and say, don't worry, it was all one big misunderstanding.'

'So what do I need to know then?'

'What do you mean?'

'Well you trained with him. And you're telling me that it might get messy. What are his weaknesses? Any long-term injuries?'

'Piotr, come on.'

'I'm being serious. Anything you can tell me?'

'You've got to walk away from this.'

'It's too late for that.'

Henio drank some more beer and stubbed out his cigarette.

'I suppose there is one thing. He had an injury, a few years back. To his right eye. He got it working on the doors. His vision on that side isn't that great. Apart from that, he's a dangerous operator. And he probably carries as well. You don't need to do this you know Piotrek. You hardly know the girl. Is it really worth getting involved? Over her flatmate?'

'It needs to be done.'

'Let me come with you. I can back you up.'

'No, I'll do this myself,' said Piotr. 'It's not a dojang matter anyway, strictly speaking.'

'You're a nutcase, you know that don't you?' Henio handed him another beer and opened one for himself. When they finished their cans Piotr walked with Henio to his car.

'You OK to drive?' said Piotr.

'I've had two beers, not two bottles of vodka,' said Henio.

He got into his car and rolled down the window. 'Listen, Piotrusz. Take my advice will you? Drop this whole thing. It's not worth it. You want to be in that food van, frying pierogi. Not in a wheelchair. Or worse.'

He drove off, leaving Piotr standing on the pavement.

PIOTR WAS SAT ON A STOOL, facing out towards the street. He sipped his soft drink, keeping an eye on the entrance to Beata's block of flats. He picked up a piece of fried chicken and took a bite out of it. It tasted like it had been sat out in the sun all day.

A few teenage boys walked in and ordered some food. They were arguing about a girl.

'That's my cousin you're talking about,' one of them said, pushing over another boy, who stumbled and knocked over a stool.

Piotr watched their reflection in the window. The two boys shoved each other, to and fro. Piotr could sense the underlying aggression and jockeying for power. Their behaviour reminded him of the wildlife programmes that his father had liked watching on TV.

He was about to take another bite out of the chicken when he saw Guzik walking up to the main door to the flats. Someone was exiting the building at the same time. Guzik sneaked in as the door was closing. Piotr picked up his drink, which was still half full, exited the restaurant, and ran across the road.

He pressed Aga and Beata's intercom button but there was no answer. He called Beata on his mobile.

'Open the main door for me,' he said, when she answered it. 'Guzik's inside. Don't let him in. And don't make a sound in there. Understand?'

The door clicked open and he ran up the stairs, glancing at the LCD display above the lift as he did so. Guzik was on the second floor already. When Piotr got to the fourth floor, he paused before peering out of the stairwell door. Guzik was making his way down the corridor towards the flat. Piotr flicked his baton open and tucked it back into his jeans. He clenched his left fist. It felt OK. He picked up his drink and headed towards the gangster.

Half an hour later Beata answered her phone. 'Piotrusz? Are you OK? Where are you?'

'I'm fine,' said Piotr, speaking in a low voice. 'Don't worry.'

'Where are you? What's happening? We heard you outside and

then some shouting and banging, like you were fighting. We were scared.'

'It's OK. It's over now. I'm going to go and see Henio soon.'

'Henio? What for?

'I need to see him, that's all.'

'I don't understand. What's happened to the loan shark? His car is still outside.'

'He's not going to use his car right now. Or hassle you this evening, so don't worry.'

'Where are you?'

'I can't explain everything right now, but don't worry. Everything's fine, I promise. Try and get some sleep. I'll call you tomorrow morning.'

Henio found Piotr by a dark blue German saloon car in the car park at Horsenden Hill. He was standing with his hands on his hips, looking down at the ground. Henio pulled up next to him in his car and rolled his window down.

'You OK?'

'Not really.'

'Where is he?'

'Where do you think?'

'In the car?'

'Yeah.'

'What? Have you lost your whoring mind?'

'Keep your voice down,' said Piotr.

'Let me see him.'

Piotr opened the boot. Henio looked at Guzik for a moment and put his hand under his nostrils before checking his pulse.

'What the hell happened?'

'I can't explain it right now. I need to get him checked out and do something with this car. And there's not much time. Have you got the replacements?'

'They're in the boot.'

They screwed the number plates off the saloon car and put the new ones on. A ringtone started playing from the boot. 'How many times has it rung?' Henio said.

'First time I've heard it.'

Henio lit a cigarette and took a long drag on it.

'What now?' said Piotr.

'I'm thinking, give me a second,' said Henio. 'I haven't seen a situation like this in a long time.' He rubbed his temples with his spare hand. 'You sure you're alright to drive?'

Piotr nodded.

'Follow me then,' said Henio, looking down at the streets at the bottom of the hill. 'We need to get him to a hospital and then we need to get rid of the car. Scratch out anything that links you to this. You never know, someone may have seen you get into it.'

Before he got behind the wheel, Henio said, 'Make sure you drive steady.'

They drove to a hospital that was ten minutes away and parked in a multi-storey car park, in a corner on the top level, where it was almost empty. Henio signalled at Piotr telling him to stay in the car until they were sure that they were alone. After they got out, they lifted Guzik from the boot and put him on one of the back seats of his car.

'Right. This is what we do,' said Henio. 'There's a little alcove before the turn off down to the A&E department. We're going to leave my car there. I'm going to drive his motor up to the A&E doors. I think there are some wheelchairs by the entrance – I was here only a couple of months ago with Ania. You're going to sit in the back to keep him upright. I'll put him into a wheelchair and push him into A&E, while you stay in the car. Then we drive back to the alcove. I get into my car, you drive his wheels again and follow me. Got it?'

When they got to the doors at A&E, Henio lost his balance dragging Guzik out of the car and almost fell over. Piotr got out to help him but Henio said, 'What are you doing? Get back in the whoring car and shut the door.'

Henio found a wheelchair and dumped Guzik onto it. He wheeled him into the hospital and stopped at the A&E front desk.

'I found him this man on a park bench,' he said. 'He's in bad shape. Maybe drugs, or maybe he banged his head. But he's sleeping and won't wake up.'

The girl at the reception desk stood up and examined Guzik.

'How long ago did you find him?'

'About half an hour ago,' said Henio, keeping his face away from a CCTV camera in the corner of the room.

'Wait here, I'm going to call someone.' She sat down, picked up the phone and put her head down. Henio saw his chance and walked out, keeping his eyes to the ground and pretending to sneeze into his hands as he passed another camera.

'I forgot how heavy that whore's son is,' he said as he got back in the car.

They made their way to a dual carriageway and started driving out of the suburbs. The road was quiet but they stuck to the speed limit. Piotr left a large gap between himself and Henio. The built up streets of houses on the side of the carriageway soon disappeared, making way for green fields marked with the occasional farmhouse as it turned into a motorway. After a few minutes they reached a stretch where there were no motorway lights. Every time he saw a vehicle approaching on the other side of the carriage, Piotr worried that he was going to see a police car that would fire up its sirens and double back to chase him down.

After driving for 20 minutes, they turned off and went down a dark country lane which twisted and turned for what seemed like an eternity to Piotr. After a while, Henio slowed down and indicated right. They drove along a stony road surrounded by tall trees. The car tyres crunched through gravel as they made their way to a small opening by a river. When they stopped, Piotr got out and noticed that the moon was brighter than usual. He realised that he had not seen the stars for a long time.

Henio had a torch. He put his lips to his fingers and flashed it at the riverbank and the ground by it. He switched it off and waited for a few minutes, listening to make sure there was no one with them. Satisfied that they were alone, Henio wiped all the door handles and the number plates with a cloth. He then wiped the handle of the boot and the whole boot ridge. Inside, he wiped the steering wheel, dashboard, gearbox, handbrake, and anything else that they may have touched.

He handed Piotr some plastic gloves and put some on himself. They let the handbrake down and pushed against both open front doors, moving the car slowly. When the front of the car touched the water, they closed the doors and pushed it some more from the rear, until it was all in the water.

They watched it sink. 'It's deep,' said Henio, in a low voice. He took a small brush out of his car and told Piotr to shine the torch at the riverbank.

There was a faint track in the mud. Henio used the brush to erase it and then kicked some gravel onto the patch of mud.

They got into Henio's car. He reversed it slowly and drove back down the path onto the road. Heading back to the motorway, he lit a cigarette and smoked in silence.

After a while, Piotr said, 'Will it stay down there?'

'It should do,' said Henio.

'So the police will never find it?'

'Probably not. But someone will find it. Eventually. But don't worry about that. Let's hope it stays down there for a few years at least.'

'How did you know about that place?' said Piotr.

Henio blew smoke out of the car window. 'I used to go fishing there.'

'I didn't know you were into fishing.'

'It was a long time ago. So, are you going to tell me what happened?'

Piotr rubbed his eyes. He stared at the road for a moment, watching the lane markings flash by. 'I'd been waiting to see if someone was going to turn up at Beata's after I'd been to the coffee shop and told them to lay off. And he did. I followed him inside. He'd taken the lift. I ran up the stairs. When I saw him outside the girls' flat, I walked down the corridor towards him. I asked him if I could help him with anything.

'He said 'no' and stood there looking at me like I was the cleaner or something. He knocked on the door again. There was no answer or sound from inside – I'd warned Beata not to answer the door. I told him I didn't think anyone was in. He knocked again, really slowly, about five times, looking at me the whole time. Like a serious psycho. There was still no answer. I told him that he needed to leave as there was no one there. He smirked at me and then asked me if he knew me from somewhere. I said he had probably got me mistaken for someone else.

'That's when I lost concentration for a bit. I was kicking myself for not staying back and waiting to see if he was going to try and knock down the door or something. I lost eye contact and looked at the door. In that split second he produced a gun and pointed it at me. He ordered me to tell Beata to open the door. All I could think of was, how did he know about Beata?

'Anyway, I stepped forward towards the door and lifted my left hand as if I was about to knock on the door. I could see that his left leg was quite far forward and close to me, so I acted straight away. I threw this drink I had in my hand in his face and trapped his arm with a forearm block.'

'Why did you have a drink?'

'I'd been waiting in a fried chicken restaurant opposite the flat.'

'Right. And what happened after that?'

'I kicked his calf so that he lost balance and slid towards me. He dropped the gun. I tried to punch him square on the bridge of his nose, but he somehow managed to cover up, and my arm trap wasn't on right. He sensed that and grabbed me around the torso and tried to throw me to the ground.

'I dropped my weight and stood my ground. I was trying to throw elbows on his neck and head to let me go. But he held on. We stumbled for a bit and I jammed my thumb into his eye socket as deep as I could. Beata's flat is really close to one of the stairwells, and it opens outwards. He lost control when I did that and we fell into the door and out onto the staircase. Somehow he managed to wriggle free and put a choke on. I put all my effort into chucking myself down a flight of stairs, I was convinced he wanted to kill me. He fell with me and cracked his head on one of the steps. He was out cold. I thought he was gone at first, but I could still feel a pulse.'

They pulled out onto the motorway. Piotr checked the wing mirror.

'And after that?' said Henio, flicking his cigarette out of the car window.

'Then I started panicking. I stood up and my first instinct was to go to the flat and tell Beata I was OK, but I realised that I needed to move him as we'd made a fair bit of noise. I jumped up the stairs, retrieved the gun, put the safety catch on it and stuck it into my belt. I stood over him for what seemed like a minute or so, thinking about what to do.'

'Where's the gun now?'

'I stuck it in the glove box.'

'Right. Then what?'

'It was still light outside and it was going to stay that way for a couple of hours at least. I remembered there was a bin room for the flats, in the basement. I checked to see if there was any blood on the stairs from his head but I couldn't see any, so I picked him up under his arms and dragged him downstairs as fast I could. We got in there and I put him right in the corner behind one of the big bins, out of sight. I found a couple of cardboard boxes and raided the recycling bin for stuff and put loads of it into the boxes. My plan was to pretend that I was doing the recycling for Beata if anyone came in. Thankfully no one did.'

'Sounds like you were thinking pretty well for someone who was panicking.'

'Yeah, well I was sweating, shallow breathing, all of it. By the time I knew it would be dark, I dragged him out through the fire exit on the ground floor. I was hoping he would have parked behind the flats. I found his keys and went outside, pressing the fob until his car flashed open. Then I went back, picked him up, firelifted him across the street and shoved him in the boot.

'So someone could have seen you,' said Henio.

'Like I said, I was panicking. That's when I called you.'

'How long were you down there?'

'Three hours maybe.'

When they pulled off the motorway, Piotr said, 'There's one thing I don't get.'

'What's that?'

'I went for him from quite a wide angle with a dummy strike from my left hand side so that I could sneak a strike in from the right. From where his bad eye is. And he saw it coming. He reacted to it in a millisecond. Unless he has superhuman reactions, then he saw it in time.'

'So?'

'Well you told me he was impaired there. That his peripheral vision wasn't that good on that side.'

'Maybe he got lucky. It happens. Or read your intentions. How do you know your dummy was convincing? You said you were panicking, right?'

'Maybe. I guess my wrist isn't in the best shape. It messed up my technique when I tried to put the arm trap on. None of this would have happened if I'd got that right. I would have knocked him out and busted his nose.'

When they pulled up at his Aunt's house, Piotr said, 'Thanks for your help. I owe you one.'

'Don't mention it. Just keep your head down, OK? You need to stay low, something is bound to come out of this. The Taxi man's going to know that it was you who did this. It won't take him long to work it out.'

'Doesn't he need evidence that I was involved?'

'What evidence? It's enough for Guzik not to report back that will raise suspicion. Man, the alarm is probably already out. Especially as you revealed yourself to them.'

'That was a bad mistake,' said Piotr.

'You don't know that for sure. It was a risk. Another time it might have made them back down, with no one getting hurt. You weren't to know.'

'I allowed it all to get personal because of Beata. I shouldn't have done that. He wouldn't have had a gun if I hadn't gone to that coffee shop. No way. He was ready in case something happened.'

'You don't know that either. He could have always carried. It's not like they don't have their own enemies. There's trouble with every gang from Albanians to Zulus in this city. Listen, I'll call you tomorrow. Try and get some sleep. Have a shot or two before you hit the sack.'

Piotr downed a beer when he got in. He crushed the empty can in his hand as he went to the drinks cabinet in the dining room and poured himself a large shot of vodka. He drank it and then had another.

Lying on his bed, he called Beata.

THE GYM WAS BASED IN A LEISURE COMPLEX. Three rings and four areas of mats spanned the ground floor. One wall was lined with a dozen punch bags of varying sizes, the one opposite with a wall of mirrors. At the end of the gym, there were pull-up bars, and sit up benches. Above them, on a mezzanine, was another conditioning area, with weights, rowing machines and treadmills, all gleaming proudly. The gym smelt of sweat and new plastic.

Piotr approached one of the staff. He was staring at some figures that were written in different colours on a whiteboard. Every few seconds he would tap something into a tablet he was holding. The tips of his dreadlocks touched a tablet as he bent his head forwards.

'Hi, I'm looking for Jacek. Is he working today?' Piotr said.

'Jacek? He's in later, for the kickboxing session,' the man said, still studying the whiteboard. 'You here to train?'

'Me? No. I'm a friend. What time does it start?'

'Seven,' said the man. 'But he's usually here half an hour before it. They'll be training in studio one tonight on the first floor as there's a BJJ session in the main hall.' He put his tablet down. 'I can't really let you in until he arrives. But I can show you around if you want. I need to get something from there anyway.'

As they walked up a staircase Piotr said, 'What kind of guys train here then?'

'All sorts really. We've got your serious MMA guys, wannabe MMA guys, then guys and girls who have either left their base art, or still train in it but they want to cross-train, see what they can pick up from others, you know what I mean? You see you can get everything you need here – classes in traditional arts; stand-up styles, a bit of wrestling, Gracie-style Ju-Jitsu, and then you can do all your cardio, conditioning here too. It's all under one roof. You don't need to go anywhere else.'

The man held a door open for Piotr. 'You do any training yourself?'

'A bit.'

'That where you got that shiner?' he said, pointing at Piotr's eye. Piotr touched his eyebrow. 'Yeah, I guess so.'

They reached the studio. 'You thinking of joining up?' said the man. 'We do monthly trials at a discounted rate. You only start paying full fees if you're happy to after the month is over.'

'I'm alright, thanks,' said Piotr. 'Is it OK if I wait outside?'

'Sure, no problem. If you change your mind then come and see me at the desk.'

Piotr leaned against the wall outside the studio and put his hands in his pockets. He watched the Brazilian Ju-Jitsu session across the hall through the studio's large windows. Piotr recognised some of the training from early MMA videos that he and his friends had watched back in Poland. He wondered if he would be able to escape a leg lock the instructor was showing the students.

Jacek turned up fifteen minutes before the lesson was due to start. He stopped still when he turned the corner and saw Piotr.

'Nice set up,' said Piotr, thumbing at the studio.

'What are you doing here?'

'I've been trying to get hold of you. What's with your phone?'

'I got a new one. Had to change the number.'

'You didn't think of telling me?'

'I haven't got round to it yet,' said Jacek, walking slowly towards the studio door.

'Listen, I need to talk to you. There's something going on.'

'Like what?'

'This isn't the right place to discuss it. When do you finish up?'

'In about an hour and a half.'

'I'll meet you after 8:30 then. In the Burger King on the corner. Is that alright with you?'

'Sure. You don't want to stay here and watch? We're working combos on the pads tonight. Nothing too fancy. It'll be a solid session though.'

'No, I'm alright thanks.'

Piotr walked back to the entrance and thanked the dreadlocked man on his way out. As he walked towards Burger King, a stream of teenagers came out of the cinema and split into different directions. A group of boys and girls were laughing and hugging each other as they walked out of the complex. Piotr couldn't remember the last time he had laughed like that.

Jacek wiped his mouth with a napkin and sucked a bit more cola through his straw.

'Man, I'd forgotten how good a Whopper is,' he said. 'You ever thought about doing burgers instead of pierogi? Everyone loves burgers. There are joints popping up everywhere.'

'No,' said Piotr, his eyes darting out to the car park.

'Damn, real good. You sure you don't want one? I'll shout you one.'

'I'm not hungry,' said Piotr, nursing an empty coffee cup. 'I had something earlier.'

'So what's up?' said Jacek, crumpling up his burger wrapper.

'Have you seen Kris recently?'

Jacek picked up some fries. 'Not for a couple of weeks, I'm so busy here, you know how it is.'

'Well, have you heard anything, has he called you about anything?'

'Like what?'

'Being threatened, followed, messages. That sort of stuff.'

'Are you on one of your paranoid trips again?'

'No, it's different this time. I may have kicked it all off again. In fact, I know I have.'

'How?'

'I put one of the Taxi man's henchmen in hospital.'

Jacek stopped chewing. 'You did what?'

Piotr sketched out his last 72 hours.

When he was done, Jacek said, 'Are the police looking into it?'

'Probably not. You know how it is. They won't give the police a sniff, so it's doubtful.'

'You worried?'

'What do you think I'm talking to you for?'

'Can I do anything to help?'

'Keep your eyes open. And warn Kris to watch out. I've tried calling him, sending texts, he hasn't responded. I don't want anyone getting hurt over this who isn't involved. This should be between me and him, but he could do anything to hurt me or anyone involved with the dojang.'

'Maybe you should go talk to him. Tell him it was just one of those things.'

'One of those things is not an explanation that's going to cut it.

209

This could mean an all out war, and we're weaker than we've ever been.'

'Damn. You need to bury the hatchet with Kris. We need everyone on this.'

A group of men walked into the restaurant. Piotr checked them out for a moment. 'Maybe,' he said. 'Listen, I'm sorry to bring this on you. I've been too lax, not listened to people. Not kept a tight rein on things. And now this. I've almost ruined everything. But believe me, if I can fix it, then I will.'

Jacek drove him back home. Piotr propped his elbow up against the passenger window. The streetlights became one long blur as they passed them.

Piotr told Jacek to drop him off about half a mile away from his Aunt's house. Jacek gave him his new number. Piotr opened the door as if he was about to get out and then closed it again.

'What's up?' said Jacek.

Piotr stared straight ahead. 'If anything happens to me, then someone needs to keep the dojang alive.'

'What do you mean?'

'You know what I mean. What Kris is running isn't part of the Kwan.'

'Why are telling me? I thought you didn't trust me anymore with everything that's happened.'

Piotr looked at him. 'Yeah, well. You're still my number two. I haven't completely given up on you. And you can be the Sabum, no problem. If you want to. If you still believe in it.'

Piotr walked down the street with his hands stuffed in his jacket pockets, looking over his shoulder every few seconds. When he was about 150 metres away from the house he slowed down and examined the street for any unfamiliar vehicles. He walked past his Aunt's house and ducked down an alley further down the street. Half way down it, he jumped over a fence into an unused and overgrown pathway. It ran between the back gardens of the houses on his street and the one parallel to it. He walked down it until he reached a tree at the back of his Aunt's property. He leaped over into the garden and let himself in through the back door.

PIOTR'S AUNT OPENED HER EYES. Piotr took hold of her hand. She looked at him and then closed her eyes for a second, as if she was trying to check if she was dreaming or not.

'I brought you some biscuits,' he said. 'The ones with the figs in them.'

Piotr took out three packets of biscuits from a carrier bag by the bed. 'Where should I put them? Here?' He pointed at her bedside table.

She shut her eyes again and nodded.

Piotr carefully moved her prayer book and rosary to one side and placed the packets on the table.

'The nurses say you had a good night.'

'I slept like a baby. It's the medication.'

'Maybe I should take some of that,' said Piotr.

Piotr's Aunt squeezed his hand. 'You should try not to worry Piotrusz. Please don't worry about me. Everything will be fine.'

'I'm trying. I really am. It's just hard.' He stood up, trying to hide his tears. 'Hey, you want some water? I'll get you a glass.'

He walked over to the other side of the bed and poured out some water into two paper cups. He put one cup on his Aunt's bedside table.

'Has Father Leszek been to see you?'

'Yes. Thank you for asking him to.'

'Don't thank me. It was really good of him to come all that way. Especially at his age.'

'He's a good priest. Do you know he was ordained almost 58 years ago? I don't know how he's gone on for so long.' She started coughing.

He helped her sit up, raising her pillows and patting her back. 'Drink some water,' he said, holding a cup up for her.

She drank a little and raised her hand to tell him that she'd had enough. 'He said that his retirement home is really nice. Almost all the other priests there have something seriously wrong with them. One of them has severe dementia. He keeps asking if the council has ended.'

'Which council is that?'

His Aunt sighed. 'Vatican II dear. Vatican II.'

A nurse came over.

'She's just been coughing a bit,' Piotr said.

'Right, well you sit up a little more sweetie to help your breathing a bit,' said the nurse. 'Anything I can get you right now?'

Piotr's Aunt shook her head. 'No thank you.'

'OK. Well you give me a buzz if you need me.'

The nurse walked away. 'They're so nice here,' Piotr's Aunt said. 'I'm lucky places like this exist.'

Piotr patted her hand. 'I'm glad you like it.'

They went for a walk in the grounds of the hospice. Piotr's Aunt held his arm and used a walking stick.

After a while she said, 'How's Beata?'

'She's fine. Busy trying to get herself a new job.'

'It was so nice to see her the other day. She's a good girl you know.'

'Yeah, I know.'

'You seem very comfortable together.'

'Alright Auntie, I know where you're going with this. But it's a little early for that sort of talk.'

'Nonsense. Your Uncle and I only got married after a few months. There's no point waiting an eternity for these sorts of things. If you love each other you should get married. People get into such a muddle about marriage these days. Waiting to save money for a big wedding, or to see if they're compatible, whatever that means. It's all ridiculous.'

When they sat down for a rest on a bench, Piotr told his Aunt that he had contacted Mr. Stablinski.

'I'm going to meet him next week at his office.'

'Now there's some good news. I'm so glad Piotrusz. What made you change your mind?

'A few things.'

'Will you still be working on your pierogi restaurant?'

'I don't know about that right now.'

'Well, you can hopefully have a bit more luck with work if Mr. Stablinski takes you on. He's an honest employer. He cares about his staff.'

As they walked back inside, they stopped to look at a bed of flowers. 'Gapczo would like it here wouldn't he?' said Piotr.

'I'm sure he would. Perhaps you can bring him here tomorrow.'

'Definitely. I'll check with the nurses, but I bet it'll be alright.'

She gazed at the blossom by her feet. She was gaunt, her skin pale and blotchy. Piotr felt as if she was shrivelling away before him. But he knew that she was content.

BEATA GOT OFF THE TRAIN and waited in line at a temporary bus stop. A man at the front of the queue was speaking to a Tube worker.

'What are all your driver mates striking for then this time?' he said. 'More money is it? Or more holidays? I wish I could strike whenever I wanted. Don't think the boss would think much of it though.'

The bus was full when it set off. Beata stood and held onto the rails as it made its way to Rayners Lane, stopping at every Underground station on the way. There were plenty of men on the bus. She thought about how one of them would have probably stood up and offered her his seat if they were back in Poland.

When she alighted at Rayners Lane, she crossed over the road, stopping and starting to avoid the incoming traffic. It was raining heavily. As she got to the other side, a car driving close to the curb splashed water that had gathered in a dip in the road all over her legs. She watched in despair as the car drove away, not noticing the two men standing near her block of flats. She fumbled in her bag for her keys as she made her way to the front door of her apartment block.

She placed the fob on her key ring against the authentication panel. As she pushed against the opening door, she felt the presence of another person behind her. Before she could pivot to see who it was, she was shoved into the corridor and pinned up against the postboxes. A man held her by the throat and put his other hand over her mouth. She recognised him as the fat bald man from Café Koncert. He was with another man that she had not seen before. She tried to scream but the bald man pressed his hand harder against her mouth.

'Keep your mouth shut bitch,' he said, his nicotine breath warming the tip of her nose. She tried to push the man's arm away and to shout out again. He pressed his forearm hard against her neck and swore at her.

The other man slapped her over the head, twice. 'Listen you little whore,' he said. 'You're being told this once, you won't be told again. We've got a message for your little chimp of a boyfriend.

He's to come and meet us at the coffee shop on Wednesday evening at 9. If he doesn't turn up, then we'll be back here again. And we won't just be talking to you. You'll be coming with us. Understand?'

'And if the police get involved, then you can forget about ever seeing your little chimp hero again,' said the bald man.

They walked out, leaving Beata in a heap on the floor, blinking tears and hyperventilating.

Piotr arrived home to find the white belts waiting outside the garage.

When he let them in, Ziggy took a large piece of cloth out of a carrier bag he had brought with him and unfolded it. He held it up, showing it to Piotr and the other students.

'This is the flag I was talking about Sabum,' he said. 'What do you think?'

'It looks perfect,' said Piotr. 'How much do you want for it?'

'Nothing. I want to donate it to the dojang. I bought my toolbox too, in case you wanted to hang it up. I've got a drill in the car.'

'We don't need all that. We can hang it off the main door every time we train.'

Piotr stood on his Uncle's work bench and hooked two ends of the flag into some grooves on the garage door. They got changed into their doboks, bowed in front of the flag and began practising their *tuls*.

Piotr taught Adam the first black belt *tul* in the garden, while Ziggy, Sebastian and Arek trained in the garage.

After two hours, Piotr called an end to the session and went into the house. He emerged with some plastic cups and two large jugs of water.

'There's something I need to tell you,' he said as they drank. 'There's been a situation. I've got entangled in something that's a little messy. So we're going to have to stay low for a bit, and I need you all to stay hyper vigilant until it blows over.'

Arek said, 'Sounds heavy. What is it?'

'It's to do with the Taxi man.'

Sebastian let out a long low whistle.

'Someone want to fill me in here?' said Ziggy.

Arek said, 'You mean you don't know?'

'No. First I've heard of him.'

'You've only been here a couple of years Ziggy,' said Piotr. 'Things have been quiet with him for a while now, so you weren't to know.'

Adam said, 'He wears a lot of Adidas, put it that way.'

'He's head of a gang here,' said Piotr. 'He's been involved in all sorts of rackets in London since at least the mid-Eighties. The story is that he was forced to leave home after killing someone he used to smuggle goods with from West Germany. The authorities were onto him and he had to bail. He came to London and took a job as a taxi driver. Since then he's always driven a taxi, that's been his front. Hence the name. He's been very discreet.

'He got back into smuggling, but joined a gang that did all sorts – robberies, a bit of protection racketeering. By the Nineties they were into drugs too. And then with the influx after 2005, he started to do some serious loan sharking.

'Anyway, we first clashed with him when he was a captain in some firm, it wasn't long after the Wall had come down. An owner of a Polish food outlet, one of the only ones in London at the time, had called in for help after the Taxi Man and his crew had targeted him for protection money. Our old Sabum and his Sabum, at the time – Wojtek Grzyb – met him and two of his gangster friends in the owner's office one night.

'The unofficial story is that one of the gangsters was killed after threatening the lives of either Grzyb or Sabum, but no one knows how, or who did it.

'Ever since then, there's been a vendetta going on. Or there was, up until a couple of years ago. The Taxi man assumed control of the gang after the killing, and the word was that he had decided to bring down the dojang in his patch, here in West London. Most of us believe that he was responsible for killing Grzyb. The police recorded it as suicide. They said he jumped in front of a train on the Tube late one night in '92. We knew different though. He was never the suicidal type, put it that way.

'It didn't end there. There were attacks and threats to new students. The Taxi Man even planted his people in the dojang. Sabum eventually discovered that one of his best students had been working for the Taxi man for years.

'We'd always retaliate. Break up some of their operations, help people out being hassled by them, that kind of thing. But we haven't heard anything for over four years now. Not a squeak. It's like he lost interest.'

'Can we still train here?' said Sebastian. 'I mean, if we're meant to be staying low and everything.'

'We can train here no problem. But we need to keep our heads down. I don't think he would even contemplate touching any of you, but you never know.'

'What about the guys that train with Kris?' said Arek.

'I've told Kris. He knows.'

They got changed and Piotr went inside. He checked his phone as he got ready to have a shower. He had several missed calls from Beata and a voicemail. He listened to it for 15 seconds and then ran out of the house in his underwear. Sebastian was about to pull away in his car. Piotr banged on his window.

'What's wrong?' said Sebastian.

'I need a lift.'

'How did they even know that you were seeing each other?' said Aga, passing Beata another tissue.

Piotr paced up and down in the kitchen. 'I don't know. I didn't tell them who I was, that's for sure. But it's not that difficult to find out. We've been seen in public before, walked down the street together.'

Aga, fighting back tears, put her hand on Beata's forearm. 'You're not even the one with the debt. This is all my fault. I'm so, so sorry.'

'This is no one's fault apart from theirs. OK?' said Piotr. 'Remember that.'

Beata wiped away some mascara that had run down her face with the back of her hands.

'How has this happened?' she said between her sobs. 'How could something like this have happened, here, in England. It's madness.'

'Shouldn't we call the police now? This has got out of control,' said Aga.

Piotr forced himself to stand still. His mind raced as he felt his anger grow. He breathed slowly through his nose for five seconds and then exhaled through his mouth for another five.

'Maybe,' he said. 'But that could be dangerous. They're not playing games. I'll have to do what they say. I don't want them hassling you anymore.'

Beata stood up, facing Piotr. 'Please, just call the police. I'm begging you.'

'It'll be OK.'

She dumped her fists on his chest. 'You said that before. Now look at us.'

Piotr held her by the elbows. 'This has to end. This is the only way.'

Piotr almost got run over as he ran from the Tube station to the site.

'You need me to buy you a new alarm clock?' said the foreman when he saw him. 'Because I can you know. I can take out the cost from your next pay packet.'

'I'm really sorry boss, I overslept,' Piotr said. 'I was up late with my Aunt at the hospice. I fell asleep by her side and then had to get a night bus home.'

'Forget I said anything,' said the foreman, waving his hand. 'Me and my whoring memory. You alright to do a shift today? You can have some time off if you need it you know. I could even keep paying you a day or two here and there.'

'Thanks, but I'd prefer to work. Helps me take my mind off things.'

'Alright. Well the offer's there.'

Piotr met Uncle and Maciek inside. They were fitting some new floorboards on the ground floor.

'How's she doing?' said Uncle.

'Not well,' said Piotr. He walked into another room to get changed into his work clothes.

Uncle followed him in. 'You OK?'

'Yeah.'

'Do they know anything more?'

218

'Not really. Could be days, weeks. Months even. She doesn't look like she can go on that long though.'

'Anything you need. You let me know. Anything.'

'Thanks.'

After lunch a builder's merchant's truck dropped off a large delivery of tiles. Piotr and Uncle moved the tiles from the street to the front garden of the house. They helped Maciek to winch them to the roof.

As they did, Piotr asked Uncle about his cousin. 'Do you know where he gets that booze from?'

'I'm not 100% sure. It's somewhere in Alperton. Maybe just down a bit from the railway station. In a back alley that's lined with garages.

'I could maybe help with that you know. If I knew about it a bit more about it.'

Uncle put down a pile of tiles on the ground and stood up, holding the small of his back. He wiped his forehead and put his hands on his hips. 'Really?' he said.

'Sure.'

'I'll see what I can find out.'

PIOTR WALKED DOWN TOWARDS ALPERTON STATION with his hood over his head, avoiding as many main streets as he could.

He passed the station and reached a boarded up pub. He turned off the main road and made his way down a side alley that was sandwiched in between a long line of garages that were facing each other.

He knocked on one of them.

'I'm listening,' he heard a voice say from inside.

'I need a ladder fixing.'

Piotr waited. A minute later the door slid half way open. He ducked underneath it. Inside, large water buckets filled the garage. Tubes ran in and out of them, into a large ceramic bath. A large copper pipe protruding from a metal barrel was dripping strong vodka into a bottle. A long line of empty ones were positioned behind it.

'How much are you looking for?' the man who had opened the door said. He was wearing white gloves and a white bib and brace overall.

'Four bottles. What's the strength?'

'It's about 65% this week. That's only an estimate though. Could be off a bit. It's eight pounds a bottle.'

Piotr took his wallet out and pulled four ten pound notes out of it. He handed them to the man. He shuffled to the back of the garage where two other men were sat, playing cards and eating peanuts. One of them put his cards down on an upside down crate and picked four bottles out of a box and handed them to him.

'Do you need a bag?' said the man.

'No,' said Piotr, taking the bottles off him and putting them in his rucksack. 'Do you mind if I ask you a question?'

'Depends on what you're asking,' said the man, handing him his change.

'How much do you make on this stuff, say, a week?'

The man lifted his head back so that he was looking down his nose at Piotr. 'We make enough,' he said.

'That's good,' said Piotr, smiling. 'So you're not scratching around for pennies.'

'Right. Are you here to rinse us?'

'No. Don't worry. I wanted to ask you a favour.'

'Yeah? I don't really like doing favours for people I don't know.'

'It's not a big one. I was hoping that you could stop selling to someone who comes here. He's a regular. Name's Wojtek.'

'I don't know the name of anyone who buys off me.'

'I didn't think you would. But he's distinctive. So you can probably pick him out from the others. He's really tall, about this high,' said Piotr holding his hand up. 'He's got thick black hair and a moustache. He also talks with a bit of a lisp. And he's got massive feet.'

The man raised his eyebrow.

'Know who I'm talking about?'

'I think so. But I'm not sure why I should stop selling to him.'

'Put it this way, he's got a kid, and a wife back home. He needs to get his life together and go back there. Sober. He's not working because of the drink and he's ruining his health. He needs help, so I'm asking you to not sell to him.'

'It's not my business what people do with their lives.'

'Think of it as helping a customer. The way he's going, he won't be in any state to buy off you soon anyway.'

'You can't come here and tell me not to sell to someone. What the hell's it got to do with you anyway? You want him to stop drinking, then you deal with it. It's not my whoring concern.'

'Sorry you feel that way. But if I find out he's still buying from you, I'll be back.'

'What sort of a whore's son are you? Strutting in here, telling us who to deal with?

'I'm only here to help,' said Piotr. 'Protecting the oppressed and the weak. If you get my drift.' He stooped under the garage door and left. The man scratched his head.

'What was all that about?' said one of the men at the back.

'I'm not sure. But I think he was Kwan.'

'Kwan?' said one of the other men. 'I've heard they don't even have a dojang in these parts anymore. He must be from out of town.'

'Or off his face on something,' said the other man who was playing cards.

'Well, he spoke like he was Kwan. And there was something in his eyes, the way he held himself. Like he meant business.'

Jacek's car was parked across the street. Piotr took Gapczo's lead off. The dog ran towards the house and up the driveway. He started barking.

Jacek was by the garage door, stacking some gym equipment against it.

'What's all this?' said Piotr.

'It's old gear I got from the gym. We were going to throw it away.'

'Why are you giving it to me?'

Jacek rested his arm on a pile of kickshields. 'I've been thinking about what you said the other night.' He patted a kickshield. 'I suppose this is a kind of peace offering.'

'Peace offering?'

'Yeah. I want to train with you. If you still trust me, that is.'

Piotr scanned the training gear. 'I never said I didn't.' He went inside the house and came out with the keys for the garage. He opened up the main door and they started carrying the equipment in. 'I can't use all this in here, there's no space for it.'

'I was thinking that it was more for the future, when we get a new hall.'

'I like your optimism.'

'It'll happen. We'll build up again. When some of the guys realise that Kris is selling them a dud, they'll be back.'

'We'll see. How much do I owe you?'

'Nothing. Like I said, we were about to chuck the whole lot. And even if I had paid for them, I wouldn't want anything for them.'

Jacek picked up a rucksack in the corner of the garage to make some space for a bag of pads.

'Careful with that,' said Piotr.

'Why? What's in it?'

'Insurance.'

'For what?'

'Something I need to take care of.'

'Is it to do with this thing with the Taxi man?'

'Might be.'

'What are you planning to do?'

Piotr sat down on his Uncle's old work bench. 'I've got to meet with him.'

'Why?'

'Because he's forced my hand. He sent me a message, through Beata. Rough up job. I need to go and see him at the coffee shop where they hang out,' Piotr pointed at the rucksack. 'The stuff in there is to get me out of trouble if I need it.'

'You've got to let me come and help you,' said Jacek.

Piotr pushed a stack of mats up against the garage wall. 'I don't know. I should do this myself. It's less risky. Anyway, the dojang is so thinly spread we can't afford something to happen to me and another black belt.'

'But you can't go alone. That's suicide.'

'It might not come to anything. He might just want to clear the decks. Maybe admit that they hurt us in the past, and with Guzik that makes it even.'

'Brother, are you even listening to yourself? You think they're going to let it go like that? If you go on your own, that's it for you. You can't trust him. You have to let me in on this. We can do this together. Have you spoken to Henio about it?'

'Not about this. But he knows about Guzik and Aga's troubles,' said Piotr.

'And?'

'And he told me to drop the whole thing. Convince Aga to pay up, forget it all and lay low.'

'That sounds like good advice to me.'

'Maybe. But it's too late for that now.'

'What's in the bag then? Hand grenades?'

'Bootleg vodka.'

'What are you going to do with that? Offer them a drink as a truce?'

'No. I was going to make some molotovs.'

'And do what with them?'

'I'm working on a plan.'

'You best work faster.'

'I'm getting there.' Piotr picked up some body armour. 'So what are these like?'

'Not bad,' said Jacek.

'Let's try one out.'

Piotr strapped the body armour to his chest and gestured at Jacek to hit him in the stomach. Jacek punched him, hard. Piotr took a couple of steps back from the force of the blow and tripped over a bag of hand pads.

'They're solid,' said Piotr. 'Well made.'

Jacek stuck his hand out and lifted his friend up. 'You've got to let me help you.'

THEY PARKED UP AT THE BOTTOM OF THE STREET, opposite a petrol station.

'What are we stopping here for?' said Jacek.

'We don't want them to know that we're here together, do we?' said Piotr.

'Fair point.'

Piotr had some sheets of paper on his lap. A map of the surrounding area was printed on them. He picked one up in each hand and compared them for a few seconds.

'What now?' said Jacek, checking the street behind them in his mirrors.

Piotr said, 'Let's run through the plan again.'

He pointed to a place on one of the maps. 'We're here.' He moved his finger up the map. 'The coffee shop backs onto the small alley, facing these houses' back gardens. Clear?'

'Clear.'

'Good. Can you see the sign on the left side of the road? The one that warns lorry drivers about the low bridge?'

Jacek squinted. 'Just about.'

'I'm going to walk down there and the coffee shop is ten metres down from there on the left. You drive down past the shop, take the first left after that and park up at the end of this cul-de-sac. Then grab the bottles and the bag and jump over this fence.' He pointed at a red circle he had drawn on the map. 'You need to get yourself over to the back of the coffee shop. Can you remember the distance from the fence?'

'60 metres.'

'Right.'

Piotr flicked through the papers and pulled out another sheet. 'Let's look at this pic that Sebastian took of the back of the shop. There's the ladder and all the big bins. See?' He passed the sheet to Jacek.

'Hopefully the bins will be near enough the ladder. You need to get on top of them and jump to the fire escape ladder. Get on the roof and crawl slowly to the other end. About five shops down. That's important. You need to crawl. And you need to be to the left of the ladder, by about six, seven metres.'

'No problem,' said Jacek.

'If I give you three rings on your mobile, you light one of the bottles and drop it near the back door. As close as you can get it.'

'Are you sure the car doesn't need to be in that back alley?'

'No way. They've got cameras at the back. They might be using them. And who knows who's hanging around there. OK, what's the jump from the roof?'

'12 metres.'

'Correct. Right, if it all goes to plan, I'll run past the fire that you start. So you need to set off the second one as you see me exit.'

'And if you don't ring?'

'Then I'll text you.' Piotr showed him his phone. 'It's all ready, all I have to do is press send. If that happens then you get back in the car, and we meet here, at this bus stop,' he said, circling his finger on another location on the map.

'And if you don't text?'

'If you don't hear from me after 20 minutes then get out of there and call the police.'

'You want me to leave you there?'

'I want you to be safe. OK, repeat all of that to me.'

After Jacek finished they did not talk anymore. Piotr pulled down the sun visor and checked his reflection in the small mirror in the middle of it. He had bags under his bloodshot eyes.

Piotr got out of the car, leaving the maps on the passenger seat. They gripped hands and Jacek held on for longer than he normally would, expecting Piotr to say something. He didn't.

'Stay safe,' said Jacek.

Piotr stuffed his hands into his jacket and started walking down the road. Jacek watched him for a few seconds and then pulled away. He gripped the steering wheel tightly, forcing himself not to look at Piotr as he drove by him. When he got to the fence, he switched the engine off and jumped out of the car, grabbing Piotr's rucksack as he did so. He leapt over the fence in one smooth movement and started running towards the back of the parade of shops.

Piotr scoped the street as he approached the coffee shop. All seemed quiet.

He took a deep breath and walked in.

The bald man was sitting in the same place as before. He was drinking a coffee and reading a Polish sports paper. There was no one else in the coffee shop apart from a girl behind the counter. She had her back to him, and was filling up the dishwasher. The shop was due to close in half an hour.

When Piotr got to the table, he said, 'You wanted to see me?'

The bald man folded his paper over and placed it towards the edge of the table. 'Take a seat.'

Piotr sat down.

'You want a coffee?'

'I'm OK.'

'Suit yourself.'

Piotr looked around the empty the café. 'So is it just you I'm meeting?'

'Who else did you want to see?'

'I thought someone else would be here too.'

'Well, I'm the only one here chief.' He gestured over to the waitress. She came over with another cup of black coffee for him.

'Will you want any more?' she said. 'I've got the dishwasher on now.'

'No, this will do,' he said. He picked up two brown sugar cubes and dropped them in his coffee and stirred it. 'So. You know why you're here?'

'Why don't you tell me,' said Piotr.

The man stopped stirring his coffee and placed the spoon on the saucer. He clasped his hands over his large stomach. 'You've got balls vigilante boy, I'll give you that. You put my friend in hospital. And he's still there. He's in a bad way. You want to tell me what happened?'

'You people seem to know a lot about me, so I'm guessing you already know what took place.'

'Cut the crap.'

'He put a gun in my face. If someone's got a finger on a trigger five inches from my temple then I'm going to do something about it if I get the chance. I was there to help a defenceless girl. He was there to intimidate. Or worse.'

The bald man sipped his coffee. 'That's it? What were you carrying with you, a sledgehammer?'

'We tussled and fell down some stairs. He cracked his head on them. Look, I'm sorry about your friend. And maybe it was my fault for coming here in the first place, but I'm not the one who lends dirty money at extortionate rates to vulnerable people. And then scares them into paying it back.'

The bald man chuckled and drank some more coffee.

Piotr heard a door click shut behind him. He turned, and felt a sharp pain in the back of his head. He dropped onto his hands and knees. A blast of pain resonated all over his neck. Everything went black.

'Get him in the back,' said the bald man.

Two men stood over Piotr. They hoisted him up by his arms and carried him through a door.

The bald man stood up and walked to the counter where the waitress was. She was sorting out some cutlery with her head down. She dropped a spoon as he approached.

'You didn't see that, did you darling?' he said. 'You understand?' She kept her head down, crouching to pick up the spoon.

He took his wallet out and opened it. 'Here, take this.' He handed her a roll of twenty pound notes.

He touched her face, but she dared not make eye contact. 'Get yourself something nice to wear,' he said.

Piotr woke up. Someone was slapping his face.

'Is he awake yet?' he heard someone say.

He opened his eyes and tried to rub them, but realised that his arms were tied behind him, to a chair. His head was pounding. He tried to move his feet but they were stuck to the chair's legs. He resisted the urge to shake his body. His mouth was taped and his chest was tied to the chair as well. He breathed in through his nostrils for five seconds and then exhaled out for another five. Three thugs were backed up by the wall in front of him. Piotr recognised one of them. He was the same man that Henio had acknowledged in the pub when they'd met to celebrate Ania's birthday. Piotr's stomach tightened.

'He's awake,' said one of the thugs.

'Call the boss,' said the bald man, from somewhere behind Piotr.

The thug closest to the door opened it and walked out, closing it behind him. A few seconds later, Piotr could hear him talking on a mobile phone.

The other two men stayed where they were. Piotr concentrated on his breathing.

A minute or so later he heard some voices outside the door and then one of the thugs came in, followed by the Taxi man.

The Taxi man grabbed a chair from the corner of the room, placed it in front of Piotr and sat on it. He took a packet of cigarettes out of his shirt pocket, lit one and blew a thick plume of smoke out through the side of his mouth.

'So the hero has arrived,' he said, smirking. 'Hasn't quite worked out for you this time though, has it?

'I guess you dropped your guard. Sitting with your back to a door. Here on your own. Or maybe you're become over-confident. Arrogant.' He took another long drag from his cigarette. 'So what are you going to do now hero? You going to break free from those binds and attack me?'

Piotr wondered if they had taken his mobile phone. He looked down at his jeans. The pocket where he usually kept it was empty. He thought about his Aunt and Beata.

'You've slipped up one time too many now,' said the Taxi man. 'Taken it one step too far. Couldn't help being the little hero. Like the loyal dumb dog, coming here to protect your bitch. How predictable.

'At least your predecessors were a bit smarter. Made them harder to kill. But you?' He sneered, shaking his head. 'I'm surprised they even let you take charge.'

Piotr felt a drop of sweat slide down his forehead.

'I suppose you really want to know what we're going to do to that slut of yours and her whore of a flatmate,' said the Taxi man. 'Well, you're never going to know.'

The Taxi man held his hand out. The thug that Piotr had recognised placed a gun on his palm. It was fitted with a silencer. The Taxi man pointed it casually at Piotr.

'You know, I never thought it would end like this. We were happy letting things take their natural course. Letting you slowly fade away. But I suppose life never ends up the way you expect it to. Does it?'

Twenty minutes had passed according to Jacek's watch. He edged to the end of the roof and looked down. There were two cars parked at the back of the shop. It was almost dark and he could see some light filtering out from the gap at the bottom of the back door. He tugged on the rucksack straps to make sure they weren't loose and carefully lowered himself down the side of the back wall. He held onto the edge of the roof with his fingers, tucked his knees up to his chest and placed the soles of his boots onto the wall. He counted to three and pushed himself off the wall.

Landing safely in between the two cars, he ran to the back wall and waited for thirty seconds. When he was satisfied that no one had heard or seen him jump, he crept up to the door and applied a little pressure to the door handle.

It was locked. He took a small multi-tool pocket knife out of the rucksack and selected one of the blades. He slipped it into the gap between the door and its frame and tinkered with the lock until it clicked open.

He pulled the door by a couple of centimetres so that he could peer through the crack. He saw a small stockroom. Beyond it, through another doorway, he heard the voice of one man talking to someone. He held the door with his foot and took a Molotov cocktail out of the rucksack and lit it. He watched the wick burn away and then threw the bottle at the windscreen of one of the cars.

The Taxi Man jumped up from his seat at the sound of the explosion.

'What the hell are you standing there scratching your balls for? Go and check it out,' he said to one of the thugs standing behind him.

As the hoodlum walked towards the back door he said, 'That back door was locked earlier. I checked it.' He took a pistol out of the back of his jeans and took some slow steps towards the open door.

'See if there's anything happening at the front,' said the Taxi man, glancing at another thug.

The Taxi man struck Piotr's face with the handle of his gun. Piotr arched backwards to try and take some of the momentum out of the strike and lost his balance. He fell to the floor. The Taxi man kicked him in the stomach.

'Who have you got out there you whore's son?'

Jacek drew his baton. He was crouched down and waiting behind the side of one of the cars. The flames gave him extra cover. A man came out pointing a handgun, scanning the scene.

Jacek waited until he began walking around the burning car. He took five long strides and smashed his baton into the back of the thug's head. He hit him again when he was on the floor, picked up his gun, and fired it into the air four times before throwing it as far as he could, away from the shop. He scrambled back to his original position and took another cocktail out of the rucksack.

Another two men ran out with their guns drawn. Jacek lit the cocktail, counted to four and threw it in their direction. One of them screamed out while the other one started firing gunshots at and over the car.

The other thug's clothes were on fire. He screamed and ran back into the building and headed straight to the toilet, trying to douse himself with water. The bald man ran into the coffee shop and ripped a fire blanket off the wall in the shop's small kitchen area. He threw it over the thug and fell on him, forcing him to the ground.

Outside, the thug who had been shooting shouted out. 'Come out you whore's son! Where are you?'

Jacek crept back up to the front of the car, staying low. He peered under the car's chassis. The thug was in the same place, but was turning from side to side every two seconds, like a pendulum. Jacek waited for his moment. When the thug was facing away, he sprung up at him, striking the thug's hands with the baton to loosen his grip on the gun. Two blows to his neck sent him reeling. He bounced against the bonnet of one of the cars on his way down before laying motionless on the ground.

'Pack up, let's get out of here,' said the Taxi man. 'Is he OK to come with us?' he said, looking at the thug on the floor.

'He's in shock, but he can move. Come on,' said the bald man, picking the thug up by the armpit. 'We've got to move.'

The Taxi man lifted his gun and pointed it at Piotr. 'So long you whore's dog,' he said.

Piotr closed his eyes. He muttered a prayer to his Guardian Angel that his mother had used to say with him when he was a child.

The room lit up.

A flurry of gunshots ricocheted off the walls. Heat stung Piotr's eyes. He started to wriggle away from a fire that had started in one end of the room. After a few seconds he felt himself being dragged from behind.

'Are you OK?' said Jacek, when they were outside.

'What?'

Jacek cupped Piotr's face. 'It's me. You're bleeding everywhere. I think your face is burnt. Hang on.' Jacek flipped open his pocket knife and sawed the rope at Piotr's legs. A siren began wailing in the distance.

'Can you run?' said Jacek as he cut the rope holding his arms and wrists.

'No idea.'

Jacek threw the rope off Piotr and helped him up, kicking the chair away. 'Come on, the police are on their way.'

They ran. Jacek held the rucksack in one hand and had his arm on Piotr's back, urging him on.

Gunshots broke out behind them. They ducked down and kept running.

THE OLD MAN ALMOST FELL OUT OF HIS FRONT DOOR as they walked up the driveway. His walking stick saved him from hitting his driveway face first.

Jacek ran forward when he saw the old man's front knee buckle.

'Are you OK Mr. Kwasniewski?' he said, helping him stand up straight. 'That's some nice recovery you made there.'

'It's thanks to my military training,' said the old man, leaning on Jacek's shoulder to regain his balance.

'Almost 68 years ago. It instilled good discipline in me. I still do my stretches first thing in the morning you know. I can touch my toes no problem.'

'I'm impressed,' said Jacek.

The pensioner brushed his hand through his wispy white hair. He peered over Jacek's shoulder. 'Are these your friends?'

'That's right, this is Adam, and that's Sebastian,' said Jacek, pointing at the two men.

'Sebastian, eh? He looks a bit young for this sort of thing.'

'He's older than he looks.'

They went inside the house and went into the sitting room, at the front of the house. Mr. Kwasniewski made some tea and served biscuits. The four men each ate a biscuit while drinking their tea.

Jacek, who was sitting near the window, peered out onto the street. He glanced at his watch. 'So they usually arrive at this time?' he said.

'Yes. They have done for the past four days,' said Mr. Kwasniewski. 'They take a break at the weekend, but they seem to be here almost every other day. Have been for over a month. I think they smoke drugs in the alleyway at the side of the house and then sit on my wall and throw litter into my front garden.

'They sometimes play loud music on their phones, and shout at each other. I dare not leave the house or even come to the window when they're here.'

'Why do they come at the same time?' said Adam.

'I've no idea,' said Mr. Kwasniewski.

'There's a college nearby,' said Jacek. 'They're spending their lunch breaks here. It's far away enough for them to not get caught smoking doobage or whatever it is they're on.'

The old man's hands shook as he put his cup down on a small table by his sofa. 'They're animals. If I was five years younger I would have sent them packing a long time ago, believe me.'

They drank some more tea and waited as Mr. Kwasniewski reminisced about his military training. Jacek looked around the room as he did so.

A picture of the Madonna of Częstochowa hung on one of the walls. Next to the mantelpiece was a large glass door cabinet with purple coloured crystal wine glasses, vodka glasses and a large decanter. On the adjacent wall was a landscape painting of some farmland in Poland. Apart from a tree and three cows by a fence, there was nothing else of note in the painting.

'You like the picture?' said Mr. Kwasniewki. 'It reminds me a bit of home. Before the war. It was so peaceful you know. We had such a carefree life. We were free, a nation reborn. We thought everything ahead of us would be good. An era of peace and prosperity. But the Lord had other plans.'

He picked up the plate of biscuits and offered them to the dojang men. 'Another one?'

They all ate another biscuit. A few minutes later, some youths arrived outside the house.

Jacek motioned Adam and Sebastian over to the window. They spied through Mr. Kwasniewski's lace curtains at the youths.

'OK,' he said. 'Ringleader. The light skinned guy with the blue baseball cap?'

'Sounds like a good shout,' said Sebastian.

'Are you sure?' said Adam.

'I think so. He's sitting in the middle of the wall and the five others seem to be focussed on him. It's subtle, but I'd say he's the big lion.'

'Did you see that?' said Jacek. 'That tall guy with the green hoodie said something and blue baseball cap pointed at him and they all laughed. And then one of the guys at the end of the wall snapped his fingers together a few times and stood up to laugh. As if he was trying to please blue baseball cap.'

Adam concentrated on the group. 'OK. I guess the only question is, does he get his hands dirty, or does he get someone else to do it?'

'Like the big guy or the tall one,' said Sebastian.

'There's only one way to find out,' said Adam, circling his neck and tightening his jaw.

'Yeah, well before it comes to that, we need to try and defuse the situation,' said Jacek.

He faced away from the window. 'Mr. Kwasniewski?'

'Yes?' said the old man, standing in the middle of the room, not daring to step forward any further.

'How many times did you say the police have spoken to them?'

'Never,' he said. 'They've come twice. Once when I called and then another time when my neighbour did, but they never get here on time. It's crazy. It's like the kids can see or hear them from a mile off. I don't know how they do it. Sometimes a couple of them hang around for longer, but they meander off before the police arrive. A patrol car slowly drives by, but they don't even get out of it. I don't know what we pay taxes for. It's a disgrace.'

Jacek examined the group for a bit longer before speaking to Adam and Sebastian. 'OK, there's seven of them today. They're laughing a lot and they're all eating junk food. They've all got the munchies. They'll be chilled out, but could get aggressive. Stay on your toes.'

'Do you boys want something a little stiffer before you go out there?' said Mr. Kwasniewski. 'I've got some nice vodka in the cabinet. I can stick it in the freezer. It will be ready to drink in ten minutes.'

'We'll have a shot to celebrate when the job's done,' said Jacek.

They walked to the front door.

'Right guys, stick to my flanks,' said Jacek. 'I'll try and speak to them all as a group rather than single out blue baseball cap and then see what their reaction is. If they start barking follow my lead. We'll have to improvise if it kicks off.'

They gripped hands and walked out of the house. Once they were near Mr. Kwasniewski's front gate, the youths noticed them.

They walked up to the gang. Jacek got close enough to force two of them to step aside, giving him the space to address the whole group.

The biggest one of the group stood closest to Jacek. He could see the detail on the stud in his ear. It sparkled, matching the shine of his teeth. He was taller than Jacek, and stronger. His pupils were dilated.

'You lost or something?' said the studded youth. He shrugged his shoulders forward, thrusting his arms down in front of his stomach. 'Can't you see this is a private conversation we're having?'

'No worries, man, no worries,' said Jacek in English, putting his hands up. 'I only wanted to ask you if you could maybe move along a bit and leave this man's wall and garden alone. He says you've been dropping rubbish in his front garden and he's old, so cleaning up isn't so easy for him.' He set his eyes on each of them briefly before saying, 'It's a polite request.'

'Can you believe what this batty boy is saying?' said the youth, turning to look at the rest of the gang.

He stared at Jacek. 'We hang out where we want. Understand?'

Blue baseball cap stood up and took three paces towards Jacek.

'What do you think you're doing gypo?' he said, standing next to his friend. He had a well-trimmed beard and a ring in his eyebrow.

'I think you and your refugee mates have got this mixed up with the gypo camp innit?' he said. The rest of the gang laughed.

'There's one in Northolt at the moment. You want me to draw you a map?' There was more laughter.

'Are you going to move or not?' said Jacek.

'Who do you think you are gypo?' said the studded youth, squaring up to Jacek.

'Nah, we ain't going nowhere. So you and your inbred brothers best get out of here and get back to your caravans.' He spat on the floor. 'This is our turf. And we'll be where we want to be. You understand?'

Jacek scanned the rest of the group and said, 'OK, if you don't want some friendly advice, then I'll give you a warning. It's best for you all if you leave now. You're invading private property, dropping litter in this man's front garden and you're a menace to the neighbourhood.'

'Alright we've heard enough,' said blue baseball cap. 'You Romanians or Kosovans, or whatever refugee camp you're from, better turn round and get out of here before we have some beef,' said blue baseball cap.

Jacek moved into a front stance, dropped his body weight slightly by bending his right knee and delivered two swift punches, one to blue baseball cap's solar plexus, the other to the chest of the biggest member of the gang, dropping them both.

As they lay doubled up on the floor he repeated his request to the other five youths. They hesitated, waiting to see what the reaction of blue baseball cap and the studded youth would be.

The bigger one got to his feet and tried throwing a punch at Jacek. Jacek ducked under it and struck him in the torso again. The youth shouted out in pain, holding his chest before dropping to his knees and rolling on the ground.

Two of the gang came over to the two youths and tried to help them to their feet. Another three stepped up to Jacek. Adam and Sebastian moved like chess pieces, positioning themselves slightly ahead of Jacek. Their silent menace was enough to make the youths back away.

'You ain't heard the last of this,' said one of them as they retreated.

'Yeah, we're gonna cut you gypos up!' said another one.

They stood and watched while the gang disappeared down the alley by Mr. Kwasniewski's house. Once they were out of sight, the dojang men made their way back down the driveway.

'Nice work boys,' said Jacek.

Back inside, Mr. Kwasniewski insisted that they stay for a drink. They each had two shots of vodka with their tea.

'We can't guarantee that they won't hassle you again,' said Jacek. 'They might try to carry out some sort of petty revenge attack. That's a common occurrence.'

Jacek gave Mr. Kwasniewski his number. 'If they come back again, call us straight away, OK?' he said.

'Thank you so much boys,' said the old man.

'It was nothing,' said Jacek.

As they were walking down the street, Mr. Kwasniewski stood in his doorway. He waved his walking stick above his head and shouted out to them.

'God bless you, and may God bless the Kwan!'

ABOUT THE AUTHOR

Marek Handzel lives in North Yorkshire in the UK with his young family. *THE DOJANG* is his first novel.

Printed in Great Britain
by Amazon